The
Capital
of
Dreams

ALSO BY HEATHER O'NEILL

The Capital of Dreams

A NOVEL

Heather O'Neill

HARPER PERENNIAL

NEW YORK • LONDON • TORONTO • SYDNEY • NEW DELHI • AUCKLAND

HARPER PERENNIAL

FIRST U.S. EDITION

Designed by Zeena Baybayan

Library of Congress Cataloging-in-Publication Data

Names: O'Neill, Heather, author.
Title: The capital of dreams : a novel / Heather O'Neill.
Description: First U.S. edition. | New York, NY : HarperPerennial, 2024.
Identifiers: LCCN 2024029659 | ISBN 9780063425996 (trade paperback) | ISBN
  9780063425989 (ebook)
Subjects: LCGFT: Fantasy fiction. | Dystopian fiction. | Novels.
Classification: LCC PR9199.4.O64 C37 2024 | DDC 813/.6--dc23/eng/20240628
LC record available at https://lccn.loc.gov/2024029659

ISBN 978-0-06-342599-6 (pbk.)

24 25 26 27 28 LBC 5 4 3 2 1

PROLOGUE

There was the sound of gunshots going off somewhere in the distance. But there was no reaction to them on the young girl's face. She was sitting in the back of a flatbed truck, between boxes of cabbage, facing the road. She looked no more than twelve, but in truth, she was fourteen years old.

Sofia was dressed in a threadbare black coat that looked as though it had seen more winters than the girl had been alive. It surely must have been passed on to her. Her hair was tied up on her head with a flowered red kerchief, a pattern that was popular with the peasants.

The truck rumbled quickly down the country roads. It seemed to react to every stone it went over. The cabbages leapt out of their boxes and fell back in. The girl looked rather precariously perched. As though one large bump might launch her right off the back of the truck. But she sat up there stoically.

She was holding a large goose in her arms. The goose remained still, only moving its neck occasionally to get a better look at where they might be going. The girl held on to the

1

goose as though it was her only possession. As though it was the only object she owned, and there was a good chance it was. People were being displaced all over the country because of the war. And they could be found clutching the most random of objects.

Her thin fingers that were gripping the goose were soft and unblemished. How was it that this girl had hands that looked as if they had never worked a single day in their lives?

Although she was dressed like a peasant, and at first glance would easily be mistaken for one, there was something about her pale face that looked refined. It looked as though it could belong only to an upper-class girl from the Capital.

She had grey eyes that were common in Elysia and thin dirty-blond hair that fell in stringy locks from her kerchief. She was not beautiful. In fact, she might have been considered plain. But her expression had a certain conceit and sophistication to it. It was this arrogance the Enemy had been so vocal about in their propaganda. The devilish, corrupt pride of the metropolitan elite, whom they wanted to destroy at all costs. But the most striking thing about her was that she was all alone. Were it not wartime, surely some adult would have been with her. But people had already begun to look away when they came across children who had been separated from everyone they loved. She was like a stray dog people avoided eye contact with. It was not at all good to look into the eyes of a broken animal. It was too much to bear. She was a million miles from anyone who could help her.

THE CHILDREN'S TRAIN

At the beginning, her mother didn't believe in the war at all. Or she wasn't afraid of it. She deliberately made provocative statements about not being afraid. She said war was good because it always created new forms of art. She thought it was particularly good for theatre. There was nothing like seeing a play right after a war.

But then the Enemy had entered the country easily and now occupied the beautiful Capital. It had upended all their lives. And in fact, all the theatres and newspapers and concert halls had been closed, as Elysian art was now illegal. Sofia's mother was at the very centre of the art world. It could be claimed that Clara Bottom was the Simone de Beauvoir of Elysia. She was the first to write in their language what it is to be a woman. That one is not born but becomes a woman, more or less. And thus, she was on the Enemy's most wanted list.

The Enemy had come to reclaim the land they had lost in a treaty after the Great War. The Capital had been spared the mass destruction the rest of the country had seen. Of

3

course, the Capital was considered sacrosanct by both sides. Now the citizens of the Capital existed in an uneasy lull in the violence, waiting to see what would happen next, while slowly building an underground resistance. Clara Bottom inserted herself right into the heart of it.

Whose idea was it that all the children should flee the Capital? From the very beginning of the Occupation, parents had asked that their children be allowed to leave to stay with relatives in the countryside. To spare them from what, exactly? the Enemy asked. But they were too afraid to answer. And then the Enemy announced that children could leave the Capital on a special train the following weekend. Sofia's mother immediately began preparations for Sofia to be on that train.

"I am not a child anymore," Sofia protested. "I don't want to be sent away with the children."

"Don't be a fool, Sofia. This is an opportunity to escape. The Enemy is letting children leave."

"You aren't leaving. I am going to stay here with you. I want to be a war hero too."

"A war hero! There are no heroes in this war."

"I am staying for the Uprising."

"Oh, you are stubborn and ridiculous, Sofia!"

"You want me to leave. You've never liked being a mother. You never wanted me to be born."

Sofia's mother was being bossy about what Sofia put in her suitcase. Sofia did not think this was fair. She never liked when her mother told her what to wear or how to act. But now she would be where her mother couldn't even see her. So why should

Sofia care? She was going to stay with some third cousins who lived in a small village. She could not even tell you whether it was a cousin of her mother's or her father's.

She asked about her new cousins.

"You'll be very good for them," her mother said. "Make sure the children pick up your accent and not the other way around. And read every night. You have to learn to have a rich vocabulary when you are young. Otherwise, it will never seem natural when you use large words later on in life. I know it's heavy, but I've put a large book in your suitcase."

"Oh, this is awful!" cried Sofia. "I am not a child. You cannot send me away with all the babies. I am needed in the Capital, just as you are!"

"This is your way out, darling. Just be a child for the duration of the train ride."

Sofia picked up her suitcase. It was heavier than she thought. She opened it again. She saw her large folklore book, *Tales from the Forests of Elysia*, inside it. She was pleased. "My book!" Sofia announced.

"Look, darling, this is the most important thing I will ever tell you." She took out the book and opened it. Sofia noticed at once that the book was different. The pages had been taken out and replaced by her mother's latest manuscript. "You are to deliver this book to the people who are meeting you at the train station. You know how valuable this is. It is my life. It is our lives. I have to get it out of the country."

"No! You've ruined my favourite book."

"Why must you be so obtuse, child? The fate of the bloody country is on your shoulders, and you're worried about a handful of fables. You say you want to be a resistance fighter. You have to get this book to people who will get it out of the country. You're the only one who can do it, Sofia. We have to get the word out to Europe. They have to know that we are like them. They can't let a civilized society filled with thinkers and artists be razed to the ground. They think we are still backwards and barbaric. They don't understand that we are nothing like the Enemy. We are like them."

"You don't love me. You love your writing first."

"Of course the book is more important than you. It's my memoir, yes. But it's more important than me. It's the celebration of an Elysian life. What are any of us except expendable during a war? It's the idea of freedom that has to be saved. It's a culture that we created. If we can keep that alive, we are all saved. Our individual fates don't matter. Don't you think about yourself. Think about the book. It has to make it out of the country."

"I can't travel with children. What if the girls from my class are there? No, I cannot get on the same train as them."

The train station was filled with mothers. Sofia believed that when a train pulled out of the station, all the mothers felt a burden lift from their shoulders. In Sofia's mind, wartime was the most wonderful time for married women in the city. They all went back to behaving like young girls. Women never actually liked being mothers; they only liked the idea of motherhood beforehand.

Her mother had taken her to the train station to see her off. She was wearing her most fashionable dress. Her mother was usually lazy when it came to anything involving paperwork, so Sofia was surprised she had managed to sign her up for this transport.

It was the only time her mother had been efficient about anything. Of course! Her mother wanted to get rid of her so she could have lovers. This wasn't about any manuscript, it was about being free of her. With her father safely in America on business, having left the country before the Occupation, her mother wanted to be a single woman. And although Sofia missed her father occasionally, her mother never seemed to. Free of a husband, she had now traded her daughter for currency on the dating market.

Sofia was surprised by the number of children on the train platform.

As the mothers began to recede, she saw she was in an enormous crowd of children. It seemed possible that at least half of them would get lost. It was hard to keep your wits about you. The children had their stops written on tags around their necks. If they were to miss their stop, they would be lost forever.

There was no one to take their hands. So they found themselves deliberately touching others so they would not feel alone. They stepped carefully on the heels of the children in front of them as they boarded; they held on to another child's scarf. You wanted to hang on to somebody.

Sofia did not like having the burden of carrying the book with her mother's manuscript in her suitcase. It meant she had to worry about the book on top of herself. She felt all the other children had been told to look out, above all things, for themselves. But she knew she was supposed to prioritize the book. She couldn't think properly. It was as though the book inside the suitcase were speaking loudly over all her thoughts. In prioritizing the book, her mother was prioritizing herself over Sofia. Sofia had a sudden urge to open the window of the train and shove the suitcase out. And be free of it.

Oh, she had had it with this war! The Enemy's persecution of artists was only giving them a ridiculous pompous view of themselves. And they had rendered going to the store a perilous adventure. How she longed for the simplicity of her former boring life in the Capital. How she wished she could be at home, drinking coffee and listening to a radio play. She would even bear school at this point. But instead, the Enemy had decided they needed their land back. They could have just asked, Sofia thought, with frustrated tears in her eyes. She straightened her shoulders. I am fourteen! she reminded herself. She was too old to weep at being separated from her mother.

When they were an hour out of the Capital, the train came to a halt. It was surrounded by trucks and soldiers. Several of the soldiers had bullhorns and told the children in their own language that they were all to debark from the train.

When they heard the bullhorns, the children had crowded up against the windows to see what was happening. But they had no impulse to get off the train. They had been told by their parents to stay on the train no matter what. They weren't supposed to get off until they had met up with loved ones.

The soldiers again instructed them all to leave the train. There were trucks that were going to take them back to the Capital to their mothers. They would be reunited with their parents. They would have delicious soup. And possibly pie. Their parents had decided they could not live without them after all. The children reacted to this with great enthusiasm.

The majority of the children came running out to the soldiers. They all pushed their way through the train doors as though they were bursting out, some falling down the steps, others happily jumping right over them. Then they lined up, pushing each other and yelling all the while, to get on the trucks. They allowed themselves to be lifted up under the armpits. They were so sure of the power of their own cuteness. They batted their eyelashes and smiled at the soldiers. They were the last of the stupid children in the country. Was being trusting a sign of stupidity?

Sofia did not line up. She stood away from the trucks and edged quietly into the forest. There was a small group of other suspicious children who took refuge there. They stood behind the trees, watching. She saw the trucks pulling away with the children crammed inside them. The oddest thing was the sound of laughter that followed behind the trucks. Like a string of tin cans attached to the bumper of a car. The children were enjoying being on the back of a truck. It was as though they were on a class field trip to an apple orchard.

She heard the voices of children in the last truck join together in song. They were singing a lullaby. They sang about a pretty girl who drowned herself after being rejected. It was a song every child in the country knew. It was a song they had learned when they were too little to properly consider its meaning. And when they grew older, they were too familiar with the words to make any sense of what they were actually singing. The words were simply the words of the song. And they made them feel young and protected and happy.

Marianna was too in love, too in love, too in love. She fell for a man who damned her to be too in love, too in love, too in love.

Sofia had never thought hard about it before. But now the absurdity of the song struck her. Everything would seem absurd from here on in, she suspected. There was no such thing as normal. Suddenly a soldier caught sight of Sofia and the group of children and called something out while pointing. The children turned and ran into the woods in different directions.

Sofia stopped to catch her breath in a small clearing in the woods. Her suitcase was still in her hand as though she were going on a holiday and not running for her life.

She sensed danger acutely. She sensed it the way an animal did. Every way she turned, the danger was standing directly behind her. She had an impulse to run, but since she didn't know which direction to go, she felt frozen on the spot. Since she had stood in the clearing for several minutes without anything happening, perhaps it made sense not to move a muscle. Maybe if she stood in place for a whole day and night, the soldiers would be far enough away from her that she could safely sneak out of the woods.

She heard the sound of footsteps breaking sticks in half. As though someone were so frustrated with their homework, they were breaking their pencil in two, again and again. Before she knew it, she was not alone in the clearing. There was a boy a few years younger standing with her. He stopped running and stared at her, panting for breath. He seemed to think he had found a safe spot since there was another child in it. His whole body relaxed. He looked at Sofia and smiled.

And there was the sound of a bullet and a terrible sinking thud. There was a black hole in the boy's forehead. He continued to stare at Sofia for a moment, as though he were wondering if they could still be friends, despite his being dead. Then his body slumped to the ground.

When his body hit the ground, she felt as though there had been an earthquake.

You had no idea how easy it was to extinguish a life until you saw it.

There was nothing anyone could do to revive that boy. There was no science or philosophy on earth that could bring him back to life. He was lying on the forest floor. While his family members back in the Capital were hoping he was safe, telling themselves he was safe.

Sofia ran. She did not believe that at this moment, her mother was worrying about whether she was safe. She was certain, instead, that her mother was worrying about the safety of her manuscript. She decided she would save herself. Maybe if she had believed her mother was worried about her, she would have stood there, like a lost child, waiting to be shot in the head too. Instead she ran away from the world of adults.

She was certain there were animals running right beside her, moving away from the danger. They weren't animals per se but were more like shadows of animals. She didn't exactly see them, but she sensed their presence and saw their black forms out of the corner of her eye. She didn't have time to turn and look at exactly what they were.

She wasn't afraid of any animals other than humans at that point. If she had seen a bear standing there, she felt she would have flung herself into its arms.

Then she was out of the woods. She was standing at another train track. She looked down at her school shoes, which were covered in mud. The soles of her feet were so painful from running, they were burning, as though she were standing on a frying pan over flames. She had to endure the pain.

There was something odd about the clouds. They seemed lower than they had been before. She felt dizzy with a new realization. She suddenly felt the opposite of weight at the end of her hand. There was a lightness at the end of her reach. And that lightness made it feel as though she might float up into the clouds like a balloon whose string had been let loose. She was horrified by what she had misplaced.

In the flurry of chaos, she had become separated from her suitcase. So many of the children had become separated from their personal belongings. They were allowed to return home, and no one would care about lost items, as long as the children were safe.

She didn't have the suitcase with her. The suitcase her mother had put her manuscript in. The manuscript Sofia was supposed to guard with her life. She knew she had no right to be running for safety without it. She had put her own life above her mother's manuscript.

She could never go back to the city. She would never be able to face her mother again. The only excuse she could possibly have for giving up the manuscript was that there was a bullet in her head. She hated her mother for a moment, for making her feel this way, for putting her in this position. For making her feel the manuscript was more valuable than her.

It wasn't as though she had any option to go back to the city. The army was moving towards the Capital to destroy everything. She knew probably more than any person in the Capital that death was coming. And it was going to be brutal and savage in a way they could not imagine. Because you could not conceive of such brutality until you had witnessed it yourself.

Sofia followed the tracks. She was so nervous. It was strange to be lost. She didn't think she had ever been lost in her whole life. She knew the city streets so well, it was impossible to get disoriented there. There were also maps on the corners of each block. They were behind glass on the walls outside subway stations. You could always stop and look and see exactly where you were. How she wished she could come across one of those maps now and stand on tippy-toes to look at it.

She turned around quickly because she felt as though she was being followed. The trees stiffened in place, like a child playing a game of freeze tag. The trees would start moving again as soon as Sofia turned her back. The sound of the stones underneath her shoes started getting louder and louder. Her footfalls sounded like a train leaving the station.

There was whispering in the air. It was like bits of conversation had been ripped from the mouths of the children from the train, like pages from a book, and like a page, the bits had been blown by the wind for several miles until they reached Sofia's ears. Perhaps there was a child who was a ventriloquist who was throwing their voice a hundred miles.

The children were whispering. They seemed to be mocking her. What could they be talking about? They were making fun of her because they were dead and she was alive. They didn't have to worry about being cold or hungry. The Enemy meant nothing to them now.

Sofia couldn't stand the idea of dying. She didn't know whether that made her a coward. But she felt that she hadn't spent enough time on earth. She hadn't had any time to properly develop a personality. She wanted, at some point, to know what it felt like to be herself.

The wind was being awful and harassing her. It kept sticking its hands in her pockets. She didn't know what it wanted. Did it want money? She never had any money in her pockets. She was a child. She had forgotten how it was always colder as soon as you left the city. She was not ready for the chill.

Sofia finally came to a station. There were crowds of country people standing at the platform being watched by soldiers. They were arguing because they wanted to take the train somewhere. But the train was late. They were waving tickets in the air.

She felt embarrassed. She was too embarrassed to tell the people she was being pursued by soldiers. They would think it was her own fault. They would look her up and down and wonder what it was about her that had caused the soldiers to dislike her so.

She saw a truck park near the station. Two older farmers stepped out of it and began to load the back with crates of cabbage that were waiting for them. They did not seem to be especially concerned by the proximity of soldiers. They were farmers. They assumed they were necessary and would be the last to be shot. The word was out that the soldiers were murdering the elite and the overeducated bourgeoisie, which probably made them think, on some level, that the Enemy had a point.

Why had her mother dressed her as though she needed to impress people at a dinner party?

There was a girl her size in an oversized, threadbare black coat and with a kerchief on her head. Sofia wore a red tam and a new coat that had been tailored in the city. She asked the girl if she wanted to trade. The girl looked surprised and was very happy with the trade. Sofia handed the girl her beret, although on cold days she would come to regret this choice. She wrapped the kerchief around her head and pulled the girl's coat around her body.

"Can you tell me where we are?" Sofia asked the girl.

"We aren't anywhere. We are just in the country."

"Which is the way to Oloman?"

"I wouldn't go that way if I were you."

The two of them stared at each other. Then the girl pointed in a direction with her finger. They turned and walked away from each other. Each girl certain the other's identity was safer than her own.

Sofia knew to be quiet; already, talking to the girl had been a risk. She knew if she opened her mouth, they would know that she was posh. Her mother had a funny way of speaking. All the girls who went to a certain elite women's college picked it up when they were there. It was an accent that gave a deliberate sneer to all their words. Sofia had heard that accent since she was a very little baby. Despite having scores of nannies who spoke in a less obviously posh accent, she had picked up that of her mother.

One of her teachers had once told her that it didn't matter whether she was intelligent or not. What mattered was that she sounded intelligent. By the time Sofia realized it was an insult, it was too late for her to say anything.

She noticed more people coming towards the station. Everybody seemed to have brought an object with them. There was a woman holding a red tea kettle covered in poppies. She had forgotten that about poor people. They were always attached to worthless objects. Whereas a rich person wouldn't even attempt to equate themselves with a priceless object.

She looked around for something she could hold in her arms. Something she could cling to as though her family's entire legacy depended on it. She was meant to hold on to her mother's suitcase with her manuscript in it.

At that moment, a white goose waddled by, craning its neck around as though it had lost track of its gaggle. Sofia leaned over and picked up the large white bird. To her surprise, it did not struggle to free itself but relaxed in her arms.

She was astonished she was not frightened of it. If she were in her apartment in the Capital and a goose walked in, everyone in the house would have run around screaming and doing everything possible to kick it out. And she would have joined them. But the minute she held the goose in her arms, she felt immeasurably calmer.

Now she was ready to pass herself off as a member of the people. They would take pity on her because she was a poor child. She went up to the farmers and asked quietly whether she could climb onto their truck and have a ride as far as Oloman. One man shrugged and hoisted both the girl and the goose onto the back of the truck.

Sofia watched as the truck pulled away from the train station and the crowds of people receded. There were people walking on the road, carrying luggage, and they moved aside for the truck, parting like water. She saw the small buildings and houses begin to fade from the side of the road, until there were no more people, or any evidence of people. And the wind grew wilder and lonelier around her.

The truck began to drive down a road that led through the forest. The forest was filled with elf trees. They grew in the country. They strangled any other trees that tried to grow there. Their branches grew outwards as much as upwards. Their branches swirled and curled. Their branches wrapped around each other as though they were in love. As though they insisted on being united. The Elysian people did not use the expression "There are no two snowflakes alike." Instead they said, "There are no two trees alike."

The tree was on the currency. On every coin was a tree whose branches reached out to the round periphery. It was rather pretty.

Sofia had not been around trees in the same way in the city. There was the occasional tree in the middle of the sidewalk. But it knew very little about anything. It was silent. It was covered in animals. There seemed to be too many birds and squirrels inside it. The trees in the park were different too. They had been planted and raised. They had had their needs catered to. They had been protected from the elements when they were little. They were timid and vain and could be knocked right out of the ground in a storm. Sometimes they had hearts and initials carved into them. Which was painful when it happened, but in later years, people would run their fingertips along the initials, and that would give the trees a strange feeling. It made them feel as though they were owned.

Here the trees were wild and alive. On the back of the truck, Sofia rode under their arched branches as bits of sunlight that made it through the foliage danced around her like gold coins, and she moved, hopefully, away from the danger.

THE HOUSE WAS WHERE WE LEFT IT

After an hour's drive, Sofia recognized a fork in the road as the one her mother turned on to go to her grandmother's house. She hollered loudly to the farmers to let her off the truck. As soon as the truck came to a halt, she set the goose to the side and jumped off. Her shoes hit the ground, and two small clouds of dust rose up around them.

She turned and looked at the back of the truck, and the goose seemed to be waiting. She could not know what he was thinking, of course. She had never tried to imagine what might be going on in a goose's head before. She held out her arms, and the goose jumped into them.

In any case, what other option did the goose have? The truck drivers were farmers. And from what she could tell, farmers murdered geese for a living. She stood holding the goose until the truck was out of sight.

Sofia placed the goose, whom she called the Goose, on the ground beside her. She rubbed her arms, as they had grown stiff from holding the Goose so securely on the back of the truck. She was afraid the Goose might run away, but he was heavy and she would need a break from carrying him. She wondered whether she should put a rope around his neck and keep him prisoner for his own good. But the Goose had a look about him that said he would not tolerate this type of behaviour.

Sofia had never had a pet in her life. Her mother had never wanted to have a cat. She'd had so many as a child. They reminded her of her own mother's house and domesticity. She said cats were supposed to be a replacement for intellectual companionship. In any case, Sofia knew nothing about farm animals. She didn't dare make any presumptions about the Goose.

It wasn't a pet. If the Goose chose to flutter off in the opposite direction, away from her, she would not try to stop him.

Sofia began to walk along the country road, and the Goose waddled behind her. When she stopped to look around, the Goose also paused. And when she began walking again, so did the Goose. She slowed her pace so the Goose could keep up with her. After they had advanced for an hour like this, she began to accept that they had an arrangement, and that they were travel companions. Which she was very pleased about because the last thing she wanted now was to be alone. She couldn't quite believe it. She was never able to get a partner at school. She was used to being rejected because she was so shy and awkward.

Sofia did not know how odd she was until she started school. It was surprising to her. She seemed to have an inability for small talk. She didn't see the point of running around after balls. She could go through the motions, but she had no natural enthusiasm for it. She didn't laugh at the things other children found funny. She didn't even realize anything amusing had occurred until she noticed others laughing.

She felt as though she were a spy. Posing as a little girl to infiltrate a group of other little girls. Perhaps she felt this way because she'd had no other friends her age before she went to school. Her mother had never set play dates for her. The sound of children playing together gave her a headache.

She did not really know what it was like to be chosen. Especially by a farm animal. That was even more unusual.

She couldn't imagine how much farther her grandmother's house was. She had only ever driven there by car. It hadn't seemed far at all. But cars were always deceptive about distance. She wondered whether she bore responsibility for the Goose. She had taken him away from wherever he was meant to be. She had given him the same lot as her.

Sofia stared at the Goose. "How are your feet?"

He looked down at them, as if to make sure they were still there. "Fine," he said.

Sofia dropped to her knees. "Thank you so much for talking to me."

"Who else would I talk to? I had half a mind to bite my tongue and not say a thing. I hope after all this, you don't intend to eat me."

"Oh no. I would never do such a thing. You are a miracle."

"Humph," the Goose answered. "I'm a miracle until you get hungry enough."

WHAT WE IMAGINED WE WERE

The country where Sofia lived was so small, it was one that foreign children would forget to name on their maps at school. Her mother had said the First Great War was the birth of the country. Until the war, the Elysian people were citizens of the Enemy country. They were disliked by the Enemy as they were a different ethnic class. They were discriminated against and mistreated.

The Elysians had traditionally lived in the forests, espousing a pantheistic view of nature. They believed the trees were alive and every living thing was filled with consciousness. The Elysians had their own cavalry, which became necessary for the Enemy in their fight on the Western Front of the Great War. Then the Elysian people engaged in a great act of treachery. In exchange for their independence, they allowed the opposing army through the Western Forest. They wanted their own country—of course they did. Their country was made up of the forest and land along the western border, the northern border (which was the only access the landlocked country had to the sea), and of course the Capital. The Enemy could keep their colder, rockier eastern land.

According to Sofia's mother and every other adult in the country, the twenty years following the Great War were a wonderful time. The country invested hugely in the arts. The Elysians wanted to be considered Western. The Capital looked very much like a sophisticated European city with all its gorgeous stone buildings. But it had several idiosyncratic touches. There were statues that represented trees and animals. The country distanced itself from its earlier feelings towards the forest. Thus its religion was relegated to folklore. Folklore books, with old Elysian tales, were bought only for children.

The country was in the vanguard of art and ideas. Nothing was boring or traditional. There was an artist who painted laughing prostitutes with black chalk. There was a ballet dancer who performed being horny. There was a tuba player who composed a symphony called *Ode to the Fart*. There was a clown who stood on a chair with a noose around his neck while reciting sins that were so mundane as to be hilarious.

The Elysian people believed they were going to be a celebrated part of European culture, although the West had promptly forgotten about them. But despite the lack of interest from any international community, they continued to create their art in the city and farm in the country. To their own delight, if no one else's.

After the end of the Great War, a new dogmatic and conservative view of national identity arose in the Enemy country. They began to advocate for the nuclear family, the supremacy of males, and pure bloodlines. Instead of a God, the Enemy believed in a great Motherland. They could not be great without Elysia. They wanted back the land Elysia had stolen from them. They built up an army in order to reclaim their former dominance. And that army grew and grew and grew.

But no one really took it very seriously until the Enemy elected a new leader. Clara and Sofia went to the movies one weekend. It was a warm spring day, and Clara wore a chic pink coat down to her ankles and a blue velvet hat. Sofia trotted along beside her in her favourite navy sailor dress and new button-up boots. They walked past all the apartment buildings to the theatre district, where lights formed constellations advertising all sorts of fictional adventures. They were at the Elf Tree Movie House to see a film about a suicidal clown when they saw the Leader for the first time in a reel before the feature.

The speech in this reel began with the charismatic Leader stating the Enemy's usual opinions about the Elysian people. The West had given the Elysians their land in order to plant the seeds of a corrupt capitalistic foreign presence, he said. The Elysian people were representative of the worst excesses of the West. He accused them of advocating pedophilia, of destroying the family unit. He said the women had no morals. They were promiscuous; all had syphilis and made the men in the country insane.

These accusations from the Enemy had become so commonplace and repetitive that they hardly made an impression. But in this speech, the Leader suddenly began attacking the arts in Elysia. He said the Elysians were degenerate and untalented and incapable of producing any art of merit. The artists celebrated the grotesque. Then there were descriptions of people in their country who epitomized the Elysians' decadence.

He had a list of the twenty most wanted people in the country. There was an image of a cabaret dancer wearing high heels and fishnets and a mask over his eyes. He was a renowned emcee who was known for his hilarious critiques of government policy.

There was also an image of a singer named Claudette, which caused shouts to emit from some members of the audience. Claudette had been a prostitute at the age of twelve but had since captured the hearts of the country. If you had a fantastic backstory in Elysia, you could be a popular singer. You didn't need talent, so much as you needed a grand personality. She was very large. She coated her sinking jowls with white pancake makeup and decorated her face with black beauty marks. It was considered very sophisticated taste indeed to find beauty in something that was conventionally ugly. Claudette had sung a song about being happy in her youth despite its being awful. It was a surprise hit that unofficially became the national anthem.

Why had the Leader called them out? How could this be? How could an artist be tried for political treason? This sent a murmur through the crowd. That was the truth that had startled everyone in the cinema. They wanted to murder Claudette for singing funny songs! They did not want access to the sea; they wanted to exterminate every one of them.

The camera swung over a massive crowd that cheered wildly at the Leader's words. And everyone in the theatre audience was terrified of this hysterical mob.

Her mother had scoffed and made loud jeers with the rest of the audience when these entertainers were put up on the screen and denounced as political enemies.

Then a photograph of Clara appeared. She normally liked photographs of herself, and she adored having her picture taken. This was not a flattering photo. She had her mouth wide open and her finger up in the air. It made her look more severe than she usually did.

Sofia looked over to her mother. She found it strange to be sitting next to someone while her image was up on the screen.

How many thoughts can fit into a second? How many angels can dance on the head of a pin? As soon as she saw her mother's face, Sofia remembered the context. Her mother was being accused of being a monster, a degenerate, a pervert. She shrank into her chair. She and her mother were quiet. Her mother stopped jeering and calling things at the screen. Clara was listening and internalizing each word the Enemy said about her. She looked as though she thought people in the theatre might listen to the Leader's accusations and attack her. Or, what was worse in Sofia's mind, look at her with disdain and contempt.

The Leader had said she was an obscene woman who hated men. She hated the family. She wanted to undermine the family as the cornerstone of modern civilized society. It was her debasement of women's virtues that had led to this degenerate art. It is for women to impose morality on society. Women need to be subservient to men or all hell breaks loose. Or there is no more virtue. Instead she wanted a world where women descended into pornography and sexual disease. She would be tried for her insidious writings.

A young woman in the front row stood up, cupped her hands around her mouth, and yelled, Leave us alone, you old pervert. All the women in the audience again began shouting at the screen together. Their voices drowned out his. But the subtitles were still there, to be read above the women's boos and heckles.

What was the plot of the main feature that followed? Neither Sofia nor her mother would ever be able to tell you.

As they left the cinema, Clara kept her head tilted so that the brim of her hat obscured her face. Usually she loved being recognized by fans. But she didn't want to discuss what had happened with any stranger.

"I didn't expect him to be so charismatic," Clara said as they walked, although she seemed to be talking to herself and not Sofia. "And the way all those people were listening to what he had to say. Without any sort of critical lens. It was terrifying."

Clara was silent the rest of the way home. Sofia did not know what to say to her mother. She could not guess what her mother was feeling or thinking. Was she afraid of the Leader, who was demanding her arrest? Were her feelings hurt? Sofia felt as though the Leader had changed everything about their reality, but she didn't know how.

As soon as they were safe in their apartment and the door was locked, Clara broke her silence. "When you are singled out by the Enemy, you must respond in kind. You must accept the challenge. You must recognize the new power and importance it gives to you. The Enemy has directed his ire towards me because my words are a threat. My words are a tool that can undermine all his hate and lies. I will show him that he cannot erase our history. As long as there is one writer with all the words and ideas of Elysia in her head, this country will flourish."

Sofia had not expected her mother to be reinvigorated and thrilled by the Leader's speech. But her mother often surprised her.

Her mother came alive when she encountered opposition. All the aches and pains of a middle-aged woman disappeared. She no longer complained about her sore breasts or dozed off mid-afternoon. She was immortal. She was twenty years younger.

Her mother's first act of resistance was to go on the radio.

When she was called on to speak on the radio, it was as though she were a general being called to battle. She paced back and forth in a flurry of activity. She looked over her notes. With a pen in one hand and a cigarette in the other.

She always dressed impeccably. No one could see her, of course. But from the tenor of her voice, one could tell she was well put together. She smelled wonderfully. She was freshly out of the bath and smelled like a bouquet of creams and hair products.

Sofia had heard the gist of her dialogue rehearsed around the apartment in the days before she went on air. But she tuned in to listen.

"The Capital is the most magical city in the world. The Capital is what it is because of every one of us. You must never leave it. You will never be able to return. It will be like a lost childhood. You will spend your life feeling nostalgic for it. Without you, our language will vanish with the wind.

"Would I die for Elysia? Yes, because I will never live anywhere else. I am nothing without Elysia.

"We will stay together and resist. And if our army is defeated and all our soldiers are gone, we will continue to resist. Everyone who stays should now be considered a soldier. We will fight them with everything we have. We will fight with kitchen knives. We will fight them with our songs. And if you don't think our music is a threat, then ask yourselves why they are trying to ban it."

Clara Bottom herself had a stake in what she was saying. She was staying in the Capital even though the Enemy had singled her out. She was in more danger than anyone, and she was staying. It was both elegant and noble.

But Clara's radio broadcast had little effect. The film reel caused the beginning of the exodus. Those who had money found passage to France and elsewhere in Europe, and some even to America. As she was walking to the grocer's, Sofia couldn't help but notice all the traffic on the streets. The cars were piled with entire families. Including grandparents. There was furniture tied on top of the cars, and the trunks were half open. There were cats on laps and dogs with their heads in the windows. There was even a car that had a large cage with birds in it. It was strange to see such a procession moving past the sleeping theatres and grand buildings.

There were also so many people on foot. They were on their way to the train station. Women were pushing perambulators with two children inside and two other children holding on. A small park was filled with people with suitcases, trampling the grass underfoot. They were all heading past the Theatre Quarter and the opera house, past the Grand Park, to the bridge and the river that would lead them on boats to the sea. They were dressed in good clothes, hoping they would be taken in as esteemed immigrants and not refugees.

Sofia's father, who was abroad, had called the Sunday night before, as was his custom. He had insisted that Clara leave with

Sofia immediately. But Clara had yelled back that he had never properly loved Elysia and that was what was wrong with their marriage to begin with.

Now Sofia stood next to her mother at the entrance of their building, watching the crowds stream down the street, feeling it was the two of them against the idiotic masses. Clara had on a fine blue coat, although in truth, her nightgown was on underneath it. Sofia still held on to the remains of her breakfast croissant, which she stuffed into her mouth. She did not feel nervous about staying put. She was at her mother's side. And there is no safer place for a child to be than with her mother.

Every stranger she saw rushing down the street seemed to be in direct disobedience to Clara's supplication. Sofia looked at her mother, to see whether her feelings were hurt and she was taking their actions personally. She seemed like an ordinary woman, and not a famed author.

It was hard for Sofia to ascertain what she was thinking. Because Clara was looking at them stoically.

No one noticed her at all. The people pushed forward as though the country were already in its past. As though someone like Clara Bottom no longer had any power over them. She had a look of disappointment, and yet not surprise. As though she had never really expected much.

It was a look Sofia was somewhat familiar with. Because she had seen her mother look at her in that way.

She was used to her mother's disappointment. So when she saw it directed at other people, she was pleased. She stood next to her mother, wearing a pretty frown on her face.

A girl her age passed by. When their eyes met, Sofia stuck out her tongue at her. And then she quickly snuck it back in as though nothing had happened. The girl looked at her with discomfort and unease. But Sofia looked away, delighted by the surge of power she felt. This was what it was like to be wicked. It took feeling as though one had the higher moral ground in life to be able to be wicked.

"You should not have said we will fight the Enemy with songs," Sofia said.

Her mother looked down at her.

"Not very practical. Unless you have a terrible voice that's off-key. That could be considered a form of torture."

"Stop, Sofia," Clara said, but Sofia saw she was smiling.

"Drop a piano from a window onto a tank."

She pulled Sofia's hat over her face to stop her.

"Tie them to a chair and read them bad poetry."

She couldn't remember making her mother laugh so hard. She was in a good mood.

POSTCARDS FROM THE WAR

When the war began, the Enemy first moved in on the countryside in the east. They set upon the area, destroying the next two seasons' crops, impoverishing the people. There had been a farmer's market in the Capital on the weekends. It was an explosion of colour. Her mother enjoyed wandering around it, selecting fruit and bouquets of flowers. But now it was empty and barren.

Farmers began to appear in the city with their bags, begging for food and shelter. There were groups of children gathered together. Sofia had no idea whether they were related. Or how it came to be that these children had neither mother nor father. They congregated around the fountains like pigeons. And like pigeons, they all sprung to their feet and began to beg for food when a person passed by.

The sight of the people on the street made the residents of the Capital more cautious and not less so. The truth was that everyone was hungry now. People were warned not to hoard food, but the warnings went unheeded. There was a mad rush for canned goods and supplies, which depleted whatever resources the grocers had. Everyone in the city lost ten pounds almost immediately.

At this point, many of the people who had remained within the country wished they had left. But this option was now an impossibility. The Enemy had closed all the borders.

There had always been homeless people in the Capital, of course. Sofia passed one homeless man on the way home from school most days. He wore a great mountain of clothes and, when it rained, a tricorn hat made out of newspaper on his head. And he had a cat that perched on his shoulder. He acted as though no one else in the world existed. There was no way he could work in a bank. His smell would be too disturbing, and of course, he would not be allowed to bring his cat.

But there were now homeless people from all walks of life in the Capital. The hotels were filled with rich families. The gymnasium where many of the popular sports tournaments were once held was turned into a temporary shelter. Cots and make-shift mattresses were laid all over the floor. Entire families slept on the floor.

The men who spent the night out on the street instead were well dressed. She saw a sixty-year-old man in an expensive black coat with a black fur collar sleeping on a bench. The parks were filled with young men who curled up on the grass at night and conversed about politics during the day.

But the country could not be considered to have fallen until the Capital had been captured. Everyone in the Capital felt they could save it. By saving the Capital, they would preserve their independence and culture. Everyone was expected to join the army.

Their idea of who could be a soldier radically changed when a famous poet named Malin Porchet enlisted. It had seemed crazy to people that a poet became a soldier. He was a poet, after all. Soldiers were young men who were too aimless to have ordinary jobs. They were third sons who hated school and lived at home. They needed order and risk. But now all the young scholars and visual artists and law students took it upon themselves to join the army and defend the city.

The president of Elysia was so different from the Enemy's Leader. He had been an actor when he was younger. He gave an almost ludicrous amount of funding to artists. He was known for being compassionate. He was sweet and pensive, lowering his head forward while considering a question. There was a deep sense of profundity and gravitas to it. It reminded people of his famous performance in the ballet of *Romeo and Juliet*, where he wept over the death of his co-star.

People liked that he was a less severe and masculine leader. They believed he was a gentle leader. They thought that having a leader who was so kind and compassionate would result in a wonderful country.

There was a famous photo of him with a fluffy black-and-white cat on his lap. This image clinched his victory. Here was a man who was not afraid to be affectionate with a cat.

At first, he promised they had nothing to worry about. The world would help them. Their allies would come to their aid. He gave emotional speeches that would make him cry. It was not, however, the best policy to have a weak leader during war-time. He seemed more terrified than anyone. The country was being taken, small town by small town. The smaller cities were all falling. People began to re-evaluate their feelings for him, as he continued to weep behind podiums.

Everyone went to see the procession of Elysian soldiers leaving for the Eastern Front. It was very much like a parade. Oh, they were so excited about parades in the Capital that there couldn't help but be an irrational aura of festivity around the event. People said that when the Enemy became aware of the number of civilians who were mobilizing, they would be frightened and retreat.

There was a band that came out in front of the procession. There had been efforts to create a national anthem. But nothing stuck. Instead, they played the song that had been written and popularized by the very large singer Claudette.

Everyone on their balconies began to take out their pots and pans and bang them in tune. The beat was infectious. The soldiers developed a hop in their step. They suddenly began to seem more like a cohesive unit. They became synchronized. The city was causing them to march off to war with a certain joy.

Women started throwing daisies at them. Some of the soldiers picked them up and tucked them into their buttonholes. The men began to be playful. They started blowing kisses at the girls.

Sofia would have liked to join in the fun, but she noticed her mother was standing quite still watching the scene. Clara reached into her pocket, pulled out a notebook, and recorded something in it. She then tucked it away, without a word, and continued to observe the crowd.

A CAT NAMED NAPOLEON

Sofia knew they would never leave. Her mother said the Capital was the love of her life. She had come to the city for the first time when she was fifteen. Her own mother, Sofia's grandmother, had thrown her father out of the country estate for cheating, so he went and purchased an enormous apartment in the Capital to feel good about himself.

Fifteen-year-old Clara went by train to visit his new apartment soon after. It was love at first sight. She realized immediately that this was where she was meant to be. She had always had a feeling she was in the wrong place. She felt ill at ease, but she had never understood why. But once she was in the city, she felt so in her own skin. She knew in that moment she should always trust her intuitions. If she did not feel right in a role, there was an alternative she was meant to seek out. She would never conform. Her father left Clara the apartment in his will. How could he not when she and the apartment so clearly belonged together?

When there was news of the army approaching the Capital, Clara was most worried about the apartment being taken away. She sat at the living room table, looking around. "They will want this apartment first. They can't know how large it is. We can't show them. They will come to see it. Because I am famous, they will think I have a beautiful apartment. I can't bear the thought of one of those ignorant brutes living here. Imagine them eating with my spoons and farting on my couch?"

To Sofia's delight, her mother announced they were going to the country to visit her grandmother, who still resided in the large rural childhood estate. Sofia jumped up and grabbed her book of folktales to read in the car.

"I wish you would read something more modern," Clara said, looking at the book.

"I wish you would not criticize everything I do."

"Good grief. You've become so contrary since the war. But I hear all the children are going quite mad. It ages children ten years."

Clara often said she'd had high hopes for Sofia because she had begun to read so early. But then, unfortunately, she had never developed as a reader.

That she was reading a children's book was particularly irksome. Clara liked to declare that she began reading serious philosophers when she was fourteen years old.

"Oh, Sofia, you can't always read children's books for the rest of your life. It will break my heart if you don't grow as a reader. There's so much out there for you to read and discover. Talking hares are a waste of time. They are there to amuse children. But they can't really teach you about the world. The modern world, Sofia! Don't you want to read books by living writers? With new ideas? Rational ideas? It's through reading that I became an adult. You can't learn anything in your enchanted forests."

Throughout this entire diatribe, Sofia looked at her mother with a blank expression on her face. When she saw that her mother had finished what she was going to say, she calmly cast her eyes back to the pages of her book and continued to read it. She would continue to read, even were she to grow carsick.

She liked that her mother disapproved of this book. It was a way for her to feel as if her reading had nothing at all to do with her mother. Which was not an easy thing to do, considering how attached her mother was to everything literary in the country. How could Sofia look at books, any pile of books, and not feel a certain resentment towards them?

And in any case, Clara was wrong. Because Sofia had evolved as a reader. It was simply that she liked to read the same book over and over. When you reread a book multiple times, you begin to find secrets in the text. You can dip your toe in the book and feel the delightful cold of the subtext.

Whenever she started a new book, it would seem like she was in a stranger's house. She was in an unfamiliar world. And she felt horribly uncomfortable.

She rather liked that no one else she knew had read the book of folktales. It had gone out of fashion. She liked the girls she met there. She felt connected to them. She was the girl in the stories.

You could prevail in this world, but you had to have pluck. She would open the book to find herself dressed in rags. And in a forest all alone. She was responsible for herself. Her family had caused her to be in her perilous state.

Mothers were never to be trusted. Many of the mothers in the tales had to give their daughters away. They had gone into debt. When their children were born, they were always spoken for. The mothers handed over their babies for gambling debts, for groceries, for clothes. For recipes and maps and keys.

Young girls who had been sent out into the world without a coin in their purse should not be judged for what they had to trade. The only thing they had were their babies.

These were the mothers whose intentions were good. The other mothers in the stories were wicked. They were mothers who lived for infanticide. They left their children in the woods for beasts to rip apart. They left them on cliffs for the weather to kill. They gave them to pirates with instructions to leave them in the sea. They gave them to hunters to slay as though they were beasts. They handed them over to travelling salesmen and told them to take them to the far reaches of the earth to abandon them.

It was then the little girl wandered around by herself. She met her true family. She encountered a blind child who could put people to sleep for a hundred years when she sang. She met a three-legged dog that was in love with a boy who beat him with a stick. But how can anyone control who they fall in love with? She met a donkey that could tell the future. But he could only foretell bad events. So he had been tied to a tree to keep him from walking up to women and telling them which of their children would never reach old age.

Sofia loved going to visit her grandmother's home. It was enormous. You could not live in a place that sprawling in the city. The grounds around the house were characterized by a bohemian, fairy tale–like squalor. All the plants and flowers had been growing there for years. They had been there since her mother was a little girl.

The garden and the house had intermingled. There were rose branches that seemed to come right out of the bricks. If you were to pull the climbing vines off the house, it would fall apart. Birds had made nests under the gables of the house. The statues were covered in moss.

Her grandmother never paid attention to her mother the way other people did. She seemed oblivious to her daughter's political leanings and her writings. Instead she treated Clara as though she were a young girl. And her mother began to act like a very young girl in the country. She sulked and complained. And she let everybody take care of her needs as though she were a child.

She never had anything good to say about her childhood. She was a polemicist. So she was either for or against specific topics.

"I have no idea how I grew up in that household and managed to be intelligent. I must be the first intelligent person born in that family in two hundred years. They are all so lazy. I can't stand being around it."

But Sofia didn't find her grandmother lazy at all. Her grandmother seemed patient instead. She had time to show Sofia many things.

That day, they went into the greenhouse to plant together. They put on large hats with wide brims and large boots. Her grandmother gave her a pair of blue gardening gloves to protect her hands because there were flowers that bit. "Flowers are not peaceful. People think because they are so pretty, they must be kind. I once had a rose bush that was so angry all the time. It would attack my friends, but I didn't know why. I think it was wicked, and there was nothing I could do about it. You have to cut their heads off or they don't grow. Maybe that's why they are so unkind. Look at these snapdragons. I plant them for the fairies."

"Do you believe in fairies?"

"Of course. Who doesn't? It's only because you live in the city that you don't see them."

"What do they look like?"

"Much bigger than you would expect. They hang around in the summer, and they never wear shoes."

Her grandmother had lunch brought out to a table in the garden. She had baked the cookies herself. The girl had assumed all pastries came from a bakery. There was a moss-covered statue of a boy, and water was trickling out of his penis. Time went slower at her grandmother's house.

The house was meant to belong to her. Her grandmother said she would leave it to her. Her mother had inherited the apartment in the city, so it was only fair that she should inherit property too. Her grandmother was sure Clara would put the house up for sale. But now, of course, the Enemy would most likely seize the property, and it would no longer be in their family at all.

"I can't bear the idea of it being lived in by a stranger. There are so many magical beings creeping around here. They would be hostile to a new owner. The beings know you. I am going to whisper to the tree creatures to protect you."

"Please don't," said Sophia.

"Why ever not?"

"Because I don't want to see a naked tree person. I would die of fright."

"When they come, you will have already seen so much horror that they won't be terrifying at all."

"Still."

Her grandmother stood up, leading Sofia to the edge of the woods. The house and garden were in a clearing. Despite being in a cloistered setting, the clearing was bright and airy, and was always bathed in a magnificent light. The light around the house became different colours during the day. It was white in the morning, greenish blue in the late afternoon. Then for a moment it turned pink before it became the colours of autumn and death, orange and red and yellow, like the dregs of orange juice that had sunk to the bottom of the glass. Sofia and her grandmother stood at the edge of the woods, looking at the trees together.

"There was once a tree that moved around in the woods," her grandmother said as they inched forward. "There are trees that are like that. They aren't really trees, though. They are a form of troll that looks like a tree. Their roots aren't that deep. They tiptoe around in the forest at night."

"Oh, how ghastly, Grandmother."

"They can be quite dangerous. If you are sitting on the roots, they can pull themselves out of the ground and strangle you. They can stay in the same spot for years. They stay in the same spot for many, many nights. Then they tiptoe closer to the house."

"How close do they come?" Sofia asked. "Please tell me they keep a respectful distance."

"I once caught one reaching through the window, trying to get to your mother's crib and snatch her out. They were always after your mother. I didn't know why the woods thought she belonged to them. I was always arguing with them about it. Maybe she really did belong to them. She certainly doesn't belong to me."

If Sofia's mother had been sitting with them, she would have told the grandmother to please stop talking nonsense. But she rarely sat with them. She went to her old room to write or read a book. Her mother found it hard to stay awake when they were in the country. The lack of stimulation made her feel as though she were already unconscious. Her body would turn itself off.

Once, they found her sleeping as though she had drunk a tiny glass of poison and collapsed. She was lying half off the couch with a book open on the ground. Although she was ordinarily a light sleeper, nothing woke her up in the country. She once told Sofia that there was nothing more physically exhausting than being bored. At the moment, there were two cats that had climbed up and were sleeping on her.

"Look into the forest. Look, really look. They will come out. The trees each have a spirit. Sometimes they sneak out of their trunks."

"How do you know it wasn't just a hunter looking for a deer?"

"You would never mistake a tree person for a hunter! You'd be much more likely to mistake one for a deer. They move in the same way. They are skittish. They move so quickly. They disappear like fleeting thoughts."

The closer she was to the trees, the more her grandmother's speech became magic. She believed, like the eldest citizens, that Elysians once spoke the language of the trees. Through time, however, the language became a more human-like one. But the trees understood every word of Elysian. And it was possible for them to whisper Elysian in your ear. The language had always been preserved specifically because of this connection to the trees.

So her grandmother spoke to the trees and asked them to take care of Sofia when the war came. For when Elysians asked the trees to hide them, the trees always would. When the children tried to climb them, they would lower their branches so they could get their footing. They offered companionship to children.

Before Elysians had their own country, they were punished for practising their religion. The Enemy regarded everything the Elysians did as slightly barbaric and grotesque. Even indecent. Their religion wasn't a religion; it was witchcraft and superstition. It was embarrassing and infantile. It was overly sexual and celebrated the basest of human instincts. The Enemy had always had a problem with the sex in the Elysian culture.

There were rituals that had been banned as pornographic. There was one where young girls and boys ran around naked in the forest, wearing wreaths with leaves in their hair and waving their arms around like branches. They consumed psychedelic berries that made the branches of the trees writhe like snakes on Medusa's head. Music was played. As soon as it stopped, the girls would rush to the nearest trees and fling their arms around them and pepper them with kisses.

In the summertime, girls would be dressed up in flouncy white dresses, and they would go down to the lake en masse to bob for apples. Their dresses would float up to the surface of the water, all around them, so that they would look, to a bird in the sky, like lily pads.

If they got an apple, it meant they would marry happily. If they didn't, well, spinsterhood or a bad marriage was on its way. Her grandmother said when she was younger, a girl in the village had drowned herself, bobbing desperately for an apple. People in the village soothed themselves by saying that the girl was most likely going to be married to someone cruel.

• • •

Clara's father had internalized the hatred towards the Elysians. He wanted nothing to do with anything traditionally Elysian. He refused to allow dishes with folkloric insignia on them. He despised when his wife told Clara folktales about the talking beasts in the woods.

He hated when Clara's mother made offerings to the woods. And when she claimed that the woods were alive, and that the trees could protect or turn against you. He did everything to turn Clara against these beliefs.

He had every intention of sending Clara abroad to be educated, but then the Great War broke out. There was nowhere on the continent that was safe. For the first time in his adult life, he was forced to stay put. That was yet another reason why Clara remembered the war affectionately. She was able to spend it with her father. They were trapped inside the apartment together. She hadn't even worried about the war and the bombings.

As Sofia and her grandmother headed back to the house, small cats, in the manner of wild hares, darted out of their way. Her grandmother had begun to allow a colony of feral cats to proliferate on her property. She had a different name for every cat in the house. And she never mixed up or forgot any of them.

Her grandmother was always having funerals for the cats. She loved them, but they were always dying tragic deaths that were, in many ways, her fault, though she never thought of these deaths that way. She closed a drawer while a cat was still inside. And it suffocated to death. She ran over a fair number of them in her car. Her grandmother never considered herself complicit in anything. Her grandmother considered herself to be the most innocent person on the planet. Because she had been cheated on by her husband, she was a tragic victim for the rest of her life.

"You know, I don't think one cat can tell the difference between itself and all other cats. Every time it sees another cat, it thinks it is looking in the mirror. Some days it is more beautiful than it remembered. And some days it isn't."

"What if it sees itself being run over by a car in the street?" Clara asked without opening her eyes.

"I imagine it interprets it as something that happened in a dream."

The cat was tearing a page out of the dictionary. It ran off with the page in its mouth. Sofia wondered which word it was looking for the definition of.

"What is that cat's name?" Sofia asked.

"Charlebois. It's the name of an army general. If I'd had a son, I was going to name him Charlebois or Napoleon. I wanted to give my child a courageous name."

"Why didn't you name me after Joan of Arc?" Clara said, sitting up and stretching.

"I named you after my mother."

"Incredible. If I were a boy, I'd have been named after Alexander the Great. But since I'm a girl, I'm named after someone with arthritis."

And unexpectedly, at least for Sofia, both women began to laugh.

Later in the afternoon, Sofia walked into the kitchen to find her mother and grandmother in a huge fight.

"You are all abandoning ship!" Clara cried. "You have no love for this country. Even if it is dying, why would you leave anybody on their deathbed? Is that the only thing you know how to do? If we all run off, there won't be a country left."

"You are staying here because you are important here. And you think you will be more important if you live through the war and experience all the horror of it. You will finally perhaps have the subject for a new book. Yes, I see that. But I think you should allow me to take Sofia with me. Even if it is just for a year. Until we are able to see how things are going."

"You will use her as a hostage. You will use her to make me come after her. And if I don't, you will tell her that I abandoned her. You will teach her that I am selfish and a whore. The way you did with my father to me. You are always trying to stop us from having lives. You will use any excuse to get us out of the Capital. Because you know the Capital represents happiness to us."

"If you are going to stay in Elysia, you should both come stay here, where at least the tress will be able to protect and hide you. Or they will do their best to, in any case."

"If you are so convinced that the trees will protect us, then why in the world are you leaving the country?"

"I am old. I have lived through one war, and I won't do it again. I can't live without my deliveries. I can't bear the austerity anymore. I need my chocolates. I want to spend my last years feeling safe."

"Do you know how it looks that my own mother is leaving the country? Especially when I have gone on the radio to tell people not to leave?"

"Who cares how anything looks when you are dead?"

"Uggh! I can't stand it. No, I'm not allowing you to take my daughter with you. Because this country will need children when the war is over. We have so much hope in that generation.

We have worked so hard to give them a country filled with art and philosophy and rational thinking. So they could be proud of where they came from. Not ashamed like I always was. Come on, Sofia. We are leaving. I will not let you be raised by this woman. She will make you old before your time."

Sofia rushed around gathering her things. She wanted to get out as soon as possible. The longer she took, the more opportunity her mother had to launch insults at her grandmother. Sofia found it insupportable to listen to her grandmother be insulted. Her grandmother seemed to her the kindest woman in the world. That her mother was accusing her of being a monster was almost impossible to stomach. It was completely screwing with her sense of everything sacred.

Her mother took her hand and pulled her as she marched with determination to the car. Because her mother was wearing heels, it gave her the effect of wobbling back and forth like a sailboat in the wind. They got to the car. Sofia scrambled into the back seat. Her grandmother leaned in the doorway of the house.

Her mother got in the car. And just as soon as she sat down, she leapt up from the seat and jumped back out. She ran back to her mother and threw herself in her arms. Sofia watched in disbelief. Everything her mother was doing was completely strange and out of the ordinary.

Her grandmother held her as though she were a child. She patted her back and murmured, "You will be okay. We will all be okay. We will see each other again. Don't worry about me. You know best. You have always known best. You have always understood the world so much better than me."

"I love you, Mama. I am sorry for everything. I'm sorry if I wasn't always there. I'm sorry if I seemed like a spoiled brat. I have always been a spoiled brat. But I love you so much, Mama."

Clara let out a loud cry. Which was shocking to Sofia. As she had very rarely heard her mother be upset or emotional in that way. Then Clara pulled herself from her mother. She ran to the car, her face covered in tears. She climbed in the car and looked straight ahead, ready to pull away from the house without looking again at her mother, as though it would kill her to see her again.

Clara didn't speak another word until they were on the highway. Her face had returned to its former dignified nonchalance. "It's a trap, that house. Every time I visit, she makes me feel as though I have to leave home all over again. I feel like a child again, and that I'm choosing my father over her. Mothers never forgive anything. Perhaps I owe her my success to some extent. It was by being the opposite of her that I became who I am."

"Imagine if I said things like that about you!"

"It would be normal, I suppose."

"You think you are a genius. And everything you do is more important than what anyone else does."

Her mother opened her mouth and lifted her hands off the steering wheel—as if to protest what Sofia had just said. But then looked as though she couldn't actually argue with what Sofia had just said.

"Oh so what?"

They both started laughing. Sofia put her hands over her mouth.

SPRINKLE ME IN ICING SUGAR

BEFORE I DIE

Sofia and her mother were walking together to a bakery in hopes of getting a loaf of bread when the air-raid sirens went off. Sofia did not know what to do. They had practised how to respond to air raids at school. They all went under their desks and put their arms over their heads. Sofia always liked those exercises. It got her out of doing tedious schoolwork. It was magical. All of a sudden, schoolwork didn't mean anything. She liked being tucked up under her desk. It was as though she was giving herself a huge hug. She had always supposed the Enemy would arrive during math class. She had no idea they might come on a Saturday. Surely the Enemy liked to enjoy Saturday as much as the next person.

The bombs made everything else silent all around her. She could not hear the words coming out of her mother's mouth. She could not hear the sound of things falling and hitting.

At that moment, there was nothing you could hear other than the sound of the bombs striking. She remembered that moment as being completely quiet. The reason was that she could not hear any of the regular noises that surrounded her.

She looked at her mother, who was yelling. But no sound reached her. No matter what her mother did with her expressions. No matter how extreme and gruesome she made them. Everyone had their mouths open, but Sofia couldn't hear any of their screaming. It was as though everyone were trying to be a gargoyle.

There were stones falling. But when they hit the ground, they silently exploded into dust, as though they were made out of snow. She saw a car quietly roll over, as though it were a bear amusing itself.

She saw windows being smashed and the shards breaking loose. And falling like a strange hailstorm. She might as well be under water. Even when she was under the water at the swimming pool, she could still hear muted grunts and squeals from above the surface. It was hard to believe anything monumental was happening. As she was most certain that history made a lot of noise.

Her mother grabbed her by the wrist. They began running. Even though her feet didn't make any noise as they were hitting the ground. No one waited for street lights or crossed in the proper place. She didn't know where they were going. Her instinct would have been to run home. If you were going to die, she thought it would be best to die with a cup of hot chocolate in your own bed.

She saw a dog barking. But his barks were the opposite of sound. What if it were possible to yell and have silence come out of your throat? And your silence was louder than all the surrounding sounds.

There was a sudden cloud of dust and debris. It had turned the corner and stepped out onto the street. Sofia closed her eyes and put her hands over her face. She had no idea where she was anymore, how far they had run, or even what direction they had gone in. When the storm subsided, she did not know where she would be. She could be in the same spot, or she might be a hundred miles away. When the cloud moved on and dissipated, she found she was still standing next to her mother.

Her mother's face was completely coated in white. It made her look like a clown. Sofia imagined she must look exactly like a clown too. She wanted to laugh, but she did not know whether they were sad clowns or jovial ones.

"You look like a clown from the Orpheum Theatre," Sofia said.

"You look like a sugared patisserie, my dear. Let's get away from here."

The street was unrecognizable now. The tops of the buildings could not be seen because of the dust, and there were stones and debris all over the street. There was a woman walking in a fur coat and bare feet. There was a woman on her knees in the middle of the street. She had a carton full of eggs, and they were all broken. She didn't want to run anymore. She just wanted to cry over the eggs.

When the sound of another fighter jet pierced the sky above them, Clara and Sofia ran into the grocer's. He led them into the back of the shop. He locked the door behind him. There were jars of peaches on a shelf. They were inching forward to the edge of the shelf, threatening to fall off. The girl hadn't seen peaches in a jar in such a while. There were small pots of jam everywhere. The grocer took a jar of peaches down from the shelf. It was sealed with a yellow rag that was itself the colour of peaches.

He took off the lid. He handed Sofia a fork. She stuck it into the jar and dug it into a peach. It was so full of flavour. She forgot about how much the small room was shaking. There was nothing she could do about that. But she could take the moment to enjoy her peaches.

When it was quiet at last, her mother took her hand and walked her through the streets.

"It's important to witness everything that happens. Not everyone will be here once the war is over. It's everyone's duty to witness as much as they can. Because we don't know who will survive to tell the story. Your job is to be a witness. You can't be too young to be a witness. It's good to be a younger witness. You'll have the memories for longer."

"But I'm frightened. I'm worried a bomb will drop on my head."

Clara paused for a moment. "Me too."

Her mother came to sleep with Sofia when there was the sound of bombing at night. Sofia's bed was small. And there was no way they could lie in it without squishing their bodies together. She would at first feel so suffocated by her mother's proximity. There was no longer any room for her to move her limbs and body. Her body was forced into the parameters of her mother's body.

Her mother's breath put her into a deep slumber. It was like an opiate. And the lingering smell of her mother's perfume and shampoo permeated the air. Her skin smelled like tobacco—it smelled like the inside of a leather purse that was used to carry around money but also makeup, like a kit of blush with a tiny mirror that showed you a tiny version of what men see when they look at you.

After a few days' respite, there was a brief noisy time of bombs being dropped. The opera house was destroyed. They did not know why an opera house would be targeted expressly. So they assumed it had to do with chance. There was great mourning for the building. The stone animals that had decorated the building lay murdered, in pieces, on the ground. It was after the bombing of the opera house that the country surrendered. The army was in disarray. They were clearly going to have to give up at some point. And nobody wished to see more of the buildings in their beautiful city demolished. The Capital and the country surrendered the next week.

It was almost a blessing that the decision to send the children away came so quickly. It didn't allow the children time to panic. It didn't allow the parents time to worry. They all had to act immediately. As long as they didn't pause, they wouldn't be able to allow their hearts to break.

There was the sound of little feet hurrying down staircases all over the city. They were all rushing out at dawn. They were trying to get to the train first. They were holding the hands of teddy bears. But some bears panicked and snatched on to the gate to stay behind. The children screamed back at the bears to come with them. But the bears did not. The scarves of the children flew behind them. The children blinked hard. Their eyes were not used to the morning breeze. Some of them were still dreaming. They fell asleep in the backs of cars.

A PHILOSOPHER HAS WHAT TO SAY

Sofia stood on the country road, with the Goose next to her, pausing for a moment to rest and observe her surroundings.

The war had caused some sounds to come loose from their origins. The sound of dogs barking travelled for miles and sometimes days. She was so used to the dissociated howling of dogs passing by her that she barely registered it or worried when she heard it.

Sometimes she heard prayers. They had gone unanswered—that was the reason they were still flying about in the wind, like old sheets of newspaper no one was going to read. Sofia felt it was inappropriate to listen to them. So she tried not to pay them any mind. "Please, please, please don't let me die. Not today. Let me at least live until my eighteenth birthday." Who were children wishing to?

"Don't let me die. I'm only seven . . . Take care of my dog. Please let my dog be safe. Please let him know I didn't want to leave him behind . . . If I stay in the same place, my mother will find me. Please let her find me."

It was also strange that so many children prayed to their mothers. When you left the city, all she could hear in the wind was mommy, mommy, mommy. They each were members of their very own monastic religion where their mothers were the one true God. But Sofia had never once prayed to her mother to come save her. If she was to pray, she would pray that she would be able to find the Black Market. She could not go back to her mother's arms. She had to find her mother's manuscript instead, and the only place she could imagine it being was at the Black Market. It was where everything illegal and forbidden and delightful ended up. It was where she could find peace again.

And for a moment, Sofia became lost in a daydream of what she would find at the Black Market. She would find a light blue hairbrush with a white rose on the back. Identical to the one her mother had always used to brush both their hair. And a silk kimono, like the one her mother used to wear all Sunday afternoon.

She would find a record of *The Swan with a Broken Neck*. It was her mother's favourite symphony. Her mother would turn the volume up on the Victrola when she put it on. The air in the apartment became thick with music. She would lie on her bed with her arms spread, as though she were on a raft, floating on the music.

And the book, of course, the book. Sofia needed to get to the Black Market.

"Do you hear that?" Sofia asked the Goose. "It's the sound of a baby crying."

They followed the sound to a rusted tin can on the side of the road that was half filled with rainwater. As she bent over to peer into the can, the water inside trembled slightly, and she heard the crying again. It had somehow settled in the water—like algae. Sofia picked up the can with her hand. She held it straight out from her, and the crying became louder and louder. Then she dumped the can out on the ground. And the crying grew faint and then disappeared.

"My feet are so sore," Sofia exclaimed. "I can barely walk anymore."

"It is all the fault of the physicists," the Goose said.

"What is the fault of the physicists?"

"For creating a world where it is so hard to get anywhere. I wish they hadn't made gravity so heavy. Otherwise, we could just float along the road."

"Physicists did not create the world; they merely explain what is already here."

"Not at all. At first everyone thought it was God. But then they realized everything had a scientific explanation and origin."

"Do you not realize that gravity existed before the theory of gravity? The apple fell on Newton's head, and then he came up with the theory of gravity."

"No. It is quite the other way around. Newton was sitting there, having nothing in particular to think about. So he was able to let his mind wander and come up with things. The second he came up with the theory of gravity, an apple, which would otherwise have been floating around, fell directly on his head."

"If that were true, then I could change the nature of the universe simply by coming up with a theory of my own."

"Are you a physicist?"

"Well, no."

"You cannot come up with rules of physics, then. You have to be a board-certified physicist to be able to write the rules."

"And what is it that you do? Other than being a goose, of course."

"I'm a public intellectual."

"Ah," she said. "Let us head this way."

"Is it in the direction of the Capital?" asked the Goose.

"No, the opposite, actually."

"You might have mistaken me for someone without a direction, but I left my farm and everything I knew with the express purpose of heading to the Capital. I am going to the Capital in order to deliver a manifesto about literature."

"Well, it's a fine time you chose to see the Capital. No one would ever say it is tourist season right now. The opera is not mounting anything new. As it has been bombed to smithereens."

"Impossible!"

"Hardly. I saw it with my own eyes. It's surprising how unremarkable it now is as rubble. It's hardly any different from a pile of rubble from a factory or a slaughterhouse."

"Monstrous! What would you call that? The aesthetics of evil. The dandification of evil. The sanitization of evil. The commodification of evil. The compartmentalization of evil. The algebraization of evil. The specification of evil. The domestication of evil."

"It's the democracy of rubble, I suppose."

"I have a proposal about literature. I have been working on it at the farm. More or less in solitude. I mean, I was surrounded by geese the whole time I was writing it. But I could not share it with them. I have spent my life nurturing a literary ability that I did not share with any other goose. And it is said that if you are in the country or a small town, then you must head to the Capital. The Capital is the Mecca for scattered geniuses."

"Where did you hear this? From a goat?"

"It is something we artists are attuned to. Like flying south in the winter."

"Oh, I too want nothing more than to return to the Capital. I live there with my mother in the most extraordinary apartment. You are welcome to come and live with us. There's always room in our apartment. We had dinner parties with thirty guests sometimes. We can't go there now. I've lost my mother's manuscript. She will be furious with me. I have to figure out what to do."

"Shall we return to where you lost it?"

"Oh no, it's impossible. There are soldiers there shooting children."

"I don't understand. There's a war on, and you think your mother will get upset at you over such a trivial thing?"

"She was very specific that I not lose it. You don't understand her relationship to her work."

"So you have no intention of returning to the Capital?"

"I shall go to the Black Market and see if my mother's manuscript is there before going back."

"Surely you can return to your mother without the book."

"You have clearly never met my mother. She expected me to get the manuscript out of the country and will be upset that I failed. Her work is more important to her than her child. Do you know that she never wanted a child at all?

"No, of course not. I know nothing at all about her."

"Well, now you do. She wrote a book in which she said that a woman who becomes a mother cannot ever be a true philosopher. And then I came along. And she always treated me as though I were an embodiment of her failings in life. She only began to be nice to me once the war broke out. Because I suddenly had a purpose in her eyes. Without the book, I will use up whatever goodwill I have earned. I can't bear for her to look at me the way she did before the war. You have no idea how much it ruins one's confidence to be despised by one's own mother."

"I thought loving their children was the one thing you could count on mothers for."

"Well, you have heard wrong. There is no one worse than a mother. They never forgive you for the pain of childbirth. As a result, they criticize everything you do."

"Hmmm. Fascinating."

"In any case, there are marvellous items at the Black Market."

"I can't imagine there will be anything I want."

"There will be a large ham covered in honey and pineapples. There will be a small cloth bag of spices that you can hold up to your nose to make yourself sneeze. And there will undoubtedly be fruit covered in chocolate. You have no idea how much chocolate improves the taste of fruit."

"I am a goose. I enjoy roots and worms."

"There will be record players and records. And you can hear a famous Elysian singer. Madame Clemence!"

"And does she have the voice of an angel?"

"Oh no. That kind of singing is not in vogue at all. She sounds more like she has a frog in her throat. Literally a frog."

"Ah, I see! Even better."

"We can get tap shoes. They must have a child-sized pair of tap shoes for you. You'll sound like a hailstorm when you walk."

"A rain of bullets?"

"Yes, I suppose. A rain of bullets."

She paused for a moment, then continued, as though undeterred. "We will be able to buy stockings. The fanciest stockings, made out of silk. With stripes or flowers on them. And it will feel as though we are dipping our legs into a bowl of whipped cream."

"What need do I have for stockings?"

"We will get you a cravat made out of silk and dyed a black as dark as the midnight sky. And when people see you wearing such a cravat, they will know you are sophisticated and serious. And they will defer to you for important philosophical questions."

"Oh, I should like that."

"They will know you are a distinguished goose. And not just a farmyard animal. No one will even think of eating you."

"Oh, yes."

"We can get ourselves cigars. You would love a cigar. You will have a large cloud of smoke that follows on top of you, protecting you from the sun. You will be in the shade."

"Yes. Yes. To remain in the shade is a proper gentlemanly activity. One doesn't want to be outside in the blazing sun like a peasant."

"And there will be books to read. The most forbidden and pornographic books will be there. There is no thrill like reading what you are not supposed to read. My mother had books, and they were filled with people who took their clothes off on every page and tried to fit their bodies together in the strangest ways. You will see when you read them. It is as though you have swallowed noodles. And the noodles feel as though they are squirming around inside you."

"That does not seem appealing."

"But that is what the Black Market is for. There are sensations you feel that are really an acquired taste. At first they will feel unpleasant and make you uncomfortable, but then you start to really like them. You can get drugs too."

"Drugs!"

"I've never tried them. I will hold a tiny spoon of cocaine to your nose. And you will inhale it, and you will feel as though you are as tall and strong as a soldier."

"Now you've gone too far. You are trying to sell me on knick-knacks and trinkets! How could any of those transitory items compare to my calling? I must go to the Capital to deliver my manifesto."

"If you wanted to go to the Capital so badly, why didn't you object to getting into the truck with me? We were clearly going in the other direction."

"I had no idea at all which direction the Capital was in. How would I know such a thing? Do you think geese are given access to maps? I'm afraid I haven't a clue where anything in the world is outside of the farmyard and the pasture of said farm and its stream. In fact, I could not say what was beyond the stream. Beyond the wet, as we liked to say. No, I was relying on you. I could see, right from the first moment, that you were from the Capital. So I thought I would accompany you, as a travel companion. Directly to the Capital."

"May I ask you a question?"

"Well, you just did."

"How did you know I am from the Capital? I am in disguise."

"Geese are very conscious of feet. They are distinguishing features. And perhaps I was already taken in by your patent leather shoes. And had concluded you were posh and had never stepped foot on a farm before. They are made for smooth concrete, marble tiles, varnished wood, plastic tiles, porcelain tiles, manicured grass in a park perhaps. But it wasn't just the shoes."

"Well, what was it? I should know, in order to avoid soldiers knowing."

"You have an attitude that I intuitively understand is one that is manufactured in the Capital. Or to put it simply, you have an air of superiority."

"I have no such thing. If you can't abide my snobbery, you should not go to the Capital then. You will find there are much grander snobs there. I am not even considered a snob."

"That is only because you are so young. You have not been able to properly develop your snobbery. But it will come. Why be ashamed of it? I aspire to being a snob myself. And every snob needs a manifesto. So there is nothing at the Black Market that is of interest to me."

"Ink, my friend! You need ink and paper to write with."

"I was going to deliver it from memory, as they say."

"You'll need bottles of black ink to express your words. Otherwise, people will think you are mad and talking to yourself."

Sofia felt the little piece of paper she was carrying in her inner pocket. She took it out for a moment and inhaled. The smell of paper reminded her of the Capital and safety. She experienced a flicker of hope, and she tucked the paper back into her coat.

À LA BOTTOM

Every home in the Capital was filled with books. Almost everyone had a writer in the family. As soon as a child learned to read, they were forced to read their aunt's or grandfather's book. And when children met in elementary school, they compared which writers they were related to.

Children often aspired to be the most famous writer in their family. Sofia did not bother. There was no point in trying. Her mother had set the bar too high.

Clara had written the country's most renowned feminist text, *Are Women People?*, when she was twenty-nine years old.

Clara was an incredible speaker. Although not everyone in the country had read her book on feminism, they had all certainly heard her speak. She was intoxicating. She was elegant and forceful. She raged against all the ways in which women were held back and underestimated.

In many ways, a person had to be angry in order to speak eloquently. Anger was an ingredient that turned language into something extraordinary and vivid.

She had a very famous speech about how different her life had been from her mother's. She spoke about how her mother knew nothing about the world, had had no choice other than to be a homemaker, had a child too young, and was at the mercy of her husband. Her mother was uneducated. And she was superstitious and religious. These were aspects of Elysian culture that were keeping women down.

She, unlike her mother, had had an extraordinary life filled with opportunity because she had rejected the antiquated notions of what an Elysian woman should be like. She would not accept this domestication. Then she uttered one of her most famous lines: I am a wolf, and I refuse to be considered a dog.

She was never intimidated by anyone. You could tell she believed she was the most intelligent person in Elysia. And since she believed this, everyone else believed it too. You believed what she said while she said it. It was wildly attractive to see such arrogance in a woman. It was a sort of novelty.

She had a shelf filled with speaking and cultural and humanitarian awards. She had seven honorary degrees. She had one from Paris too. This was the one she was most proud of. It was very difficult for Elysians to be taken seriously beyond their country's borders. She had impressed the French. This had happened during a quiet news cycle. It became legendary, as some events inexplicably do.

She was invited to participate in government discussions about allocations of funding to grant organizations. She was on the jury for the annual Clara Bottom Prize, established for promising young women thinkers.

There was a way of dressing—particularly wearing a tan coat with the collar popped up—that was referred to as dressing à la

Bottom. To complete this look, young girls carried books in their hands and smoked cigarettes. They studied and went to university. Clara Bottom had made it incredibly chic to be an intellectual.

Sofia lived with her mother and father in the enormous penthouse apartment that Sofia's grandfather had bought in one of the oldest buildings on one of the most glamorous blocks in the Capital.

Everything in the apartment was expensive and noteworthy. The walls were covered in paintings by artists of some renown in their country. And the furniture was carved by the finest Elysian craftsmen from the turn of the last century. Even the plants in the flat were famous. There was a fern Clara had brought back from Paris. She had been having lunch with the president and his wife. She had commented on how lovely a fern hanging from their ceiling was. The president's wife immediately had it taken down and packaged up for her. Now it took up half the kitchen and shed leaves over everything. Guests always pointed to it and said, "Is this the president of France's fern?"

"It's a nuisance, isn't it?" Clara would reply, indicating perhaps that the French had nothing on the Elysians.

Her mother was very conscious of being a public figure. She always dressed up. No matter how simple the errand she was going on, she spent the time it took to doll herself up. Every moment of her life was important. A trip to the marketplace was a special event. Anyone who ran into her at the marketplace came away feeling that life was very glamorous.

She was short, which she corrected by wearing heels everywhere, and buxom, which she accentuated by wearing form-fitting skirts and jackets. She had jet-black hair she wore in a fashionable bun and to which she pinned the most elaborate hats. Her mother always put herself together so elegantly, it seemed as though she had been born in the outfit she had on.

It wasn't that her mother was the most beautiful woman in the room, but she commanded the most attention.

She was followed by a trail of cigarette smoke. It was as though the cigarette smoke were a fine fur shawl she wore around herself. In almost every memory Sofia had of her mother, she was standing in a storm cloud of cigarette smoke, picking bits of tobacco off her tongue with her fingernails.

Clara Bottom was called on to speak on all sorts of political matters. She often publicly lamented being the only woman who was called on to speak. But Sofia knew she loved it. And after giving a speech, her mother was always in a such a good mood that she was sweeter with Sofia, for a time.

BABES IN THE WOODS

When Sofia arrived with the Goose at her grandmother's house, she wanted to collapse on the doorstep, she was so relieved. They had finally arrived at a house Sofia could relax in and feel safe. She would have preferred that her grandmother be home, of course, but she had left the country months before. So when Sofia and the Goose entered her grandmother's house, she was shocked by the disorder it was in. There were piles of clothes on the shelves and floor. There were dirty dishes all over the sinks and counters.

It smelled different too. Her grandmother had always had a particular smell of lavender and herbs. It made her happy and relaxed. But now the house smelled rank, of rotten food, smelly feet, and cigarette smoke.

Before she could make sense of it, there were two boys, slightly older than her, standing in front of her in the kitchen.

The larger dark-haired boy was dressed in the most peculiar outfit. He was wearing an older man's suit that was much too big for him. It was also very strange to see a child dressed as an adult. It gave him an air of superiority. Sofia realized at that moment that he must have got the suit out of one of the closets. It was one of her grandfather's suits. Her grandmother never threw anything away. She had a sentimental attachment to everything. She thought all objects had souls.

The other boy was fair and had a softer, gentler face. He was wearing a green blouse and slacks. These belonged to her grandmother. He had cut the bottoms of the slacks with a pair of scissors, and they had a raggedy edge. She noticed he also had on a pair of her grandmother's grey silk slippers with roses embroidered on the toes and kitten heels. He slid across the kitchen floor with them. He seemed to be enjoying the clothes.

"My name is Abelard," said the boy in her grandmother's clothes. "And this is the inimitable Balthazar."

"And just who the fuck are you?" Balthazar asked. "This is private property."

"I am Sofia. This is my house."

The boys looked at each other uncomfortably.

"Bullshit. You can't come in here. It belongs to us," said Balthazar.

"This does not belong to you at all. It belongs to my grandmother."

"Your grandmother is not here," Balthazar said. "There is no one here but us. So it doesn't belong to her. If the soldiers are seizing everyone's homes, nobody's home belongs to them anymore."

"What indeed is a grandmother?" said Abelard. "If you want to stay with us, there will be less food. We will have to divide it up another way."

"But she has a goose. We can make a meal out of it. And soup that will last four days."

At that, the Goose began to squawk.

"You can't eat him. He's extremely intelligent," Sofia said, stepping in front of the Goose.

"He is your pet?"

"I am not a pet!"

"He is not a pet. We are companions. We have decided to travel together."

"You know," Balthazar said, "I am beginning to think you are not quite right in the head."

"That fascinates me," Abelard interjected. "That in itself is a reason to let her stay. I am intrigued by madness. I often think of myself as being afflicted by a certain lunacy."

"You aren't mad at all," Balthazar sneered. "You're desperate for attention. And you'll do anything to stand out."

"We can't throw her out if this is her grandmother's house," Abelard said excitedly. "She's bound to become angry. She'll feel hard done by. She'll turn us in."

"We would have to kill her," Balthazar said. "I'm not there yet. And she has a certain charm. She travels with a goose."

Sofia had always been too shy to engage with boys. Especially boys her age. Whenever they came close to her, it always seemed to remind her that she was a girl. As though that were something distasteful. Now here they were.

A boy once came up to her on the way home from school. He was holding his fist out in front of him. Not in a threatening way. More like it was on fire and he was trying to keep it away from the rest of his body. He stepped in front of her. Opened his fist and tossed a large spider on her. It fell onto Sofia's coat. Squiggled around hysterically as though it were looking for its limbs.

Sofia had a horror of bugs, the way children who had grown up in the city did. And she shook and began screaming wildly. And for a week afterwards, she kept checking her body, never able to be absolutely sure the spider was not somewhere on her.

And now, she had the distinct feeling, there was a spider creeping around the crevices of her body. Perhaps in one of her pockets. Perhaps in her stocking. And she was certain the boys had put it there.

These strange boys did not seem to be intimidated by Sofia. They did not seem to be upset in any way that they were in the presence of a girl. They did not seem at all unnerved. They stared at her.

She and the Goose sat next to each other, completely immobile and prim. There could be no unaccounted-for movements with their arms and legs. They were always being judged. It seemed safer to remain as still as mannequins in a store window. How physically demanding and awkward it was to allow yourself to be judged. As a girl, you always felt like an unwelcome guest. Even if you were in your own house.

She looked at the Goose. He was holding his head up as high as was humanly possible. He was obviously under strain. She wondered whether he was trying to pass himself off as a swan.

Seeing the Goose's terrible insecurity made her wonder if her own insecurity was causing the Goose to feel this way. And that made her want to be stronger.

The Goose said to Sofia, "Your shoes are untied."

Even though they were not, Sofia bent down to pretend that she was tying them. At this point, the Goose craned his neck so he could whisper into her ear with his beak.

"Tell them your parents are coming, and they will throw them in prison for trespassing. Say your father lifted pianos for a living when he was younger so they will think him very big. Tell them you have two giant dogs that despise strangers and will surely rip their throats out. You cannot allow boys to stay in this house. They will make your life hell."

"How did you know to get off the train if you are not a spy?" Balthazar asked, interrupting them. "Did you know all the children were going to be executed?"

"Were they all executed? How do you know?" Sofia asked back.

"Abelard understands the Enemy language and overheard some of the soldiers talking."

"One of the cooks at my orphanage spoke the language. She used to let me have beet soup. It was hard to disguise because it always left my lips so red."

"Where are all the trains with the adults going, then?"

"To the Enemy country."

"Why?"

"To take people to work in camps. But they should really just allow themselves to be thrown in a mass grave. They are going to have to work in mines."

"But a lot of them looked too fancy to go into mines."

"I think that's the point. It's some sort of re-education. They are supposed to get rid of their bourgeois sensibilities."

"Are you hungry?" Abelard interrupted.

"Yes, I'm starving."

"Well, I do have something I want you to try. It's a soup I whipped together with some herbs from the yard."

Sofia devoured it with a large spoon. She tried to control herself, but she simply could not. She felt herself turn into an animal.

She shovelled the food into her mouth. She snatched at the bread as though the boys might take it from her. But they were staring at her with no desire to intervene, calmly smoking cigarettes. She dunked the bread viciously into the soup. Then moved her head close to the bowl to shove what was left into her mouth as quickly as she could.

"Were you on a train from the Capital too?" Sofia asked.

"Oh no, my lady," Balthazar answered. "We were not. We met on the way out of Shumus. It was bombed to smithereens last month. It was an extraordinary sight."

"City hall was knocked down," Abelard said. "The bell on top of it fell down and landed on people. Their legs were sticking out from under it, like cockroaches underneath a shoe. Like it had knocked out a whole group of witches, all at once."

He crawled under the table and stuck his legs out, as if to demonstrate. Then he quickly scrambled back out to finish his description.

"There was a cradle in the middle of the road. I saw a baby sleeping so peacefully inside it that I let it be."

"They didn't even spare the babies?" Sofia asked.

"Nobody was spared," Balthazar said matter-of-factly. "There were people who had been evacuated from the hospital. You could tell because they were all in pajamas, as though a slumber party had been interrupted."

She felt frightened. That they were able to wax poetic on such horrifying sights meant they had seen and become accustomed to almost anything.

"They rounded up everyone. I fled the city on my motorbike, and I met Abelard on the road."

"And we have been together ever since."

The country had put so much effort into creating newspapers and presses and radio shows. And now here she was, hearing about the war from two boys in her grandparents' clothing.

"Look how you're eating. What must they think of you?" the Goose nagged in her ear. "I'm so embarrassed to be with you. I am mortified. I mean, we are their guests."

Sofia yawned, her mouth stretching wide and crooked like that of a sleepy lion. She was too tired to be offended by what the Goose was saying. His words floated around her head but were unable to get in. Like words of people passing on the street outside the window. Almost minutes after she had finished her bowl of food, she was overcome by a need to sleep. She couldn't sit on the chair. And her head began snapping up on her neck, as though she had come up with a scientific revelation.

Abelard took her bowl from in front of her. "I expect you'll be wanting to go to sleep."

Sofia went to spend the night with the Goose in her mother's old childhood bed, in a room filled with forbidden books.

"I don't like it here," the Goose said in the dark. He raised both his wings and stood up on his tippy-toes. And then lowered himself again slowly. "It isn't safe. I don't like these boys at all."

"Boys always make bad first impressions."

"All I know is that you promised me we were on our way to the Black Market—and here we are in an old lady's house. It has the smell of an old person. It smells like mothballs and faded perfume and mould. With some lavender."

"I don't mind it," Sofia said. She was happy to find the room still smelled the way her grandmother's house usually did. She changed into one of her mother's old nightgowns, which she found hanging in the closet, and the aroma of the familiar surrounded her.

The smell of the boys had changed the atmosphere in the rest of the house. Their musk had seeped into everything. It was marking the territory the way dogs did. The smell emanated from their greasy hair. From their dirty toes. They had made the living room smell like so many different things. It smelled like the lake. It smelled like stones that had been lying in the sun. It smelled like smoke. It smelled so much closer to death than a girl did.

She thought that soon the smell of the Capital would leave her body. She too would smell like animal turds and gunpowder.

"How long will we stay here?" the Goose asked when they climbed in bed.

"At least for a little while. The Enemy are probably looking for children to shoot now. Perhaps they get a compensation, the way farmers give hunters rewards for killing wolves."

"I thought children were a protected class."

"You thought wrong. It's positively criminal to be a child right now. Anyway, this is our house."

"You say this is our house. But it isn't. Is it? Not anymore. Because the country isn't ours. It isn't theirs either. Can't you see? Everything is suspicious. You can't trust the chairs. You can't trust the carpets. They look so familiar, you could swear you were in your home. But you are not. And it is time for you to leave. You always have to keep on the move during a war. You must keep marching. There is nowhere safe. So we keep to the road. In activity. We can't sit here like sitting ducks."

"I will have to stand up to the boys in the morning. I will let them know who is boss. That's how you deal with men."

"Where in the world did you ever get this idea?"

"My mother lectured on it at the Bibliothèque Nationale."

"What makes sense in a library does not always make sense in the real world. Why should you even listen to your mother at this point? She was the one who sent you off on a train to be murdered."

"You don't have to be frightened of them. They are only boys. They are acting like men, but really they are almost the same age as me. And besides, they are clearly from poor backgrounds. They will listen to me because I am from the Capital. And I am more educated and more worldly. They know this is my house. I will have to be very firm with them."

"Ah, you think they are going to want to reinstate your relationship before the war? You think they will gracefully accept that you come from a wealthy family? That your mother would never let you play with them? That before the war, you would be communicating with them only to give them orders, to get rid of your trash or mop your stairwell floors? This is a war. You can't trust any of your old hierarchies. In fact, I think having been a posh child might work against you."

"You think I am a snob?"

"We established this, yes."

"Well, you are a snob too."

"Absolutely. I don't want to have anything to do with those boys. I have no qualms with admitting I am superior to them. I consider myself an intellectual. And they are part of the proletariat. It is up to me to understand their condition since they are too stupid to do it themselves."

"Goodnight."

"Goodnight."

• • •

In the morning, Sofia washed her dress and hung it up to dry in the bathroom. She put on a large sweater over her nightgown and walked into the living room. She was able to take stock of how ramshackle and disorderly the house had become. This was natural because the house was extremely cluttered and filled with items. Her grandmother had been a great collector. Particularly when her husband was cheating. The more she tried to repress his cheating, the more objects she purchased. When Sofia picked a porcelain bulldog off the floor, she felt a sense of longing for her grandmother so intense, she thought she might keel over and die from it.

The house was not only messy but also suffused with tobacco smoke. The boys seemed to have only very recently taken up smoking. There was something awkward in their gestures as they smoked. It made it seem as though they were pretending to smoke instead of actually smoking.

They had come across her grandmother's pile of cigarette cartons. The cartons that had a winking woman in a sailor hat on the label. She purchased them in bulk from the Capital. The boys smoked the thin cigarettes as though the supply were infinite. And they would never run out. Or perhaps it was like with candy, where they thought they had to shove as much as possible in their mouths before it was taken away.

Balthazar took enormous inhales with a cigarette pinched between his thumb and forefinger, then stood with the smoke in his chest and exhaled. Abelard waved his cigarette in the air around him, as though he were making circles with a ribbon. Sofia had seen him admiring himself in a mirror while smoking.

That evening, Balthazar arrived at the table dressed in nothing other than a green velvet housecoat, while Abelard wore a blue silk dress whose neckline fell below his nipples. Sofia was back in her own dress, tailored for her size. After eating, Balthazar retreated to the basement. He came back with a bottle of wine. Sofia knew it was a very expensive bottle that her grandmother was saving for a grand occasion, but she said nothing. Balthazar poured them all drinks, and he and Abelard polished off their glasses quickly, while Sofia carefully sipped hers.

"There's a rule we have that you cannot miss your mother and start weeping once you are drunk," Abelard said.

"All right," Sofia answered.

"Will that be hard for you?" he asked. "Do you miss your mother? I adored my own mother."

"He doesn't know his mother," Balthazar said. "He was living in an orphanage when the war broke out."

"My mother was a prostitute and my father was a travelling thief," Abelard confided.

"He isn't ashamed in the least," Balthazar scoffed, lighting another cigarette. "In fact, he's proud of his heritage. He can't shut up about it."

"My mother was murdered. She loved me, though."

"You were so young when she died that you can't know anything about it."

"There are some things you just know. She was wild about me. Everyone in her family told her to put me in an orphanage. But she didn't listen to them. I was the light of her life. She thought she could make enough money and would be able to raise me properly. She went out every night, meeting different men. But she was so beautiful."

"How do you know she was beautiful?" Balthazar demanded.

"She was so beautiful it made men angry."

"How so?"

"They were furious she didn't belong to them. There was nothing they could do to win her love. Because her heart was already taken, by me. They would beg her to stay longer, to spend the night with them. But she had to get home to feed me. One man was so enraged she was leaving that he slit her throat. It snowed for seven days after she died. That is a fact."

"Who told you?"

"It's in the almanacs. At the orphanage I was told that the day I arrived, there was a terrible blizzard. They almost didn't hear the knocker because the wind was so loud. Can you imagine such a thing? They might have left me on the doorstep. I would have been a block of ice."

"Oh, I've had more than enough of your fairy tales. You talk like that about your mother because you never got a chance to know her. And what about you?" Balthazar said, addressing Sofia. "What's your opinion of your mother?"

"My mother is a well-known writer."

"I don't believe it for a minute. What did she write?"

"*The Rights and Importance of Women in the Modern Age*."

"I've never heard of it."

"I have," said Abelard.

"You have not."

"And how about you?" Sofia said, not wanting to go into her feelings towards her mother. "Don't you miss your mother at all?"

"Not in the slightest," Balthazar answered. "I'm happy never to have to see her face again. I hated living at home. I hated always being cooped up. I hated being forced to go to school every day. To be honest, at the beginning, the war eliminated certain things that drove me crazy."

Sofia wondered whether hating your family made it easier for you to survive the war.

"Maybe things will be okay," Sofia suddenly said, as if to change the subject from mothers once and for all. "Maybe they only shot the children who ran from the train. Maybe we'll be able to return to life as it was before."

"I've seen things you've never seen before," Balthazar said, shaking his head. "The Capital hasn't really got the worst of the fighting yet. They started killing everyone in my town. I saw a young girl spit on a soldier who whistled at her. They hanged her from a lamppost. Everyone could see up her skirt after that. That was the first murder I saw. If I close my eyes, I can still see her hanging there. It's like she's in my head. Clear, like I'm watching a movie. And when I close my eyes, it's as though the theatre goes dark and she comes up on the screen again. Hanging. I don't think I'll ever be curious about what happens under a woman's skirt ever again. It ruined that for me. Probably for the best."

Abelard opened his mouth as if to add some sort of anecdote of his own, but then shook his head and shrugged.

"Until they invade and destroy the Capital, and everyone in it," Balthazar concluded, "the war is not over; in fact, it has hardly even begun."

PORTRAIT OF AN UGLY CHILD

Clara and Sofia were walking down the bombed streets back to their apartment with the collars of their black coats turned up. When they saw a group of Elysian citizens who were now dressed in the Enemy's uniform, Clara stopped dead in her tracks and gave them a look of disgust that Sofia had never seen before. She took Sofia's hand and turned in the opposite direction to take another street home.

"You'll begin to see that people who had no purpose before and were losers and pests will rise up during the war. When a war begins, you see who is a partisan or a collaborator."

"My teacher last year seemed like a collaborator."

"Why would you say that?"

"He always sent girls to sit in the corner and wear the dunce cap. But you could tell he wished he could punish us harder."

"We have a habit of sending failed philosophers off to teach children. It turns them into nihilists."

"What happens to collaborators once the war is over?"

"Collaborators are hanged at the end of the war."

"There's no future in it, then?"

"They are worse than the Enemy."

"I would like to be a member of the resistance, then."

"You already are," Clara said and looked down at her daughter. "I would never raise a collaborator. Of course you are part of the resistance."

And Sofia was so pleased that her mother assumed she had inherited her fierce traits. They were members of the resistance! She thanked the war for a brief secret moment. Because before the war, she was certain her mother had often treated her as a collaborator, someone intent on destroying her freedom. Sofia reminisced on the awful way things used to be.

Her mother resented her for having been a baby. And she did not forgive Sofia for having been a difficult birth. "You took so long to come out of me. You didn't put any effort into it. It was as though you couldn't imagine there was a world out here. You just wanted to stay inside me for as long as possible. You have to make your own way in the world. You can't live off someone else. It's the definition of being a parasite."

She said that having a baby had made her profoundly stupid. She said her intellect couldn't possibly recover for another seven years. But she told Sofia that she should not under any circumstances feel guilty about it. Her mother was clear that guilt was the most useless of all emotions in a woman.

There was a story from Sofia's infancy, from a time she herself could not remember, that Clara loved to tell. She once crawled into her mother's office and destroyed all her papers. She knocked over a stack of papers and ripped them to pieces, sticking them into her mouth. She picked up a jar of ink from her mother's desk and took a swig from it. She had to be rushed to the doctor at the time.

Sofia hated when her mother told this story. She felt she was blaming her for something Sofia had done when she was a baby. She did not like the memories her mother selected to keep for her. They made her seem as though she had been born dour and judgmental. It was hard not to feel that your personality was shaped by the memories your mother gave to you. And her mother was a writer. She could have presented Sofia with a personality that was luminous and pretty. Instead her mother had stuck her with a personality that wasn't quite hers.

Clara Bottom liked to tell these stories about Sofia because she found them to be important for her image. Yes, she had become a mother. But she hadn't become a sad, pathetic sack of a woman who allowed herself to regress in order to care for her baby. No. On the contrary, she had fought against the absurd tyranny of her baby. She, unlike other women, would not be outwitted by a child—she would not raise her child's status above her own.

And what was a better metaphor for this than an image of baby Sofia eating Clara's manuscript pages and drinking her mother's ink?

She sometimes felt that black ink was still inside her, coursing through her veins. Especially when she was mad at her mother. She felt her heart pump black, inky blood through her body.

She felt she was physically distant from her mother. There were ways in which children were physically intimate with their mother's bodies. Other children would climb on their mothers' laps without permission and yell up at them while they were speaking to others. She had even watched children disappear under their mothers' skirts. As though a mother's private world were a circus tent for them to hide inside. Sofia would never have that audacity. She did not have that kind of access to her mother's body. Although she would stand close to her, her mother kept her distance, as though they were strangers on a lift or the subway.

Sofia spent ample amounts of time in front of the mirror. She would stare at herself, trying to figure out whether there was a way to conceive of her own face as pretty. She could never figure out this riddle. She was often alarmed by how much time had passed while she was standing and staring at the mirror. It was as though she had disappeared into Narnia. She was mesmerized by the question of her own ugliness.

Once she noticed the sun had gone down while she was staring in the mirror. She pulled away from the glass. She had been staring at it so closely, she had blurred vision afterwards and lost all depth perception and walked into a wall.

She wished she had some manner by which to distinguish herself. She was neither ugly nor pretty. She was neither smart nor stupid. She was only smart enough to realize her lack of intelligence. She was profoundly aware of what she wasn't. She wished she had a talent. She wished there was something special about her.

At the beginning of the school year, when calling out the names in class, the teacher said, "You must be intelligent because of who your mother is. You'll have to help the other girls out." Sofia felt her cheeks suddenly catch fire. She knew she could never live up to these expectations. She thought the other girls in the classroom must hate her. They would all figure out she was not exceptional, and they would ridicule her for it. This was so unfair! None of the other girls had to prove they were exceptional. They were allowed to be ordinary. They all arrived in matching navy jackets with red piping along the hoods and berets tilted at exactly the same angle. And they all seemed content in a manner that perplexed Sofia.

She would seem like a complete idiot if she was compared to her mother. She did as little as possible to draw attention to herself. Once a ribbon fell from the end of her plait, and Sofia did not move an inch to retrieve it. She let the ribbon sit on the tip of her patent leather shoe. She managed to become invisible while still being in the classroom.

As an only child, she had an oddly formal way of acting. She had been to so many dinner parties where she was the sole child present. She was capable of niceties but had no idea how to express herself otherwise.

She was in the cafeteria and sat at a table next to a group of girls. "How are you today? Are you enjoying the pudding?" The girls all looked at her quizzically, then one of them said, "We are fine."

For the rest of the lunch she said nothing at all, but sat at the edge of the table, too mortified to eat.

There was a poem about hares that they were forced to memorize. Each girl had to go to the front of the class and recite it. It wasn't boring at all, though. They each made some sort of mistake in their recitation that caused all the other girls to jeer and call out. While the teacher banged her ruler on the table, demanding that they settle down. The hare in each girl's mind was a slippery, elusive thing.

But when Sofia went up to the front of the class, she found herself unable to recite a word of the poem. The whole class became quiet looking at her. The girls were too embarrassed for her to bother uttering a sound. She made them cringe so hard, it felt as if they might disappear, leaving only the pile of their uniforms on the chairs, and stockings and shoes under the desks. They wished she wasn't in their classroom. They didn't like to be reminded that there were awkward and defective girls in the world. Ones like Sofia, who looked at the floor as tears dropped out of her eyes, for a hare she had no words to describe. And who didn't know when she ought to return to her desk. Not when they were in school, learning to all be the same.

Sofia's constant sense of shame was palpable. She knew it caused the other girls to keep their distance from her. Shame was considered contagious. At that age, children considered negative qualities to be catching. They didn't want to spend time with her and afterwards find themselves horrified and humiliated by their own presence. So they kept their respectful distance.

Sofia brought her report card home for her mother to see. There wasn't anything wrong with the marks. They were not extraordinary, but at the same time, she hadn't done badly in any of her subjects. Her teacher wrote on her report card that she performed adequately. That word, "adequately," had stoked her mother's rage. Her mother thought you should be the best or the worst at something. Never simply adequate.

"It frustrates me every time I see your report cards. I never thought I would have a child who didn't do well in school. I always had the highest marks in class. It was so easy for me. I loved doing better than all the boys. I suppose you inherited your father's intellectual slowness. But nonetheless, it frustrates me that you can't excel in a single thing."

Sofia went to her room and sat on the side of her bed. She had no idea what it meant to excel in something, or even what she might excel in. Her mother had pronounced her ordinary. And being ordinary meant you did not stick out. And if you didn't stick out, then you were invisible. And if you were invisible, could you really be said to exist?

Sofia was certain she had been made to feel worse than any of the other children in her class, even the ones who had failed their subjects. She thought her mother would have preferred that. Sofia knew her mother would have appreciated if she had come home with all Fs. That would be unusual. It would make for a delightful dinner party story—how the country's leading intellectual had a child who couldn't make heads or tails of grade school.

Sofia took up the clarinet in part because her mother, like many people in the country, had a fondness for the instrument. Some ten years before, a clarinet player from their country had gone to Europe and been declared the greatest clarinet player in the world by a newspaper in Belgium. It gave everyone in the country a whiff of pride, and they went out and bought his albums and made him a national hero. In high school, when it came to choosing an instrument, everyone wanted to play the clarinet.

But then Sofia came to really like playing the clarinet. There was something so melancholy about the song of the instrument. Its sound was not fancy or pretty, but sad in the loveliest way. She thought, This is how I would sing if I were a bird. She knew there were other children in her class who were more naturally talented than she was. But it didn't mean she could not learn to play as well as she possibly could.

She spent an hour one night mastering a tune by a famed national composer, until her mother threw open the door of her bedroom. "For the love of God, will you stop massacring that piece? You're giving me a migraine, and I will never be able to ever listen to it again."

After that, Sofia felt like a loser whenever she picked up the clarinet and couldn't wait for the day when she didn't have to play it anymore.

A NAKED GIRL IS ALWAYS PRICELESS

While staying at her grandmother's house with the boys, Sofia reflected on how little time she had spent apart from her mother in her whole life. Before, when she went into the bathroom in the morning, she would walk over a soft carpet of tights and underwear that her mother had kicked off messily before getting into the bathtub, and that no one had got around to picking up yet. It was like moss on the floor. If her mother were an animal, Sofia would say she was in her natural habitat. Her mother's perfume and cigarettes were still absorbed in her dress. She missed the wonderful stink of home.

The boys would try the radio every day, to see if there was information about the war that was going on beyond their purview. Sofia was afraid of hearing her mother's voice on the air, but there was the same radio play on a loop all day and every day. It was clear the Enemy had taken over the airwaves, preventing any news from being transmitted to people in this country, and also neighbouring ones.

"They've gone too far," Balthazar said. "The other countries don't know what is happening. They don't understand about the internment camps. They don't know about the executions. When word gets out about the atrocities being perpetrated against a pacifist, educated people, they will come to rescue us. When the war is over, the first thing to do is make immediate friends with the liberators."

Sofia fell quiet. Her mother's book would have relayed to the outside world what a precious culture was being destroyed. If she had been able to get it out of the country. The world couldn't put faces to the people. The world had forgotten how civilized they were. Her mother had spent so many years working on making the country appear civilized and modern and forward-thinking. And wasn't it exactly for this moment? Wasn't it for a moment like this? Wasn't it so that others would see them as human and come and rescue them?

The boys slept together in her grandmother's enormous bed. It was an old-fashioned bed that had been passed down for several generations. It was meant for large families to sleep in all together. But her grandmother had only one child, and her husband had left her. So she had always slept in the giant bed by herself. When Sofia was little, one of her favourite things was to jump into bed with her grandmother. The mattress was so soft, and the purple comforter was stuffed with goose feathers. You would feel warm almost instantly when you got into it.

It was strange to see the boys in her grandmother's bed. They sometimes passed out fully clothed. And other times they were naked.

• • •

Balthazar had chosen those of her grandfather's clothes he felt most comfortable in and proceeded to wear that outfit every day. He began to smell rather rancid. Especially since he slept in his clothes. Sometimes simply hanging his jacket from the bedframe before flopping into the bed. But he didn't care what the others thought of his smell, since he could not smell himself.

Abelard dressed rather extravagantly. He was wearing a purple jacket that had belonged to her grandmother and a pair of black trousers that had belonged to her grandfather. He had tied a silk scarf in the most dramatic fashion around his neck. He had pushed his blond hair straight up into the air. He was very vain about his hair. He said they ought to invent a sort of blondish oil paint and call it Abelard Yellow.

At night he said a prayer by the side of the bed that his hair would never fall out of his head. "I need my hair because I want to be able to play twenty-five-year-old men until my fifties." Sofia was confused about what god he was praying to. It seemed alarming. He had grown up in an orphanage. That was why he was so versed in the old ways.

He was magnificent during a game of charades one evening. "Show her some of your impressions," Balthazar said. "Surprise us with one of your animals."

Abelard began to gallop and neigh around the living room, in what was clearly a rendering of a horse. It was so realistic. It was uncanny. It was almost as though he had been possessed by the spirit of a horse. The other children knew exactly what he was trying to be. But they refrained from guessing because they didn't want the performance to end.

Sofia was stricken by how real his imitation was. It was

as though he had suddenly transformed, as if by magic, into a horse. She found it unnerving. But she had always had a fancy for theatre—a propensity to suspend her disbelief.

When they went back to their room, the Goose grew immediately more relaxed. He flung himself onto the bed like a shirt tossed off a hanger. He let his neck hang over his body. The Goose would go over the events of the day. But he would spin them in the most negative way. He didn't see anything worthy in either of the boys' personalities. The Goose gave a very cutting analysis of Abelard's performance when they were in bed together.

"Abelard is preposterous. Someone needs to tell him he has no talent. He is embarrassing himself. Imagine he does begin performing for the liberating army? He will embarrass the whole country. They'll think we don't know anything about the thespian arts."

"What does it matter if he is untalented? But I don't think he is."

One afternoon, Abelard brought out a clarinet that he had found in a closet. "Who knows how to play?" he yelled.

Sofia held the clarinet to her mouth. She began to play a very simple children's tune they all knew from when they were little.

The Goose had never heard anyone play the clarinet before. The Goose was shocked that she was able to create such a pretty tune. It sounded so familiar to him. He felt so raw and emotional. It was the language of geese, but so polished and sweet.

He wondered why he had tried to say anything in human tongue. He had thought it was more sophisticated. Because he alone, among all the other geese, was able to speak human, he elevated it in his mind. But now he heard his mother tongue and realized how beautiful it was. He opened his mouth and began to sing along in his own language.

The others began to laugh and look at him with delight and amazement. But also condescension. And when he noticed the hint of ridicule, he immediately stopped singing. He clamped his mouth shut and moved to the corner. Noticing the Goose's pain, Sofia instantly stopped playing her song.

"Perhaps when the war is over, we can return to my farm and you can play that tune to the geese there. I can assure you, you will have an appreciative audience. Although who's to say which of the old geese will be there. Every day is a war for me. You wonder who has disappeared. Which of your friends have been killed. Do you realize that being an animal always implies being in an occupied country? You don't even have the slightest idea about what my day-to-day reality is like. You couldn't begin to fathom it. You have no idea what it is like to wonder whether one of your very best friends has been turned into a sandwich."

Sofia looked at him. She started to laugh. A shout of laughter burst out of her—as though she were drinking laughter, had choked on it, and had spit it out. Then she began laughing in earnest.

She could tell the Goose didn't find it funny. She tried to restrain herself. But the very act of trying not to laugh made her want to laugh even more. There were times when she forgot the Goose was actually a goose!

Balthazar was somehow excused from doing any housework. One day he stood up and announced, "I have to go work on my shot."

Sofia's blood ran cold when he came out of the bedroom with a gun in his hand. She was certain he was about to shoot her or the Goose. But instead he began moving around the living room, taking figurines off the shelf. He headed outside, and Abelard and Sofia both ran after him.

He placed a porcelain ballerina on the fence and walked about fifteen feet back from it. He aimed. Sofia didn't say anything. She thought the figurine had a chance. She was so lithe and skinny. There seemed to be no possibility the bullet would hit her. She would whisk out of the way. A bullet is so heavy and lugubrious and dull and stupid. How could it approach and destroy something so pretty? Even though she was frozen in porcelain, she always seemed to be dancing. She was on tiptoe, frozen in place—moving—and she would possibly dodge out of the bullet's way. But the bullet struck her violently, severing all her limbs at once.

Sofia went and picked up the pieces of the porcelain statue. She put them in her pockets quickly. She intended to glue them back together. She wondered what state of mind the ballerina was in now that she was shattered in so many pieces. Any broken bone was particularly devastating to a ballerina. But to have every part of you broken. How must that feel? To be holding your nose in your hand. To be looking at your foot and see that three of your toes are gone. To have to pick up your cheek from the ground and stick it back into your face like a puzzle piece!

Ballerinas were already hopelessly neurotic. A friend of Sofia's mother's was always threatening to kill the launderer, who she was convinced shrank her leotard and had ruined a performance and got her a bad review in a newspaper while on tour.

Balthazar proceeded to massacre the other figurines. Sofia found herself asking him where he had got the gun.

"On the Black Market," he answered.

"Where is it? Is it nearby?"

"Who knows. It was on the side of a road. We weren't look-ing for it. We just drove and came upon it."

"So south of here?"

"Yes, south of here. Who wants to know? Are you building a case against me for when the liberators come?"

Sofia hurried to her grandfather's old desk. She picked up the large pad on top, stuck it under her arm, and grabbed a pen. She walked back to Balthazar. She sat on a large rock near him and began to sketch the territory around her as best she could. She had a map of the city on her wall at home that she had made herself. She drew maps of all the neighbourhood spots she knew. She was quite good at it, she found. She put in all the little details. Even her mother looked at the maps and said, "That's unusually concise."

When she was done her new map, she held it up to Balthazar. "So the Black Market, might be on any of the roads south of here. Might it be the Lorgus Pass?"

"The Black Market! What in the world do you know about the Black Market? You look too young to be able to go to the Black Market."

"I'm only two years younger than you."

"Well, it isn't about age, is it? It's about maturity. I am far beyond my years, which anyone would be able to see."

"I've gone to the Black Market in the Capital myself."

"Liar."

"I know exactly how to negotiate."

"Liar."

"I've carried items from the Black Market on the metro."

"Liar."

"I've carried them right past guards."

"Liar."

"Even though they smelled."

"Liar."

"And the dogs were barking at me because they smelled the sausages."

"Liar."

She stamped her foot. She had finished her story. She was determined to get to the end of her lie once she had started it. He had taken the wind out of her with his assertion that she was a liar, and each additional sentence felt harder and harder. They sounded ludicrous even to her own ears. You can believe your own lies only if the person you are telling them to believes them too.

"It's for the deviants," Balthazar said smiling, clearly including himself as one. "What in the world could a person like you want from the Black Market? It's where adults go to find what they have lost and are missing. Coffee and alcohol and dirty pictures. And weapons and drugs. And pretty undergarments for developed bodies. If you know what I mean. Tell me what you have to trade on the Black Market, and I will tell you where it is. You can't go empty-handed."

It had not occurred to her that even if she made it to the Black Market and they had her mother's book, they would expect something in exchange for it.

"Well, if you weren't so clueless and stopped destroying things in the house, I would have items to trade at the Black Market. Those ballerinas are each worth more money than your parents make in a month."

As if on cue, Balthazar aimed and shot the last solo ballerina. Sofia's body jolted when he did it.

"Why did you do that?" she yelled.

Balthazar gestured for Sofia to follow as he strode into the house. He walked into the kitchen and then bent down beneath the sink and emerged with a wooden box. Sofia recognized the chest of silver utensils immediately. It had been a wedding gift to her mother from her father's side of the family. They were made of Elysian silver. Balthazar opened the lid. Clearly some of the utensils were missing. They were trading this family heirloom away piece by piece.

Sofia instinctively reached for the box, but Balthazar slammed it shut, nearly crushing one of her fingers. And then he placed his elbows on it and looked at her with a smirk.

"Well, I think you should give me at least a tablespoon," Sofia said.

"Sorry, these utensils need to be traded for arms. You cannot trade them for lipstick or perfume. That is a waste. If you were an older, more attractive woman, I would give you a spoon for that. But it won't do you any good at all. Trade your goose for whatever it is you seem desperate for."

Sofia looked around the house. Her eyes fell upon a painting. It was a small oil painting of a nude young woman by Arturo Zersat. His works were famous because he went into brothels and painted teenage prostitutes. All the elite wanted to have one on their wall.

"That painting is the object that is worth the most money in the house."

"It isn't even good."

Sofia walked over to the painting. She had never thought much of it before, but now, while looking at it, she felt she was looking at herself. There was an uncanny resemblance. She was the same age as the young girl in the painting. The girl had a sultry look on her face, but her body had not yet reached puberty. There was something of her conundrum that Sofia related to. She stood in front of the painting and positioned her body to match that of the girl.

For the first time, Sofia realized how a piece of art changes every time you approach it. There is an age at which you suddenly become aware of the hidden subtexts that are right in front of your eyes but still entirely invisible. There was sex and darkness everywhere.

Was the painting vulnerable or violent? She could not say. It was the power and arrogance of victimhood. She imagined how terrifying an army of such girls would be. She would join them. They would kill together.

Perversity is an acquired taste, her mother had once told her. And Sofia internalized her mother's comment, right at that moment. Because it was truly the most beautiful and valuable item in the house.

And there was no way this would not fetch a pretty penny on the Black Market.

"You can keep your spoons," she said haughtily.

She went into her mother's room. She pulled one of her mother's childhood books off the shelf, opened it, and stuck her head inside and inhaled.

She wished she had her mother's manuscript now. She would arise immediately, fully formed from the page. That was the power writers had. When you read them, the author was right there with you, sharing their ideas. As though they had been invited over for tea.

Her mother would appear before her. In a beige coat and a fur collar. She would be smoking a cigarette. How Sofia missed the smell of her mother's tobacco, which had perfumed everything in the apartment. It sank deep into the chairs and the pages of books. Even her body. Her skin and hair and clothes always carried the scent.

If she had the manuscript, Sofia was certain she could hold it up to her nose and smell the cigarettes on the pages. And were she to read the words, swirls of smoke would surround her.

How she wished she could read those words. She would choose a particularly severe passage. One that condemned women for not seizing their own destiny, for being terrified of their own independence, and for waiting for men to come rescue them from their lives.

When Sofia returned to the living room, Balthazar looked at her with a loaded sneer. She didn't know what it meant, but then he looked over her shoulder.

It was as though she read his mind because she turned and looked at the Zersat painting. The girl in the painting, who had thought herself so defiant, who gave a look that indicated no one could touch her, whose body seemed possessed of sexuality that was unknowable, had been defiled. The boys had scribbled a coarse patch of pubic hair on her body with a black pen.

It changed everything about the painting. The girl seemed trapped and miserable. She looked tawdry and disillusioned. She looked like someone the Enemy would drag out onto the street and shoot in the back of the head. They had spoiled a masterpiece.

Sofia turned and saw that Balthazar was pleased. He enjoyed watching people react to his cruelty. It was the point of it. To see the pain he was capable of causing. It was like an artist stepping back and admiring his own work. That was what he thrived on. He had developed a taste for it during the war. If he had lived in the Capital, he surely would have been a collaborator.

Sofia felt as though she too had been defiled in some way. She felt like a broken thing. An insect. A speck of mud. A monster. A deformation. Someone who should be in hiding. Someone without worth. A person who ought to be rubbed out with the eraser at the end of a pencil. He made her feel unworthy.

It was as though she were less than the boys. Because she was a girl. But also because she was unattractive to them. They were unable to see any worth in her. She was a distorted, imperfect male. If she were older and more beautiful, she would have some sort of power and dignity. But they had no interest in her as a sexual being. So they did not know the point of her.

Abelard was under the table. She loathed that. He was a coward. He was equally guilty, but he wanted to act as though he wasn't. She considered Abelard to be in the position of all the civilians in the Enemy country. Who would arrive and move into their homes. To reap the spoils of war without feeling complicit in any way. They closed their eyes. They gave no orders. But they were the ones who profited off the war.

Their apartments would be occupied by people who believed themselves pure and untouched by violence.

Sofia looked from Balthazar to Abelard. "You have gone too far. You have destroyed a masterpiece. You will be tried for treason when the war ends. You will be hanged as war profiteers and collaborators. I have many connections in the Capital, and you can rest assured I will turn you in."

With that, she stormed off to her room.

"Are you frightened?" Sofia asked the Goose as they were lying in bed.

"I am always frightened. I am always in a state of abject terror. Why should right now be any different?"

"Don't be. You'll see, the Black Market will be wonderful."

"For you, but what is in it for me?"

Sofia whispered into the Goose's ear all the marvellous things she hoped to find at the Black Market.

There would be many things for sale. She would not want any of these. She only wanted her mother's manuscript. But she couldn't help dreaming about the other delightful items that might be up for sale.

She liked the idea they still existed somewhere. And even if the Capital was destroyed, it hardly mattered. Because all these things continued to exist, somewhere, wandering around in the country. Like a circus caravan that would unpack its trunks of marvels for children in various spots.

They would have a jewellery box. And when it opened, the sound of her doorbell would come out. There would be a tambourine, and when you shook it, the sound of girls laughing on the bus would erupt from it. There would be a salt shaker that made the sound of her father's wristwatch when she held it up to her ear. There would be a perfume that smelled like the bakery next door to her apartment in the Capital. There would be a crystal that captured the way the dawn looked in the city.

There would be postcards of the Capital and its stars. And it would be as though they were sent from a faraway country, known as the past. Was there ever any road that brought you to the past? If there was, it would be treacherous and difficult to find. Almost impossible, some would say. And yet, that was where she intended to go.

THE MERMAIDS WHO LOST

THEIR VOICES

That night in her grandmother's house, Sofia had a
dream that she had arrived at the Black Market.
She saw a large table. It was in the middle of a
barren field. But it was clear that despite the landscape, there were people feasting and drinking at the table.
Over top of the table was a large black banner attached to
a stick on either side. She could see the letters painted in
white on the sign. They said: BLACK MARKET.

There was a woman sitting at the table. She had the
same physique as Sofia's mother. But she was wearing a
black felt hat tilted over one eye, so Sofia couldn't make out
her face. She was laughing like her mother. She had her
legs crossed underneath her chair like her mother. She was
dressed like her mother when she was getting ready to give
a speech.

Sofia ran and ran towards the table. But it never seemed
to get any closer. She couldn't get close enough to see
whether it was her mother, and whether she was still alive.

• • •

Sofia and the Goose walked into the kitchen the next morning, and Balthazar and Abelard were sitting quietly at the table, as though they were expecting them.

"We've come to a conclusion," Balthazar announced.

"I don't know if I would exactly call it a conclusion," Abelard said.

"What would you call it? A decision?"

"No. No. Not that."

"We think it's because of you, Sofia, that the war happened to begin with. The Enemy came because they were furious at the wealthy. Look at this house. It could fit three families in it. But it was occupied by one old lady." Balthazar paused and then looked at Sofia. "We will have to ask you to leave."

Sofia had not expected this. "I'm not going to leave. This is my house!"

"Hmmm," Balthazar said with a smile. "I thought you might say that."

"It's my house. If you find you can't stand me, then *you* will have to leave."

Abelard leaned his elbow on the table and put his chin in his hand. He looked at her with his large eyes, which he blinked in a bewitching manner. Sofia was momentarily hypnotized by his curious expression.

"It is a beautiful home," he said. "I never thought I would find myself staying in such a place."

At that moment, Balthazar came around behind her and put a black cloth bag over her head. She began struggling wildly. She wouldn't let the boys get a hold of her. She was thrashing her arms and legs in every which way she could. The Goose came to her aid. He started biting the arms of the boys, and Sofia managed to pull the bag off her head.

Balthazar grabbed the Goose by the neck and lifted it in the air. The Goose stopped gobbling and began instead to emit gasping, squawking sounds.

"Stop moving, or I will shoot this fucking goose in the head," Balthazar said.

And Sofia did. She straightened up her body and sat upright on the floor. Balthazar put the bird down. Abelard put the black bag back over her head.

Sofia was on the back of a speeding motorcycle behind Abelard. The Goose was attached in a basket on the side. Although she could not confirm this with her eyes because she still had the black bag over her head. Her hands were tied behind her back. She called out to the Goose to see if he was still there, and he gobbled back.

It was peculiar to be in this darkness. She tried to make sense of the sounds. She wasn't sure whether she was supposed to make sense of them. But in the darkness, the woods began to take on different properties. She couldn't help but believe what her senses, other than her eyes, were telling her.

There was a tree that pulled its roots out of the ground, like a child pulling its feet out of rubber boots. And it began to run along beside her. There were grey horses galloping ahead. A fat bear roared from the roadside. There were birds that were flying beside her head.

After the motorcycle stopped, Abelard untied them and pulled the black bag off her face. She stared all around her at the unknown road. Abelard tossed Sofia her bag, in which they had allowed her to pack her clarinet and silver knife, as though these two things would save her from the wilderness. She had also rolled up the map she had drawn, which, although rudimentary, was her most practical possession now. And she had in her inside pocket her important piece of paper, which she stroked with her hand for a moment, as though checking to see that her heart was still there. After Abelard had driven away, Sofia and the Goose stood on the side of the road, looking up and down it. She held up her map, trying to determine where they might be.

She inhaled deeply. In the Capital, Sofia had lived in a neighbour-hood whose streets were lined with expensive shops. And she was quite sure she could tell where she was on the street while wearing a blindfold. Because of the different smells. She would be able to tell whether she was in front of the bakery or the restaurant or the café.

What in the world did nature smell like other than nature? It smelled like mud all the time. There was the smell of blackness and boots and skinned knees. It smelled like garbage and potato peels. The air smelled cold. It smelled of bare hands. It smelled like the inside of a coat. It smelled the way her hands did after holding a fistful of coins. It smelled like cracks in the wall.

It smelled like a bucket of brass doorknobs. It smelled like the footprints of horses. It smelled like steel wool. It smelled like leather boots and gunpowder and running water.

It smelled like a tin that had first stored tea, but then later, so many things. It had been used to store letters and safety pins. The air smelled like rulers and the graphite of a pencil trying to record its trajectory towards infinity. Is there a difference between infinity and nothingness? It smelled like cherry pits when you spit them out on the street. It smelled like a smack in the face. It smelled like a split lip. It smelled like black thread.

The Goose, meanwhile, looked at his big webbed feet in an aggravated sort of way. Because he was a goose, he decided to have a tantrum. "I wonder if I didn't make a mistake in coming with you," he said suddenly. "I should have gone straight to the Capital."

"Oh, certainly. You would be someone's delicious soup right now."

"I am not simply a goose. I am a speaking goose. And I have sophisticated ideas. I left the farm precisely because no one could hear me over the racket. I was looking for a child. An intelligent child who needed tutelage. Who would offer me secure lodgings in exchange. You stole me from the future I was supposed to have. I should be living in a very large house. I should have a nursery. Why can't I have a nursery? I deserve to have a nursery.

"Why can't I have walls that are covered in murals? It doesn't take any effort to find a muralist. Muralists are always looking for work. I should like to have furniture with a French name, like an armoire or a divan. I doubt you have ever even heard of such things."

"There's a war on. It's not really my fault. If we were in the Capital, I would provide you with everything you need. I would give you a wonderful life. We could go to the park and eat boiled eggs. I could take you for chocolat chaud at a café that has paintings of girls holding umbrellas on the walls. We could go to the cinema. I assure you, I am a very cultured child. When we get to the Black Market, I will provide you everything you need."

"I apologize, Sofia. I did not mean to take my frustrations out on you. Perhaps we should just go to the Capital, then?"

"The war is about taking away everything special in the country. They don't think we deserve it. But the Black Market will be filled with everything they took away. When we get to the

Black Market, we can drink milky coffee. Oh, it's so much better with milk. And we can sit across from each other and have conversations about all manner of things. There are subjects that are so much easier to talk about over a milky cup of coffee. It makes you talk about what is right and wrong in the world."

"So you didn't know the difference between right and wrong before you started putting milk in your coffee?"

"Correct."

"Well, sometimes I wonder whether you haven't chosen to deliberately derail me with your tales of hocus-pocus and the Black Market. You decided to be our navigator. You have led me so far from my original destination."

"I am trying my best. You didn't exactly help defend me against the boys. You could have said something too."

"Men are not afraid of a goose's rage. And they use it as an excuse to wring our necks. My neck is the most elegant thing about me. It is what allows me to express myself. It moves and looks in so many directions. It is what makes my movements not only functional but also meaningful. It means I am. My life has meaning. I have a soul and not only a purpose. But men look at my neck and all they can think about is putting their hands around it and killing me. And they believe that is its primary purpose. My neck is there for them to wring, and is consenting to be wrung. It is their natural right to wring it. I know there are people who consider a swan a more dignified creature than a goose."

"I believe it is well established."

"It is *debated*."

"Well, there is no ballet called *Goose Lake*, is there?"

"You are wrong. You have a rudimentary knowledge of art. It is normal for children to appreciate classical notions of beauty.

Because your knowledge is not evolved yet. You will see when you get around twenty years old that all those ideas will seem boring to you. They were meant to sing you to sleep as a baby. And then you will see that things you once found banal, grotesque, frightening, odd, unsavoury will be where you find deeper beauty, for lack of a better word.

"A goose is a metaphor for these times. Everyone is trudging through the mud. Marching. Marching. Like geese always have. You don't hear about swans trudging through the mud, do you?"

"Why on earth would they when they can fly?"

"The swan is an ideal. But the goose must walk among men."

"Beautifully said."

"Thank you," the Goose said. "I am delighted to be freed from those boys. But of course, if I'm honest, you were rather harsh with them. Those criticisms are likely to stick with them. The wounds will grow infected. The gangrene will set in, and it will consume them. Is that the way your mother spoke to you? Is that where you learned it from?"

"Unfortunately, yes. She would criticize me. And her comments stayed with me. Like something I swallowed but couldn't digest. They are more like magic spells being cast on you. She will tell you that you are boring. And then you will be worried for years that you are boring. You won't want to say anything for years. She effectively damns you to boringness."

"Mothers are always cursing their children, aren't they?"

"They are supposed to love you unconditionally, but in truth, everything you do annoys them. They complain about the way you raise your spoon to your mouth."

"Nobody is really born free."

"No. The umbilical cord is like a chain that is never truly cut."

"It's terrible to imprint on your mother. Geese imprint on other geese. But not necessarily their mothers. Sometimes they imprint on other things. I knew a goose that had imprinted on a cow. He was always wandering off towards the pasture and would graze with the cows. They ignored him, but he accepted that as his fate. Even though he would have been so much better off coming to join the flock. There was another goose I knew that imprinted on a car. He was always standing in the middle of the road, honking away. Until he was run over. A ridiculous and tragic death."

"And who or what did you imprint on?"

"Nobody and nothing. I was always independent, you see."

Sofia laughed. She too felt independent of her mother suddenly. She felt strangely good about herself. She had erupted. It had had consequences. The boys had kicked her out. But they had thrown her out because she had made them throw her out. And she knew that part of her had wanted to be evicted. Because she had realized that even though she loved her grandmother's house, she did not want it. The boys were right that it was not her house. No, what she needed now was at the Black Market.

The sky suddenly darkened. Sofia and the Goose both ran for cover behind a bush in the ditch. Sofia was so frightened that she felt as though she were under water and couldn't breathe. She thought this might be her last moment.

She regretted only half listening to her mother most of the time. One afternoon she was sitting in the bathtub when her mother came in to stare in the fogged mirror and began offering Sofia some astute idea about the world. As she was speaking, Sofia had lowered herself under the water. So her ears filled up with water. And her mother's voice sounded like a whale singing somewhere in the ocean depths.

Then the sky became light again, and Sofia realized that what she had been frightened by was simply a passing cloud. As she pulled herself out of the ditch, she thought she would get her mother's memoir back. She would get to the Black Market. She would have all the missing words and ideas her mother had meant to share with her.

Hunger led Sofia off the road and deeper into the woods. She followed the sound of food like a little beast now. She perked up her ears, and they led her to water. The stream sounded like someone dropping sugar cubes into a cup of tea. The murmuring of the water sounded like voices at a restaurant. The gurgling sounded like a cash register being run up. She closed her eyes, and the sound of the water summoned the Capital to her mind.

"Are we going to catch a fish or what?" the Goose inquired.

Sofia opened her eyes. They were the grey shade of underwater stones.

The Goose was a great help fishing. He swam around and dunked his head under the water as his butt shook in the air above. It was as though someone underneath the deep had grabbed his neck and was throttling him. But then he reversed himself and cried out: "There's a school of fish moving that way. Go cut them off by the rock!" She ran over to see. She climbed up onto a large rock, lay on her stomach, and hung her face over the water to see what there was to see. She could not see anything other than her reflection. It looked so murky under the water, but then it seemed to become clearer. As though someone were rubbing fog off a bathroom mirror. Then she realized she wasn't looking at her reflection at all.

What she had seen made her body begin to quiver so violently. She picked up the Goose and held him in her arms.

Once she was looking in a pond in the city for a mermaid. Her mother scoffed, "What do you think, they dump mermaids in there like goldfish?" And Sofia had felt embarrassed. Her cheeks had flushed like they were the temperature of tea right before you drank it and it wouldn't burn your tongue. She was determined never to mention mermaids again. It was at that moment that she stopped believing in mermaids.

It was not a mermaid she saw in the water now. It was a girl lying on her back with her arms spread. She was fully dressed, except she was wearing only one shoe. She looked as though she was on a class expedition. She was wearing a pinafore with a red scarf around her neck.

When Sofia saw the dead body, everything stood still. She was suddenly out of time. She was in a state of shock. She looked all around her. Nothing was moving. She was the only thing still alive. Everything around her was frozen and incapable of movement. The birds in the sky were motionless. The water had stopped moving. There was a leaf that was suspended mid-flight. The trees had ceased to rustle. And were now absolutely quiet and still.

Then the water began to move again, taking the mermaid away. And then an entire school of uniformed girls came down the river and passed by. It was as though they were all deep in sleep. Some were lying on their bellies, looking into the depths of the water. Some were staring at the birds above them. Some had closed their eyes and were dreaming. The red ribbons danced around their necks like goldfish. There was one girl who passed close to Sofia's feet by the bank. There was a bullet hole in her forehead and the girl was looking straight up at it.

MOTHERHOOD IS A DISGUISE

One day, soon after the Enemy occupied the Capital, everyone in the city was ordered to go to one of a number of addresses and register for a new identity card. More or less everyone registered their name, occupation, and ethnic background.

Sofia went with Clara. Her mother signed her married name, which she never used publicly, and listed her occupation as housewife. Sofia was surprised. If there was one thing her mother loved more than being a writer, it was telling people she was a writer. That was how Sofia knew the country was in terrible danger.

Clara took her papers and documentation out of her purse. Officially, her lie seemed to hold up.

They asked her what her husband's occupation was. She said he was a salesman. He was in another city on business at the moment. The soldier stared at her. Perhaps he was thinking, She is not a housewife at all.

• • •

Now that the country was occupied, Sofia's mother began to take her everywhere she went. She never did this before. She said being a mother made a woman invisible. Whereas before the idea of being invisible made her feel horrible, now it was something she wanted.

She filled a grocery basket with her jewels and put a pile of potatoes on top. So it looked as though they were very ordinary people.

Sofia watched her mother try to pass herself off as an ordinary person. It seemed ridiculous. She knew her mother did not like to leave the house without her fur coat. She had bought the fur coat with the money she had won from an essay competition. When people looked at her coat, she felt they were acknowledging her writing. She put on a plain black coat. She tied a red kerchief with white polka dots around her head and fastened a perfect giant bow just to the left of her forehead.

"Whatever you do, when we go out, don't act as if I'm a very famous figure."

"I don't know that I ever do."

"No, I suppose you don't. One day you'll see the importance of your mother."

"I am looking at a woman in a red kerchief who is about to sell her jewels to get a piece of ham."

"Well, when you put it like that, there's a certain down-and-out glamour to it, don't you think? I'm like a heroine in a French naturalist novel."

She was counting on Sofia to make her look drab. When a group of soldiers passed, her mother turned to her and said, "Walk swiftly. Don't stop and declare your love to a cat or something like that."

"Okay, don't stop and tell me the history of every building and which poet once took a dump inside of it."

And her mother laughed. Since the war, her mother had begun to find the things she said funny. That or she had become funnier. But she didn't think it was that. She thought her mother listened to what she said now.

They walked by the long lineup to the grocery store. Her mother found it humiliating to purchase anything with ration coupons. Her mother could not stand waiting in line.

"They want us to wait in line for nothing. Our waiting has no purpose outside of itself. We are waiting to wait. They want us to believe our time has no inherent value. They want us to learn to be obedient with no reward. We are supposed to learn to thank them for nothing. As though nothingness has an inherent value."

Waiting in line was far too democratic for her. Everyone was treated exactly the same in a line.

"They want me to wait in line with dishwashers and concierges so I know I have achieved nothing that sets me apart. In any case, I cannot be seen in line. Imagine how depressing it would be to witness your country's greatest writer in line for bologna. It's too much for morale. You must go for me. No one has any opinions about you or thinks anything about you."

They went to a jewellery shop whose windows were now filled with empty display boxes. Sofia's mother quickly pushed her through the jangling door. The jeweller's wife waved for them to go through a small door at the back of the store. Since the war began, Sofia was always learning about doors that led to secret dingy rooms.

Her mother dumped her bag onto the table. "These are really elegant pieces. They were gifts to me. From people in foreign countries, when I travelled."

Sofia wanted nothing more than to put on the glasses of the jeweller. They had round magnifying lenses on them. His eyes were enormous. Sofia thought if she had such a pair of glasses, she would crawl around on her knees. And make conversation with ants and grasshoppers.

Her mother lit a cigarette. "I know it's normal to rob somebody, but not too much. We have nothing. The money in the bank was frozen. I didn't keep anything in my mattress. Those of us who are modern suffered first."

"Are you aware these pearls are fake?"

"No. But they were a gift from the ambassador. I should have known, shouldn't I?"

"The one who went to prison years ago?"

"Yes. How much will you give me for this watch? It belonged to my father."

"That I can give you something for. And that ring on your finger. Perhaps you don't want to part with it. But I can tell you it is very valuable."

Her wedding ring was so ostentatious. It didn't suit her parents' marriage.

Her mother often left her wedding ring on the soap dish on the back of the sink. Once it fell down the drain and she announced it was irretrievably lost. But the maids sprang into action and managed to rescue it from the drainpipe. Sofia could not say her mother was happy when it was retrieved. She simply shrugged, smiled weakly, and put it back on her finger.

"Take it," Clara said. "If a soldier sees it, he'll take it for his future wife. What am I supposed to do with it anyhow? What other people are doing? Swallow it and then crap it out? I can't act in that manner. I've had it."

She took the pile of money. She folded it and put it some-where underneath her skirt.

"And the soldiers are taking everything good for themselves. They don't even appreciate what they are using. They've never tasted pâté de foie in their lives. Now they eat it out of the can with a large spoon. They are bringing back stockings to women who live in the countryside. Can you imagine? What are they going to do? Milk the cows in silk stockings? The poor women will freeze to death."

Her mother could have sent one of the maids to buy them treats and delicacies from the Black Market. She had always sent them to run errands before the war. But this was something she needed to do herself now.

"I have to assume the risk myself. I can't ask anyone else to do it for me. They are trying to make us believe that things we adore are of no value and can be sacrificed. First they will take away our coffee. Then they will ask us to give up our freedom. Our books."

She stopped to look in the mirror before leaving, applying her makeup. She didn't resort to her usual colour palette, which was bright red lipstick and white powder underneath pink blush. Instead she applied makeup that was designed to look as though she was not wearing makeup. She put on a light peach lipstick that was similar to her lip colour. And a gentle brushing of blush over her cheeks to make it appear as though she'd been in the sun.

"Why can't I go to the Black Market with you?" Sofia asked.

"It's secret, darling. Please don't be an idiot. They know I am safe to sell to. I am already a dangerous person. They trust me. I would never turn anyone in. I would rather kill myself."

"I would not give them up either."

"Of course you would. You won't know how to resist torture. How could you? You've never suffered a moment in your life."

Sofia tried to picture what the Black Market looked like. She could not imagine where it was. It couldn't be far because her mother went there on the subway. She had heard the Black Market was underground. The girl pondered whether it was right beneath her feet. She passed a sewer grate and wanted to bend down and peer through the holes to see whether the market was there. She imagined it was in a black truck that moved around like the puppet show. Or maybe it was like a travelling theatre troupe.

When her mother came back from the Black Market, she had a large bag of coffee in her coat. She smelled so strongly of rich coffee, Sofia wanted to put her face into her mother's lapel and inhale her. She did not know if the coffee was particularly pungent, or if she hadn't smelled it in so long that she was no longer used to it.

"I was terrified riding the bus home. I thought everyone around me must be smelling the coffee on me. I got off the bus three stops early when it became crowded."

They ate a roll of sausage. They made no preparations. Sofia's mother took a knife, sliced large chunks of sausage, and handed them to Sofia. They both devoured it, like two dogs who needed nothing more in the world. She and her mother had never been so close.

She opened a jar of jam. Before she spread it on the bread, she stuck a spoonful in her mouth. Sofia was so surprised at just how good these things tasted. She thought they tasted much, much better than they ever had before the war. She felt she had never tasted fruit before. She used to eat while thinking of other things. She did not pay attention to the food. Now her mouth and body were completely focused on the jam. Sofia wondered if jam had always tasted this good, or if it was that food on the Black Market tasted better in general. Or if disobedience was a sort of spice in itself.

One day her mother brought home a book from the Black Market. "This was just written! Can you believe it! There's such a perfect feeling reading something that has just come out from a writer who is alive and well. You get to be one of its first readers. Our reactions will be historic."

She read the book out loud. It wasn't a fanciful story, as Sofia was hoping. But rather a manifesto about how to go about writing poetry while under occupation. When she was done, she tossed it into the fire. It lit up in an explosive way. Sparks began popping out of it. Embers started leaping out of the fireplace. Like tiny bombs. Mother and daughter grabbed the hems of their skirts and pulled them away from the fire.

All she knew about the Black Market was that it seemed to possess everything her mother desired. It would have her smell hanging like a cloud over it. It would have her thrill for being alive like an electric field in the air. It would be carpeted with her old stockings. Her mother's book might be there.

HUNGER GLOWS IN THE DARK

S ofia and the Goose walked for three days. Her feet were always sore. She fantasized about having new feet. She fantasized about passing by a store that sold feet. She would choose a new pair. They would be a tiny bit smaller. She would lift them up to see whether there were warts underneath. She would wiggle the toes. She would unscrew her feet and put the new ones on. But that was an absurd fantasy.

They walked away from the forest and through the fields where the Elysian peasants farmed. In this area she believed she was more or less safe. It seemed the Enemy did not necessarily think there was anything the matter with peasants. They didn't have affiliations with anybody. The peasants had stopped fighting back after the Enemy had razed the countryside. Her mother had said there were peasants who were entirely disgusted by the draft. They had gone into hiding, and some had even been arrested for opposing it. They had traces of Enemy blood themselves. And it was said they wanted the Enemy to take over. They

even agreed with some of the propaganda about citizens in the
Capital.

One night Sofia and the Goose walked through a field of
moon dandelions. It was the witching hour. As the sky darkened,
the dandelions began to glow like tiny satellites. They appeared
like the breath of children against a closed window. As she walked
through the moon dandelions, they erupted and their seeds rose
in the air, swirling and waltzing their way up into the darkening
and darkening sky until they affixed themselves like stars to the
firmament.

Every peasant they came across looked at them with suspicion. She didn't even think they spoke the same language. There
were some parts of the country, especially farther from the forest
and close to the eastern border, that spoke in the Enemy tongue.

It had not occurred to her that even if she were to trick the
Enemy into thinking she was a peasant, the peasants themselves
would not be tricked, or they would not want to hide or protect her.

She noticed an old lady wearing a large army coat from an Elysian soldier. She saw another farmer with an officer's hat. When
the soldiers had been killed, the peasants must have arrived like
vultures to clean them of their clothes. She wondered whether
there were photographs of strange children in the pockets of the
coat. The photographs of the soldier's children who were living
like memories the old lady had stolen, in her pocket.

There was a child sitting on top of a truck with no wheels. He
had on a gas mask. It made him look like a strange, uncanny bird.
Another group of children emerged from the truck. They were
also wearing gas masks. They looked so unlike the children who

had been with her on the train. The ones who were dressed in elegant clothing and had tears on their cheeks as the train pulled away.

What kind of child was Sofia now? Was she an elegant child from the train? Or was she a carrion bird?

Everyone was feasting off the spoils of the Capital. But they were hungry. It gave an evil glint to their eyes. Before the war, Sofia had never known anyone who was hungry. But now everyone was hungry. Hunger was new to her. As it was to most people in the city.

Although the Goose was able to find worms and grubs to eat, he sensed the hunger of others.

"This land has a very strange, vicious appetite. I can hear its belly grumbling. When you are raised to be eaten, like I am, you sense hunger from far off. That is how I first know that a wolf is near. I don't hear the subtle sounds of paws snapping twigs. I don't see it slinking around. I sense it. I sense its hunger. It transforms the atmosphere around it. It's like time slows down. It makes things quiet. You feel as though you are in a net already. You feel as though your decency has been stripped away from you. Nothing you believe to be important about yourself is important. You feel yourself stripped of meaning. It is a cold place to be. Do you feel it now?"

Sofia did feel it now. She felt naked. It was a desperate feeling. It was different from the feeling of the Enemy being close by. This was a feeling coming from her own people.

The hunger was such in this part of the country that she felt she was in as much danger as the Goose. The Goose had always said she was privileged because she did not have to worry about being eaten. She did not know what it was like to envision her body parcelled into different edible portions. She imagined a drawing of her naked body on a chart at the butcher shop. There were small darts along the legs and arms. With descriptions of them. People would come in the shop and point to her belly. Then the butcher would go put it in a sheet of newsprint and hand it to a complete stranger.

She imagined her heart being bitten into like an apple by a child, and then the child would walk around with two hearts beating in his chest. Like a marching game with two children who make sure their feet are in sync. And the child would fall in love with twice as many people as possible.

She knew it was not good to visualize horrific possibilities during a war. You could deal only with the danger at hand. It served only to make you like a frightened animal. Like a deer or a hare that can't move at all.

On the outskirts of a village, they walked through a doorway into a house that had a variety of walls destroyed. Most of the house was in rubble, and the ceiling had collapsed. She found a pile of potatoes in the larder. Her mother used to mash her potatoes more lightly than anybody else in the world. She served them to Sofia in a small porcelain bowl that had pink roses all around the rim. She liked to have mashed potatoes all on their own. As though they were a delicacy.

Now she bit into the boiled potato and it tasted like ashes, mud, lead pencil, and chalk.

When she was little, she always had her very own plates and bowls and cutlery. They were smaller and daintier and more decorated than those the adults ate off of. She had a small baby spoon. She used it to eat sherbet with. She could never decide which she preferred, ice cream or sherbet. She liked the bright colours of sherbet but the texture of ice cream. Ice cream seemed to sit on her tongue longer. It stayed a brief while to have a relationship and tell a little story.

She saw an armoire still standing in the midst of the rubble, with its doors open and the glass from its panes all broken. Surrounding the armoire were shards of china plates and cups. Then she looked into the armoire and saw on the top shelf one single teacup and spoon. Sitting daintily. As though there had been no devastation. As though they were expecting someone to pick them up and serve delicious scalding tea.

It was miraculous to see objects so refined here. It was surreal almost. It was hard to believe that once the teacup would not have been out of place at all. But in a world that entirely resembled it.

It was an artifact from a world that seemed to have existed many lifetimes before.

Then the teacup began to tremble. Although the armoire was perfectly still. And nothing else in the rubble was stirring. It shook violently.

"It's the soldiers. They are coming. The fine china can detect their movements. Let's go back to the trees!" she yelled to the Goose. But before she ran, she picked up the teacup and spoon and wrapped them in an extra sweater in her bag and tucked the bundle in securely.

She had to enter the edge of the forest to hide from the soldiers. It was a moonless forest without stars. She and the Goose couldn't see their hands or feet in front of their faces. The dark reality of the woods all around her became apparent. Each tree trunk bristling with pine needles—like the fur around the cuff of a wolf's neck, sticking straight up.

They suddenly, from the ground, a glowing dome appeared. The light was so soft, it didn't startle her in any way. Or make her feel afraid. It had the same glow as a small night lamp in the corner of her bedroom at home.

But how could that be? How could it be possible? How could someone have plugged in a lamp in the forest? Would they have plugged it into a tree? For a brief moment, Sofia's notion of the scientific universe expanded. She thought she would like to bring a record player out into the woods, plug it into a tree, and listen to the Elysian Children's Orchestra in the darkness.

Then a hundred mushrooms all around them began glowing. They were standing in a clearing in the woods, and they were surrounded by fairy mushrooms. They seemed to change wattage and colour, and so the light moved like an astral phenomenon, like the northern lights.

"It's a fairy circle," Sofia said, clasping her hands together.

"I have never seen anything so beautiful," the Goose said.

Sofia had finished a jar of water she'd brought along. She stopped for a moment and yanked up a large clump of soil with phosphorescent mushrooms sticking out of it. And she stuffed it in the jar and put the jar in her bag. They slept next to its glow.

She had a dream she was lost in the forest. But then she began to hear some noises. She followed the sounds and ended up at a clearing. There were small lights wrapped around the tree branches. There was a tent constructed of colourful bedsheets, sewn together in a quilt. In front of the entrance to the tent was a wooden sign on a stand on which were carved the words "Black Market."

Sofia pushed aside the fabric fold that served as a door and walked inside. There were tables covered in forbidden goods. Sofia ran up to them. She was surprised to recognize so many items.

There was a statuette of a naked woman. It had been on her mother's windowsill for as long as she could remember. What was it doing here? She began to look furtively and anxiously through the objects on the tables. There was a hairbrush she recognized. All its bristles were bent and wrecked. But she preferred it to any other brush. It was carved out of wood and had an apple painted on the back. Clara had had it since she was a child.

Then she saw a copy of her mother's book. She felt so relieved. All her problems in the world disappeared. She was thrilled. She reached out to grab it, but she woke up at the same moment. Her arms were above her head. Her hands were as empty as they had been the day she was born. She grasped at the emptiness. It seemed as though the universe was filled with darkness. There was nothing out there in the universe, no life, other than the one earth. And this was completely overwhelming. She felt how tiny she was in relationship to the rest of the universe. She rolled over and grasped the Goose in her arms. This way she felt larger at least. She wiped the tears on her face into the Goose's feathers.

THE WOLVES DANCED

ON THE CEILING

They ended up walking along a road that went through the forest again. She began to hear the trees whispering and talking to one another. They took the wind and turned it into words. They were able to communicate with one another as though through a telegraph wire. They knew what was happening throughout the country.

Sofia didn't know why the trees were so noisy until she was on a hill and was able to see the road beneath her. It was the road that led to the Capital.

The road in the distance began to grow black. As though there was a black flood coming down it. It was as though the grey dirt road were being covered with tar. She knew soon enough that it was troops of soldiers. She had never seen so many before. She had thought the Elysian soldiers in the Capital constituted a sizable army. She had thought that they would have hope against the Enemy. But now she realized that Balthazar had been right. The Capital didn't stand a chance against the black flood that was heading towards them. It extended as far as the eye could see.

Why were so many troops going to the Capital? She knew. She knew. She knew.

"The Uprising," she whispered.

There were airplanes in the sky. They were all headed towards the Capital. They had to be warplanes.

If she had got the book out of the country, perhaps they would still have had a chance. Perhaps the countries on the other side of the forest would have come to their aid when they read the book. They would have helped the resistance. She wondered whether she had single-handedly lost the war for her country. But how could that be possible? She was just a tiny girl. And then she thought if that was possible, it meant she had power as an individual.

She wondered whether she ought to go back to the Capital. She was so homesick. She had never expected to feel this desperate to be in the familiarity of her own home. She thought homesickness was something other children felt, not her. She just wanted to run back to the Capital. It didn't matter if it was captured. She went to the road. She stood on it, staring in the direction of the city.

"I want to go home!" Sofia suddenly cried out.

"You're not making any sense. You have to be realistic. I've been around more death and slaughter than you have. And it is a very magnetic pull. It's like a black hole."

She had once been given a cast-iron lantern with wolves carved into its sides. It was an expensive gift from one of her mother's friends. They had picked it up while travelling in the Enemy country. Trinkets from that country were always peculiar. They had a vaguely medieval aesthetic that everyone had abandoned so long ago. Her mother lit a candle in the middle of the lantern. And then she spun it. And the room was filled with wolves. As though a group of them had leapt out of the woods. They were circling the small fire, wanting to pounce on whoever was being protected by its glow. Sofia cowered on her bed. She was upset that her mother had let some villainous force out into her world.

The sky above the city was filled with wolves. There were wolves on the rooftops. Crawling all over the place like alley cats.

She thought of running back to her mother, regardless of the danger. She wanted a lesser but more familiar safety. But she could not face her mother without the book. Her mother would be thinking that the book was safe. Her mother would be imagining she was going to be immortal. Her mother would die terrified but with a feeling of vindication. Sofia could not take that away from her.

"If you were about to be shot in the head, what would you think of?"

"That question makes no sense to me because geese do not get shot in the head."

"Well, if you were about to get your head chopped off."

"I would be thinking, This fucking dimwit is the cause of my demise. How pathetic. And isn't that how everything goes? The stupid win in the end."

A WARTIME LULLABY

As they began to live under Occupation, Sofia's relationship with her mother changed.

Sofia had never spent much time with her mother in the daylight before the war. She didn't even know who her mother might be in the mornings. But when she woke up one day, she was surprised to hear her mother in the kitchen. And she was even more surprised to see her up and dressed. Wide awake, ready for the day.

"Come along, Sofia. Have a little something to eat, then we will go out into the world. Get your clothes on."

She had never been her mother's primary companion. Ever. When they were together, her mother was perpetually focused on finding someone else to talk to. At which point Sofia was abandoned.

The change in Clara's diet also seemed to make her more awake and alive. Before the war, she had existed on a diet of rich pastries and bowls of milky coffee. And she was often in a sugar-induced deep sleep after snacking on a large mille-feuille. Now she existed primarily on stale bread and tea and the occasional spoonful of Black Market jam.

Sofia was helping the maid clean the kitchen floor. When Clara walked in, kicked off her shoes, and picked up a rag. Sofia looked up. "What are you doing? Are you going to scrub with us!"

"What are you laughing at? Do you think I can't clean floors like everybody else? If I could, I would have a photographer record this moment. I want people to know that when the war came, I was down on my hands and knees with the working women of this country, trying to save it."

She tried to get down on her hands and knees, but then her stockinged feet came in contact with a puddle of soapy water. She began flailing her body around like a first-time skater on an ice-skating rink. Sofia and the maid stared at her as her body struck one angle after another, trying to restore balance. It was startling to see.

"Careful!" Clara said. "If I fall to the ground, my ass will cause this building to fall to the ground, even though the bombs didn't."

"Yes," Sofia said. "It's a pity the photographers aren't here to capture Clara Bottom as Everywoman."

Clara had a loud laugh at this. She tossed her soapy rag at Sofia. Who screamed when it landed in her lap.

To Sofia's surprise, Clara had baked a little cake for her birthday. She was dressed in her father's green velvet housecoat, with a silk kerchief covered in rose blossoms on her head. While Sofia sat in her old sailor's dress, which now had holes under the armpits. Clara held the small lopsided cake, smeared with blue icing, out to her on a round tray. Sofia knew immediately that it had been baked by her mother and not the maid. It was too pathetic to have been concocted by the maid.

Her mother took out a little music box, wound it up, and put it on the table.

"I have a need to walk by myself. I miss that feeling of independence. I just want to be a young woman in the Capital, up to no good. It'll be like when I snuck into nightclubs when I was a teenager. How exciting it was! To be in the city! I wanted to do everything I wasn't supposed to do. We had such wild moves. I didn't know any of the steps at first. But I learned them in no time at all."

It wasn't often that her mother reminisced like this. She didn't believe in women being all reverent of their younger days, as though they were the high point of their lives. She thought a woman wasn't even in her prime until she was in her fifties and had reached menopause.

"Show me," Sofia said, standing in front of her mother with her arms akimbo—demanding things as though she were a soldier.

Clara looked at Sofia. She held her in her arms and began dancing with her. Sofia stood on her tippy-toes. Her mother was not a tall woman, but Sofia's head still rested on her soft breasts.

Sofia could not remember the last time her mother had held her in her arms. Outside, the sound of a loudspeaker warned the citizens that curfew had begun and it was time to get inside.

THE FOG WEARS GREY STOCKINGS

When Sofia and the Goose awoke, fog was everywhere. It was thick all around her. She couldn't make out anything. It was as though she were in a fishbowl with filthy glass she could not see out of. The clouds had come down from the sky and settled in for a nap. They weren't going to rise until noon.

The pair set off walking, nonetheless. But they had to walk slowly and be completely aware. The ground didn't really appear until they set their feet down on it. She had to believe with each step that the road was there. They had no idea what was surrounding them. They could not even make out the trees.

When the fog was very thick like this, it was normal for people to put off going to work until it lifted. It made rational sense to do this, since the fog could be so disorienting and lead to terrible accidents. But there was the other reason too. You might encounter a creature made out of fog.

The fog was so odd and heavy in Elysia. Parts of it ripped off and formed little pockets that refused to dissipate.

The fog would disguise itself as corporeal earthly forms. It could retain these forms for hours. Enough to terrify you. It would always be best to lock yourself inside.

Her grandmother had all sorts of stories about the fog getting into her house. She said she walked into the kitchen one morning. She saw a pale girl sitting at the kitchen table. She had only one arm. But then her hand reached out of nowhere. Picked up a glass of milk and lifted it to her lips.

Sofia took a scarf and wrapped it around her mouth and nose, and she fished a handkerchief out of her bag and wrapped it around the Goose's face. They moved through the fog together. Like two very odd bandits.

"Whatever you do, don't open your mouth and scream. That is how they get in. Don't let them know you are afraid. Just ignore them. Let's look straight ahead. We'll keep marching forward and never slow our pace. I think noticing them gives them their power."

The fog began to clear. Thankfully the road seemed to be empty up ahead. The fog was attaching itself to the trees, which knit it into various forms.

As Sofia and the Goose hurried on, all the trees had turned black. Their roots were feeding off the dead of the country. They had been drawn with India ink by a hand that suffered from shell shock. The thin trees against the sky looked like cracks in porcelain cups that had been repaired.

They seemed wicked and unkind. It was intolerable for Sofia to have to listen to their hostile ranting as she walked. She passed them as though she were passing a jail cell with dangerous men luring at her from behind the bars.

"Shut up. Prissy thing. So far from the Capital now. She's afraid of us. She thinks we are going to eat her. Prejudices. Stupid thinking. If you're going to treat us as though we're dangerous, then we might as well be vicious."

The fog made it hard to see anything. Sofia began relying on her other senses. There was the sound of a baby crying. She began to follow it. Perhaps it had crawled off by itself. There was a cradle on the side of the road. That was where the crying was coming from. Sofia spread her arms out in front of her. She so wanted to save something, someone. She so wanted to be a war hero.

She saw a form moving and twisting under a pink baby blanket that was trimmed with white lace. She grabbed the end of it and yanked it off to free the baby. But to her horror, underneath the blanket was a crow that opened its beak and squawked and fluttered its wings viciously, then burst up into the sky.

As it rose, the sky began to fill with other crows. They were flying up out of baby cradles all over that town. It quickly became night.

With the night, the fog finally dissipated. They found themselves standing near a rusted hull of a car several feet from the road. It had been there quite a while, as vines had climbed through holes in the bottom of the car and wrapped themselves around the steering wheel. Sofia and the Goose climbed into the back seat and curled up together. She turned off her brain like a light. She fell into a deep, dreamless sleep. It was the type of nap one has in a coffin.

Sofia was awoken by the sound of gurgling water: a rumbling, mumbling noise that was approaching. As though she were in the husk of a ship that had slipped out to sea. As the noise grew louder and closer, she realized it was the sound not of water but of voices. Crowds of people were approaching. And every now and then a louder cry erupted from the assemblage of voices, and when it did, the voices all around quieted down temporarily. They slowly began to rise afterwards, like water filling up in a bathtub.

Sofia peeked up at the rear-view mirror to see a large group of citizens from her country being led by soldiers. They were a well-dressed group, relatively. They seemed to have been recently evacuated from their homes. Many were carrying luggage and expensive items that were worthless for survival. Sofia and the Goose remained frozen in each other's arms, crouched beneath the seat.

Sofia and the Goose stayed in the car for several hours, until they were certain the group had long past. As they walked along the road, they continued to come across all sorts of articles that seemed to have been abandoned by the group. They stopped to look at a painting that had been left by the side of the road, leaning against a tree. Sofia and the Goose crouched down to look at it. It was of a very sophisticated girl with red hair and green eyes. She had a fierce, proud look in her eyes.

Sofia stared at the painting, waiting to see if the proud expression would change, whether the eyes would reveal any sadness or fear. Whether her mouth would appear to have a frown on it.

But there was no change. Sofia stood up and began to move on. The proud simply do not survive wartime, she thought.

She came across a long scarf hanging from a bush, and she quickly wrapped it around her own neck. She kept an eye open for something to eat, and finally came across a can of milk. She viciously stabbed the lid with her knife and suckled eagerly from the can. As though she were a famished baby. She offered some to the Goose, who shook his head in disgust.

Sofia and the Goose stood at a group of signs on the road. "Let's go to Abeu Ivor," she declared. She pointed to the words "Abeu Ivor" on one of the signs, thinking of a postcard she'd received before the Occupation.

"Why?"

"My friend Celeste is there."

"Do you imagine this town has somehow managed to escape the war?"

"She might put us up. She'll be happy to see me. If she didn't want to see me, she would not have sent me a postcard from there."

"The town will be swarming with soldiers. It's too dangerous to go there."

"Yes, but she is in love with one of them. She knows soldiers. She'll tell them not to hurt us."

"You are suggesting we put our fates in the hands of a traitor."

"Well, yes. Why not?"

"How do you know this girl?"

"She was our maid."

THE PATRON SAINT OF

YOUNG GIRLS IN HIGH HEELS

Celeste's aunt had worked for them before. And she was efficient and quite wonderful. She had become pregnant. She recommended that her sixteen-year-old niece come work for them. The minute Celeste showed up at their door, it was clear they could never fire her. She was too vulnerable, but she didn't know she was vulnerable. And that made her even more so. She was dreamy. She was too young and frivolous for the job.

She had features that were elfin-like. She had an enormous forehead. She had very large eyes and ears that stuck out of the side of her head, but her other features seemed so tiny. She was so thin it made her hands and feet seem slightly too big for her limbs. She had blond bangs that she was able to wear down to her nose but could still see through. Sofia had known other girls who had attempted this hairstyle in the Capital. But they ended up not being able to see through their bangs and walking into walls and tripping over furniture.

Celeste was pretty in a way that other children find pretty. When adults looked at her, they would never think there might be something extraordinary about the girl. She was so thin. She seemed as though she had just run in from being caught in the rain. She was pretty in a way that made you think you were the only one who considered her pretty. And having this knowledge made you feel protective of her.

She also had a very beautiful frown. Which was of great value during wartime.

Celeste did silly things that she insisted made her work better. But there was really only evidence to the contrary. She danced around to ballet while doing the dusting. She did little pas de chat in the living room. She had taken ballet lessons, surprising for a girl of her class. She was still able to take them on Saturdays. She often announced that dancing was her life and she would end up on stage one day. Even though Sofia was a child, she knew this aspiration of Celeste's was beyond the girl's reach.

She knew this because her mother didn't pay Celeste's dancing any mind. And if her mother didn't appreciate Celeste's dancing, really how good could it be? Her mother was a great fan of the ballet, and she treated Celeste's dancing as an annoyance. Something that made her presence in the house too loud.

Whereas the other maids and housekeepers had left because of the threat of the invasion, Celeste kept returning. Even if she wasn't going to be paid proper wages, she arrived to have something to eat. Celeste was one of those skinny young people who could seemingly devour any kind of food. And remain as thin as a pencil. Sofia's mother, once concerned about her intake, had taken her to the doctor to see whether she had worms.

Although Celeste was only a few years older than Sofia, she already belonged too much to the land of adults. Girls from poorer neighbourhoods grew up faster. She seemed to be more of an adult than a child. But an odd sort of adult. One who did not have any common sense and made terrible decisions.

One day Celeste was in the bath in the main bathroom. She was whistling a tune that was unfamiliar. No one said anything. Everyone became very quiet. The tune had a different melodic structure that was not recognizable to them. It had to be a refrain from the Enemy's country. It was like seeing an invasive flower in a garden. Of course it was beautiful, but who knew how it would proliferate. It might strangle all the other flowers and suck so many nutrients from the earth, it would make it barren.

Sofia always wished Celeste had not whistled that tune. Celeste said she had learned it hanging around soldiers she thought were handsome, and she didn't care what anyone said.

Sofia's mother had once told her that Celeste wasn't that stupid; she simply preoccupied herself with stupid things.

When Celeste disappeared, Sofia's mother spent the day on the telephone trying to find out what had happened to her. She got dressed and said she was going over to Celeste's home to see if she could find something out. Sofia imagined that Celeste was just with friends. But her mother told her there was indeed reason to worry. Celeste's father, who worked at a meatpacking facility, had joined the resistance.

When Clara came back, her face was red and she looked out of breath. She told Sofia the entire family had been arrested. Sofia sat down on the kitchen chair to hear her mother's story. Even during a war, people could be shocked over and over again by everyday cruelty.

HEATHER O'NEILL

Sofia knew people could be arrested and immediately shot for working with the resistance. But she did not know their families and children also could be. Strangely, this comforted her. It meant her mother's book was dangerous for her too. And since she could immediately be shot in the head because of it, did it not follow that she was in part co-authoring it?

It had struck Clara and Sofia as odd to see the postcard. They were mystified to see it in the mailbox. They had received no letters at all in so long. It was from Celeste. She said she was in love. She was living in the town of Abeu Ivor.

They did not know what to make of this postcard at all. It seemed as though she was not acknowledging that a war was going on, nor did she say what had happened to her family or how she'd escaped. It was no different from the types of postcards they used to receive before the war. When people had simple concerns and went on holidays. And worried about whether they were giving their children special enough childhoods. It was a mystery why Celeste had sent such a picturesque postcard during wartime. Her mother found it troubling.

But Sofia was pleased that Celeste was thinking of them. She tucked the postcard away in the inside pocket of her coat. She wanted to hold on to it. There was something about Celeste she had always found intriguing. She had knowledge about what it was like to be an older girl. The postcard was sent from the strange, vulnerable world of older adolescence.

• • •

"If she was your maid," said the Goose, "then you are especially a fool to go see her. The tables have been reversed now. She has all the power. She will force you to be her maid. We will never be able to endure the humiliation. Or I for one won't be. I'd honestly rather be soup."

Sofia was slightly worried the Goose might have a point. Perhaps Celeste had developed some sort of class consciousness during the war. But she doubted it. She didn't seem like the type.

"No, no, you have it all wrong. We were always very nice to her. Too nice, really. She hardly did any work at all. She will be very happy to see me. You will fall in love with Celeste. I used to be so smitten with her. I sometimes wished I could grow up to be a man. So I could marry Celeste."

"We have to be wary of other human beings."

"Celeste isn't a human being at all. She's more like a pretty white goat. If you could imagine a goat riding a bicycle and going to the grocery store. And up on its hind legs, dancing to the radio."

"I cannot. But I do see your point. There are girls who are kind. Occasionally I think it's because they are too silly to be cruel."

ADRIFT IN FORMALDEHYDE

When they reached Abeu Ivor, it was evident that the tiny city had been bombed. There were no human victims she could see. The ambulances had already come and gone. The first thing they did was to remove the bodies. You couldn't get anything done with bodies around.

The strangest thing was how there were objects that were completely out of place.

There were objects that were never meant to be on the street.

There was a beautiful rocking horse in the middle of the road. Who did the horse belong to now? Had it escaped? Had it been liberated from the child who previously owned it? Was it now wild?

There was a doll whose crown was cracked in half. You couldn't tell if she was attractive. She had no eyes to see. The eyes of the doll were still back in the house, witnessing the past. There was a chest of drawers. One of the three drawers was open, and there were ladies' undergarments all over the ground. There was a single pair of blue silk underwear hanging from a branch of a tree. It was as though a piece of the sky had torn off on the branch.

They passed the sweet shop. The window had been blown out. There were bits of glass all over the ground. It made a crackling sound as they walked, as though the world were on fire.

There was nothing left of the town. It had been burnt into a pile of black rubble. The smell of the burning went so deep into Sofia's lungs, it affected her too much. Everything she smelled for the next several weeks would reek of smoke. Even flowers.

There was no chance that she would find Celeste. Whoever was in this town had obviously had to leave. "Oh no, no, no, no, no," cried Sofia. "I just wanted to see someone from home."

She knew it was a hospital because it had a red cross in a white circle out front. Part of the eastern wall had collapsed, but otherwise, it was rather miraculously intact. It was clear the army had been there at some point in the recent past. There were tire marks all over the front. The wheels of all the vehicles had made barren whatever possible garden was there. Sofia did not believe the soldiers were returning. Not for a while. They had already ransacked the building. From what she could tell, their raison d'être was to go around laying waste to places.

"Let's go into the hospital," she said to the Goose. "Maybe we can find some food and blankets. If it's empty, we can sleep there and continue to the Black Market in the morning."

"Wherever it may be," added the Goose, tired himself.

There was a swimming pool behind the hospital. It was rather pretty, with white and blue tiles all over the bottom. But it hadn't been maintained. The surface was covered with leaves and a small pond of floating scum. And when she looked at the bottom, she could see there were leaves that had sunk down there. There was also a wheelchair that had perhaps fallen in during some shenanigans.

The Goose didn't mind the state the pond was in at all. He climbed in almost immediately and seemed to fall into a stupor. As though he had forgotten for a moment all about Sofia and the war and had gone back to the simpler state of being a goose.

Sofia decided to go and look around inside. She had never been in such a large building unsupervised before. It seemed impossible that a building this size could be empty. She kept expecting a soldier to appear, or an abandoned patient with missing limbs and bandages on their eyes. And if it was empty and had truly been abandoned to its ghosts, what would they be like? Would she encounter a coughing ghost of a child who had died of influenza? Or the ghost of a woman who had died in childbirth, scouring the hospital for her baby? It gave Sofia chills.

"Stop it!" she whispered harshly to her imagination.

The first room she walked into was an amphitheatre. There were chairs around a small podium in the middle and glass cabinets on all the walls. The cabinet drawers contained the most remarkable specimens. This was what the human body was made up of. But it was kept on the inside. She came to a section with jars of fetuses. They looked like the drawings of trolls that were in the fairy tale book her mother had ripped apart. It was hard to accept that these babies had grown in the uteruses of women. They seemed to have grown underground with the roots of trees.

Perhaps these weren't the fetuses of babies at all. Maybe they were the babies of trolls that had been discovered in the woods. They were killed but then kept in formaldehyde for the scientific community to examine.

• • •

Sofia called out to ask if there was anyone in the hospital, but there was no answer. The building did not have the anaesthetic smell of cleaning products that most hospitals had. Instead there was a musky smell of male perspiration.

Everywhere she wandered, there was evidence a large group of men had been there.

She walked into the cafeteria. There were dirty plates all over the tables. There was the stench of food that had rotted many days before. She opened the fridge door to encounter a putrid smell and heaps of mouldy food swarming with tiny bugs. She slammed the door shut so quickly, it seemed to shake the whole building.

She looked in the large fireplace to discover the fire had long since been put out. It didn't radiate any heat at all.

She came across ashtrays that were overflowing with cigarette butts. She came across makeshift ashtrays too. She opened up what appeared to be a cookie tin and found it filled with cigarette butts.

The most evidence that men had been there was in the bathroom. There was a pile of newspapers in the Enemy language stacked up next to the toilet. She picked one up. From the photographs on the front page, it seemed as though they were having the very opposite headlines as her country. Elysian newspapers had sadder and sadder headlines. The Enemy's paper had a photograph of people tossing their hats in the air, with triumphant grins on their faces.

She found a book on the edge of the sink. She walked to it immediately. There had been an order to destroy all the books. So she was surprised there was one hanging around where soldiers had been. As soon as she held it up, she saw it was in the Enemy language. There was a drawing of a man on a boat in gold on the cover. She had somehow assumed that since they had ordered all the books in her country destroyed, they also didn't publish any of their own.

There was a pile of dog turds in the hallway. There had been dogs here.

She found a small wing of rooms on the top floor. This was a wing where patients with terminal conditions most likely once stayed.

The rooms had a more permanent feel. When patients entered into them, they were meant to stay there until the end of their lives. They were much more like rooms in a hotel than a hospital. They were quaint. They seemed very feminine.

Sofia walked into one. The wallpaper was a light pink with a pattern of roses that were a slightly darker pink. There was a round mirror on the wall. And there was a small dressing table underneath that had cat figurines on it and a rusted gold-plated box filled with makeup. The bed was still a hospital one, but it was disguised by a floral comforter and a pile of about ten pillows with frilly covers.

Even though the room managed to look very homey, it was still in a state of disorder. It was apparent that men had been staying in these more decorated rooms too. There was a pile of dirty plates next to the bed. And Sofia would find out in the coming days that there were more dirty dishes under the bed. Someone had been in the habit of eating in bed and then simply pushing the dishes underneath it and forgetting about them.

There was an abandoned pair of men's army boots with holes in the soles in the corner of the room, and a man's hat was on the windowsill. And there was a broken tobacco pipe on the nightstand. The mattress had a dent in the middle, as though an unexpectedly large man had lain down on it.

Sofia figured it was probably the more elite officers who had stayed in these rooms.

Whenever she saw a faucet, she was in the habit of turning it. At the beginning of their journey, water had still occasionally come out of them. But the infrastructure of this small city was completely destroyed, so it was unlikely any water would come out of the faucets in the hospital. She liked to turn them on just the same.

She turned on the faucet, and nothing at all came out. Then came a hollow, maniacal woman's laugh. Sofia hurriedly shut the faucet. It seemed that laughter was far more horrific than sobbing during wartime.

"I wish you wouldn't do that," said the Goose. "It's perverse. Nothing good ever comes out of those pipes."

They thought no one was in the hospital. Because there wasn't the sound of anyone moving around. She called out loudly. There wasn't a response from anyone. She and the Goose took a peek in each room. The beds were all disorderly and empty. There didn't seem to be anyone there at all.

When the sun went down, she walked around the hospital to see whether there was a light on in any of the windows. She assumed every human was as addicted to light as she was. They wouldn't be able to resist turning one on.

There was no evidence anyone else was in the building. She

wasn't sure why she continued checking. She felt a presence. But since she was in a hospital, she thought she might be feeling the presence of a ghost.

She took the little paper she had been guarding so carefully out of her pocket and placed it on the windowsill, where it might dry out in the morning sun. She fell asleep in the pink room.

Sofia woke up with a horrible start. There was something that felt very much like a tarantula crawling across her stomach. She shuddered with horror. She didn't want to look but couldn't help it. She seemed to need to have concrete proof. She sat against the wall, looking on in terror at the bedcovers, which were bundled up at the foot of the bed. She was thinking that perhaps she had imagined the sensation of a giant spider crawling across her body when she saw a figure sneak out on multiple legs from under the bedcovers.

But it wasn't a spider at all. It was a small, delicate hand. It crawled out from under the covers. It stretched out, looking to touch someone, looking around for Sofia. It moved to the right and then the left. It went as far as its arm would allow it to extend. Then, reacting to its limitations, it paused. Of course it wasn't going to remain immobile, but she quite hoped it would. The hand abruptly moved into reverse and disappeared under the blankets. When it appeared again, this time it brought the rest of the body with it.

It was a girl with strawberry-blond hair. Her hair was thin and straight but in a great tangle, especially on the back of her head, where it seemed to have formed into a giant mat. She was pale. Her eyes had huge bags underneath them. They were so puffy it seemed as though she couldn't open them. When she smiled, her eyes squinted.

Like most people when interrupted in the middle of a deep sleep, she smiled broadly and hopefully. She smiled as though she were in love.

It took Sofia a moment to accept that she was a human being. She was so sure she was a fairy creature who had come from the woods.

"Celeste!" Sofia exclaimed.

Celeste was wearing a long white nightgown that went to her feet. She had on one silk sock, and her other foot was bare.

They all sat down in the small kitchen in their wing. To Sofia's absolute delight, there were cans of food on the shelves. "The soldiers left quickly, but they are coming back. They always have food."

Sofia opened a large can she had found on the kitchen shelves, and it was filled with a mushy spaghetti with sauce. She dumped it into a pot and put it on the gas stove. When the blue flame licked out of the range, she was so surprised she jumped. It was then that Celeste told Sofia and the Goose the story of how she came to live in the hospital. She had to be shaken awake three times during the story. Despite it being the story of the most harrowing adventure of her life, she seemed to lose interest in it. As she spun her noodles around her fork, it began to hypnotize her. Her head slipped, as though off her neck, and fell forward into the spaghetti. She sat up again abruptly. She continued the story, albeit with spaghetti sauce on the tip of her nose and her eyebrows.

"They barged into our apartment building. It was so hot that night that I was sleeping on my balcony. They didn't see me there. They made my mother and father get dressed while they pointed guns at their heads. They had to change right in front of the soldiers. When I saw that, I knew it doesn't matter if you get dressed during wartime. It doesn't matter if you are naked.

"I climbed down the fire escape in my nightgown. I would have got away. Or I would have at least got away from the square and the audience. But I saw them take my mother out the door of the building. They were pushing her and yelling at her. I had never seen anyone treat my mother that way. Everybody loved my mother.

"I saw my mother being dragged into a truck. When I cried out, she turned and saw me and she looked horrified. And she yelled, Run, Celeste! Run! But that was all she told me. She didn't say where I should run to, so I stayed right there. Everybody stopped and looked at me. I was in the square with my bare feet and my nightgown.

"A soldier came and asked me to get in his car. He said, You don't want to see this ugliness. I'll protect you. The thing I will never forget is the expression on my mother's face when she saw me being taken away from her. I wish she hadn't been upset. I wish she hadn't seen it. That was the worst. Why do mothers have to get so upset?"

Celeste lit up a cigarette. She had taken up smoking, like the boys at Sofia's grandmother's house. She took a drag and held the cigarette between her fingers, forgetting about it as it burned down to the filter and singed her skin. The ashes fell into her noodles without her noticing or caring.

"I was very, very sad about my mother. But the soldiers who took me swore they were not the ones who had killed her. They said it was other soldiers. They said: There are bad soldiers and good soldiers. It must have been the bad soldiers who murdered my dear mother.

"I tried not to cry too much. I knew if I cried too much, they would get tired of me and throw me out. Then I would be murdered too. I cried for three days. They gave me some whisky in my milk. It was the only way I could fall asleep. The whisky made me fall asleep, but I felt even worse the next morning when I woke up. I thought I would die from missing my mother so much.

"I really started thinking I would have been better off dead. I would have much preferred to be murdered with my family. Then I would not have known what was happening to us all. Actually, I would have preferred to be shot around the dining room table. Then we would have all died with our heads in our bowls of soup."

Sofia and the Goose took a moment to visualize this peculiar scene that Celeste had created for them. The symmetry of it was fascinating.

"That's when one of the soldiers gave me medicine. He said I would be able to think about my mother as much as I wanted. But I wouldn't be sad at all."

She began taking the pills every day. It made her popular with the soldiers, who were also interested in seeing such a tiny girl knock herself out. They believed all girls should be inebriated all the time. They were much funnier in bed. It was lovely when they stumbled on their way home. They did very amusing things. They slid off their chairs and ended up on the ground. They sucked their cheeks in to look like a fish and then kissed you. They put your face in both palms and declared that you were beautiful. They said they loved you.

"I stayed with them for three months. I was meant to go with them when they left. But I fell into a deep sleep. I took more medicine than usual. I think I was asleep for three days straight. When I woke up, everyone was gone. I was so surprised. One of the officers was so in love with me. He said he wanted to marry me. He is coming back for me."

"You don't speak the same language. You can't really know what he said," Sofia reasoned.

"If they weren't coming back, they would not have left their belongings."

And later, Celeste showed her an operating room that was filled with large, unmanageable tanks of gasoline. It was like looking over the deck of a ship at an ocean of sharks. Their presence was so sinister to Sofia that she shut the door quickly.

In Sofia's folklore book, there was a story about a woman who put fly tape all over her porch. There was a little skinny girl standing on the porch in the morning. Her feet were stuck to the floor. Celeste reminded Sofia of one of these fairies.

One of the objections to traditional fables in her country was that they all seemed to be about sex and rape; although no one could put their finger on where in the story the sexual act had actually happened. Her mother had particularly despised these stories. She didn't understand how reading about the repeated degradation of girls was suitable entertainment for anybody. But Sofia found them comforting, especially now. These horrific fairy tales now seemed to have a context and to make sense. Especially since she was going through adolescence without her mother.

One day, Celeste spent the entire afternoon in the backyard with her arms spread to both sides. She told Sofia she wanted to know what it felt like to be a tree. But she could never be a tree. Sofia knew that staying in the hospital forever was not an option. The soldiers would obviously return. Each day she woke up feeling a little more desperate, knowing her luck might run out and the soldiers might arrive. And anyway, she needed to keep moving. She wanted to get to the Black Market. She wanted Celeste to come along with her. But she knew she couldn't ask her just yet.

She looked at Celeste, with her arms spread, as though nothing in the world could touch her. But Sofia felt the opposite.

Sofia felt the constant sense of being followed. It was painful to be this aware of your surroundings.

Now she understood what those animals in the forest were feeling. Previously, she had considered them paranoid. They looked around, sensed nothing, and then scurried off. But now she knew what they were sensing.

She thought she could make out the heartbeat of a soldier nearby. It was ferocious. She knew it was the heart in her chest that was actually beating. But it was beating in a way it never had before. So she seemed to think it had to be the heart of a soldier that was rocking her insides.

She felt a different sort of coldness in the air. It smelled like copper. As though she were holding two fists of pennies up to her face. It was the smell of a male hand up against her mouth.

Every sound was amplified. The sticks beneath her shoes snapped. As though she were standing on ice that was cracking and she was about to fall through.

Celeste showed Sofia her medicine bag. She did not want to share the pills with anyone. She was as protective with the bag as a dog was with treats. But Sofia had no desire to touch the pills because she saw the effect they had on Celeste. She looked beatific when she gazed into the bag. It was an enormous bag that the few remaining pill bottles rolled around at the bottom of. Sofia couldn't imagine Celeste carrying it if it were full. Sofia once gave her a plate, and it fell through Celeste's hands and smashed on the floor. "I'm sorry. It was too heavy." There were still a couple of full bottles among the empty ones. They could not last forever, although Celeste seemed unconcerned about that. She had become dependent on these pills while she was with the soldiers. They had been able to hold her captive with them. But now she had these magical pills and was free of the soldiers.

A peculiar state came over Celeste right after she got high. It was as though her brain were a toilet and she had just flushed it.

"Look at my hands." She held them up for Sofia to look at. "Can you see through them?"

"No."

"You can't? They look like they are made of the same material as clouds. Like the steam on the surface of a mirror after you take a warm bath. I'm afraid to blow on them or they will disappear."

She was standing with her hands against the window, and she was breathing steam on it. "I feel that if I have a perfect enough thought in my head, I will be able to exhale frost on the window."

She was staring into her cup while sitting outside. When Sofia sat next to her, she held up the cup. There was a leaf floating in it. "I'm afraid to move. I want to take a sip, but I don't want to upset the sea in my cup and have the ship sink and all its poor passengers slip away to an untimely death."

Celeste was humming a song. It sounded so pretty and forlorn. It was familiar to Sofia and began to strike emotional nostalgic chords in her body. Sofia searched her brain for the composer. Then she realized all at once that Celeste was humming the tune to a cola commercial that used to play on the radio.

She came out of her room wrapped in a blanket. She spent the whole day wrapped in it as though she were in a cocoon. She categorically refused to take it off, despite the bottom being covered in dirt and debris.

There was something ethereal and transparent about Celeste. She always reminded Sofia of the moon when it came out during the day.

She nodded off on the couch with a cigarette between her fingers. Sofia hurried over and plucked it from her. There were already two cigarette burn holes in the beautiful light blue nightgown she was wearing. She remained with her hand out, as though preparing to take a drag. As though she had paused for a brief moment in a conversation to collect her thoughts. And the moment she opened her eyes, she would deliver something profound.

She nodded off everywhere, very much like a cat. She curled up in an armchair. The chair seemed like a large hand that was holding and admiring Thumbelina. She folded her limbs up, like the petals of a flower that were closing at night. And she would fall asleep in nooks and crannies. She once offered to wash the dishes. They then found her headfirst in the sink as though she were in the midst of being swallowed by a whale.

Sofia went to talk to Celeste, but when she entered the bedroom, she found her holding the Goose in her arms. Unlike the boys, Celeste showed great affection for the Goose.

"You are so beautiful. You remind me of laundry. When the laundry comes back, you hold it in front of your face and you can't believe it. All the stains are gone away. You would never know a meatball fell on me. You would never know I had my period.

"I saw you dunk your head in the pool, and it was the most wonderful thing. It was as though I was at the Olympics. Do you remember that time the gymnast Lydia Meusla was expected to win bronze at the Olympics. And everyone was so excited that our country would finally win a medal. But then she slipped and broke her ankle. You reminded me of her when you stuck your butt up in the air like that."

Sofia got very worried when Celeste began to make a fuss about his neck. She knew it was his greatest desire to be told he had all the attributes of a swan.

"Your neck is so beautiful. It's so long. I wish I could have a long neck like that. I've been told I have a long neck. But it's not like yours. You have a neck that was meant to wear pearls. My mother always said I had to hold my head up high so it would accentuate my neck. But my neck is nothing like yours. It's extraordinary. Is it longer than goose necks should be? When I first saw you, I was certain you were a swan."

The Goose stretched his neck upwards as she spoke and rocked from one foot to the other, intoxicated by Celeste's compliments. Obviously, she knew just the words he delighted in hearing.

Sofia was worried that were Celeste to leave, the Goose might decide to go with her. When she could not find the Goose, she would go to Celeste's room and often find the two of them napping together. She thought Celeste did nap like an animal. So that was perhaps why the Goose wanted to do it with her. Once, Sofia walked into the bathroom. Celeste and the Goose were both sleeping in the bathtub, curled around each other like twins in a womb.

It was odd to her that the Goose seemed so relaxed around Celeste. She asked him about it when he was waddling out of the swimming pool. He shook his body, and an arc of water droplets spun around his head like a halo.

"She reminds me of the Goose Girl, who was tasked with looking after the geese on the farm. They both had the same *je ne sais quoi*. The same insouciance."

"I can put up with you saying almost anything, but I cannot bear to hear you speak in French."

"*À ton goût*," the Goose said as he shook all the water off his feathers.

Sofia couldn't really blame the Goose for being smitten with Celeste, as she was too. As each day went by, she became more and more attached to her, and frightened about being separated and being on her own without a human companion again.

The Goose began to elect to stay in the hospital more often when Sofia went to scavenge in the town. Although she was a very wealthy child from an important family, she often remarked that people seemed to favour the delightful lower-class Celeste above her. When they walked down the street together, people called out joyfully to Celeste. A delivery boy took his hands off the handlebars and put both to his mouth, kissed them, and then flung his kiss at Celeste. Celeste reached out with her hand, snatched the kiss out of mid-air with her fist, and put it in her pocket. When she walked into the butcher shop, the owner opened his fat arms to her, as though she were his granddaughter.

Celeste was never worried about the future. That was what made her such an enticing child. She lived in the moment. What was more beautiful than being a girl who lived in the moment? It was like watching a pigeon hopping around in traffic. Or a cat darting across rooftops.

But Sofia was constantly preoccupied with the future. She knew they could not stay in the hospital.

Even the cans of food were getting low. She had come to realize how fast cans of food disappeared when that was all you were living off. They emptied so quickly, leaving behind cans like bullet casings on the floor. Even though she was doing most of the eating on her own. She ate far more than Celeste, who, although she had once had a ravenous appetite, now seemed to exist happily on air.

Celeste seemed not at all concerned about the food running out. Sofia went hunting for other cans. It was somewhat less daunting than fishing or hunting for hares. At least there would be no fighting when she chanced upon them. It would only be unconditional surrender.

She tucked her paper into her coat pocket. She dared not go outside without it on her. Sofia quite liked going through the debris of the town. The village had not been completely pillaged and picked through yet. She stopped at a large house without a wall. She was so preoccupied with examining the labels on old cans of beer that she didn't hear anyone approach until a voice spoke up.

"She's death herself, the girl who lives up there. I think even the Enemy were afraid of her. That's why they didn't take her with them."

Sofia sat up to see an older woman with a large scab on her nose and missing teeth. She had a large backpack filled with objects she was scavenging too.

"She was up there, you know," the woman continued. "A lot of us saw her. Even with all that was going on, she wasn't hard to miss. She was standing up on top of the roof, and she was watching everything. And she was still watching everything. And she was still watching everything. And she was still watching everybody get killed. There wasn't any feeling in her at all. Now that's a sign of the devil, isn't it?"

"She's not the devil! She was our maid from when we lived in the Capital."

"Well, if you're vouching for her, stay away from me! I don't want nothing to do with you. They say it's you lot from the Capital who started this war with your arrogant ways. But I'd move on before the soldiers come back this way. They have no mercy on this town."

Sofia was so disturbed by this information, she forgot to ask the woman for directions to the Black Market. She would know something about it. Then Sofia could get away from here. She had to get away from here.

She was surprised when her mother first told her that the Black Market was not always in the same place. It was like a travelling circus. The Capital circus toured all over the country before returning home. Naturally, they travelled so others had access to them. But they also travelled in order to collect the best performers in the country. The ones who hadn't had the where-withal to come to the Capital themselves.

Sofia knew this because every time she saw the circus again, it would include a strange performer from the far-flung regions of the country.

Once there was a girl about her age who wore a sparkling white leotard and rode her bicycle across a high wire.

They had to travel to faraway places to find poor people who had been neglected in this peculiar manner. No mother had worried about this child dying. Sometimes neglect can help you discover your potential.

The Black Market was like this. It travelled in order to become richer. She wished for a moment the Black Market would just come to her. Or come for Celeste at least, and turn her into a dancer and not a monster.

BALLET FOR A SWAN

WITH A BROKEN NECK

I t took some pressure from Sofia for Celeste to talk about what exactly had happened in Abeu Ivor.

"The town was occupied, but then a garrison of our soldiers arrived to liberate it. I was so surprised to see them, I called out, My God, we thought you had all disappeared into thin air.

"My Enemy officer told me that they once came up against a troop of our soldiers. And they all disappeared into the woods. And they never came out. They sent soldiers to follow them, and THEY never came out of the woods. Since then, his men have been superstitious about the woods and don't want to have anything to do with them. And I said that in the olden days, Elysians believed that trees could come to life. And they would take the form of people, but odd people, who appeared only when death was near or you were in mortal danger. But that really, nobody believes that anymore. And he looked concerned when I told him that.

"But of course, the Enemy had the advantage because the hospital was up here on the hill like a fortified castle. They just went ahead and put missiles up on the roof. And they launched them on the soldiers. And the whole city below. They blew everything up. Nobody stood a chance. I tried not to see it. I kept the curtains in my room closed. I had to plug my ears too. There was so much banging. Louder than the bombing in the Capital. Much louder."

"Where are they now?" Sofia asked.

"The Enemy soldiers had to join the procession heading towards the Capital. Our soldiers—those who were still alive—ran off to somewhere. I do hope your mother was already dead by the time they arrived. I heard a lot of mothers took poison when they found out their children hadn't crossed the border. It would be sad to know your mother was shot in the head. She was so pretty."

The thought of someone she knew well being shot to death seemed to evoke only a fleeting sense of melancholy in Celeste. As though it made her suddenly wistful for an easier time. Sofia realized it was because she had seen her own mother being taken off to be killed. It had made her immune to death. Everything paled next to that horror. She wasn't afraid of her own death either.

Celeste, it seemed, was a girl who could not live without her mother. Maybe that was a weakness that came with having a mother who was too sweet and spoiled her with nonsense and affection. Sofia knew the way she was raised made it impossible for her to act the way Celeste was now.

She would not lie about and let herself mope around because her mother was dead. Her mother didn't believe in such extravagant shows of affection. She had raised her daughter to be a survivor. She had raised her to be a soldier. She had raised her to know when she should put herself first. Sofia knew there was a point when she would have to leave Celeste behind.

• • •

"What happened to your feet?"

Sofia was surprised she didn't immediately snatch them away so Celeste couldn't look at them. She wanted Celeste to see them.

"It's from walking in fancy shoes."

"Your feet are so interesting—I could look at them for hours. They don't look real. They look like a monster's feet. A tiny, adorable monster. I wish I had a bronzed pair of your feet. So I could put them on a shelf as a way to always remember you."

Celeste then reached into her pocket and took out two slim blue silk stockings. She pulled each one onto Sofia's feet. When Sofia looked down, she believed they looked lovely.

"Where did you get these stockings? I thought they were impossible to find."

In times of war, stockings are always the first thing that goes missing.

"I got them at the Black Market, of course."

Sofia let out a gasp at the mention of the Black Market. She felt her heart fall off a windowsill and plummet ten storeys. "Can you tell me how far from here it is?"

"To be honest, I can't be sure. It was a church in the middle of nowhere. Isn't it peculiar how everything is in the middle of nowhere now?"

"Nothing is in the middle of nowhere. What road did you go down?"

"The one that leads down the hill. The winding one."

She touched the window as she pointed to the road. She was looking at the window as though it were a painting and not something to look through.

173

It took some level of prying and cajoling to get any concrete details about the Black Market from Celeste. It made Sofia feel sneaky, but she persisted. She walked up behind Celeste and began stroking her hair and speaking in the soft voice of a kind elementary school teacher.

"Try to remember what you saw on the way. It's fun. It's like a sort of game. Lie down and close your eyes. If you imagine some place in your mind and you concentrate on it long enough, you end up being right there, as though you are in a dream."

Celeste found this to be an appealing activity. She was generally averse to anything that involved getting out of bed. So she welcomed this activity, which required her to lie in bed and close her eyes.

"Shall we go to the same place, then?" asked Celeste, having already closed her eyes.

Sofia could immediately tell from the thickness of the air in the room that Celeste had fallen asleep. She breathed the air in deeply, and when she exhaled it, it was filled with the air of her dreams. It was a thick, swampy air. The ground was soft in her dreams. Your feet sank into the ground as though it were mud. It didn't matter if you were standing on a cement surface or a carpet in a living room.

Sofia moved her shoulder gently against Celeste's. Celeste's body roused. It was like pulling an unconscious drowning body out of the water and resuscitating it.

"Oh, right," Celeste said. "I was somewhere else for a second."

"We got into one of the cars. Look out the window of the car and tell me what you see."

"I see trees. So many big trees. I don't think I have ever seen trees that big before. If we were to stand on either side of a tree

THE CAPITAL OF DREAMS

and wrap our arms around the trunk, we wouldn't be able to hold hands."

"That must be the Ancient Southern Forest Ridge. I knew it was near this town."

"To get to the Black Market, we continued down that road. There was nothing but trees. Oh, wait. There was an unusual bridge we crossed. There were statues of two giant green women holding hands. And our car drove underneath them. Everyone in the car remarked on how beautiful they were. Which surprised me because I didn't think they liked the things we built, since they spent so much time blowing them up."

"That's Moldia."

"It was Moldia. It was all destroyed. We drove through it. Then we continued down that road. I don't think I saw anything else that wasn't broken on that road. But at the end of it we came to a green church."

"It was painted green?"

"Yes. It was very small. And it was made out of wood. It was painted white. And there were leaves painted on the front of it. At first I thought it was ivy that was covering the front of the church. But when I got there, I looked and saw the leaves were painted on it."

"Moldia was once very religious. They decorate their churches with flowers and plants there. It's to commemorate the Virgin Mother."

"You know so much about everything, Sofia. That's because it was important for your mother. Did you know that Clara paid for my ballet lessons?"

"Oh!" said Sofia, who had never understood how Celeste had been able to afford those classes.

"My mother would take me to the classes on Saturdays, and afterwards we would eat ice cream. It was wonderful for both of us. I took ballet classes for two years at the Children's Conservatory. The one next to the library? I know some exquisite ballet moves. I can present them later."

Sofia's little map no longer fit all the details. She found a large piece of thick paper in one of the storage rooms. She unfolded it on a large table. The paper was as big as she was. She could lie on the paper, outline her body with a pencil, and then cut it out. She wondered whether she needed a map as large as the country itself. She worked on it with a charcoal pencil she had found in an operating room. Celeste sat down next to her and ran her fingertip along one of the rivers.

Celeste wiped her finger under her nose. It left a smudge, like a black moustache. Sofia was too shy to tell her she had a moustache on her face and should wipe it off. When they returned to their room and Sofia went to the bathroom, she was surprised when she saw her reflection. She, too, had a black moustache under her nose.

It was easy for Sofia to assume that Celeste would forget about the ballet presentation. She sometimes forgot what she was talking about in the middle of a sentence. It was as though her thought had popped like a soap bubble. But to the surprise of Sofia and the Goose, she arrived in the visitors room, where they were sitting that evening, in a costume of sorts.

She was wearing a pale blue bathing suit over a pair of lavender leotards with holes in them. She had tied a curtain panel from the bathroom around her waist like a skirt. It was a peculiar outfit indeed. But what was most peculiar was that she had gone to such an effort.

She stood there, perfectly erect with her feet turned out to the side. She turned her face down slightly. She put her arms akimbo and placed her fingertips prettily on her hips. They all waited for what came next for a long couple of minutes. But Celeste remained frozen in place.

Sofia jumped up and hurried over to wind the music box. She put it on. There was the scratching noise. As though someone was trapped in a coffin and trying to claw their way out. Or a mouse was trying to make a hole in a cereal box. And then a piano note filled the room. Like feeling a single drop of rain. Sofia put her palm out and looked up at the ceiling, whereupon there was a soft sudden downpour of notes.

Celeste began to rock her body back and forth while leaping from foot to foot. It was a pas de chat. A move that seemed eminently appropriate for her. She pranced about on her toes in a very small circumference. If she had taken ballet another several years, she would have been permitted a larger circumference. She then put one foot forward, positioned her arms in front of her. As though she were reaching out to hug someone who was retreating from her, as though on a boat, and she then executed a pirouette. Her legs clicked together like knitting needles.

Celeste was by no means a professional dancer of any kind, or especially talented. But that day, she showed them something ephemeral. She embodied ordinary fleeting girlhood. She was born to be carefree. She was born to laugh at other people's jokes. She was born to leap screaming off of diving boards. She was born to read romantic novels on the bus and almost miss her stop.

There was something about her spirit, the spirit of every girl, that was so, so beautiful.

This was what they imagined she was like when she was isolated in the square that day. When she tiptoed out into the square wearing a nightgown and in bare feet. She had given a similar dance performance.

Now she also seemed to understand how beautiful she was. This was why the officers had lifted her up and carried her off, and had taken her to a place where they could dress her up and touch her body. Why they decided they could not, would not shoot her in the head. It was why they decided they wanted to keep her like a pet. So they could look and look and look at her.

That was when her personality was still lit up.

Looking at Celeste, Sofia couldn't help but be reminded of the porcelain figurines Balthazar had lined up on the fence for execution.

Later, Sofia chanced upon the Goose at the end of the hallway. He was so lost in thought he didn't notice her. He was swaying around with his wings in the air and his neck winding around strangely. She could not make heads or tails of what he was doing. But then he began to spin, and she realized he was dancing ballet. In imitation of what Celeste had been doing earlier. He tried to stand on the tip of his webbed foot, but then stumbled and fell to the floor. He sat on the floor like a ballerina taking a moment offstage—at the side of a class.

She wondered whether Celeste had in fact given him some of her pills. But she wasn't sure a goose could survive pills that had been invented for human pain. It seemed more likely the Goose had got high through osmosis. She did not have a complete knowledge of the way a goose's mind worked. They moved in flocks. And when they were in a flock, they moved as one body. They shared parts of their brains with one another. She thought it must be what soldiers felt like. They never quite knew if they were pulling the trigger of their own volition, or if it was the group doing it.

"We have to leave before the Enemy returns," Sofia said to the Goose, hoping he had not lost sight of their mission.

"Oh, what a bore. We are living in a grand mansion and we have patrons. It is so comfortable and joyous. All we have to do in return is be our pretty little selves."

"I feel as though no one here is remembering the early work of my mother. She said girls have been conditioned to believe they have no agency, so they always turn to men to solve their problems. But solving problems is what makes a girl a person. We can't call on men to save us. Or we will never be real people."

"I remind you again, this is the woman who sent you off on a train to be murdered," said the Goose. "Whether she knew that you were being sent off to be murdered is hardly the point. Whatever the intent, had you stayed on that train, you would be dead. So your mother is homicidal and does not have your best interests at heart. Let's go with the prevalent philosophy in this hospital."

"My mother was opposed to thinking as a group. She always said you have to make sure you are thinking your own thoughts, and not those of someone else."

"Oh, who could ever keep up with your mother's standards? She probably simply said these outrageous things to pay the bills. Why not take a moment and just relax? Take the easy route. It wears the body down. We are good."

"We have to eventually move on. What about the Black Market and the Capital? And your bottle of ink and your manifestos?"

"Oh, Sofia, don't you know dreams make a person absolutely miserable in life? You can't enjoy today because you're worried what effect it will have on tomorrow. Why? Tomorrow never actually comes, Sofia. Have you considered that?"

Celeste began to run out of her drugs. She became twisted up inside. She seemed to be desperate for something. She had a look on her face as though she'd had a striking realization. As though she had remembered her child was all alone waiting for her at a train station and she had no way to get to her. She looked as though she was afraid of all the things that ordinary people were concerned about during wartime but that had never bothered her before.

Sofia had believed Celeste was immune to what was happening in the country. But now that she was sober, it became clear how volatile Celeste actually was. It made sense she had become addicted to sleeping pills. She could hardly bear this reality.

The cruellest thing about withdrawal was the realization that one had to go through life wide awake and conscious of what was happening.

Celeste's problems returned to her brain, one by one, like birds returning after being frightened. They settled down and began picking at her thoughts again. Like tiny drills trying to hit a genuine source of anxiety. One that might bubble over the whole day. All she wanted was to be able to experience that numbness once again. It was as though she wanted to pour bleach on her brain to erase all the dirty thoughts.

Celeste left the hospital later that day. Sofia kept waiting for her to come back. She couldn't figure out where she had gone. Celeste never went for long walks. She was too frightened by the prospect of having to walk all the way back. She didn't like to be in the sun very long because it would burn her skin and make her feel dizzy.

Sofia went outside looking for her. She found her sitting on a large stone. She was weeping profusely. It looked as though she was doing all the crying she had put aside for the past months. Sofia hadn't thought Celeste was capable of these intense, enormous emotions. As though her sadness were a frozen ice cap, and as it melted, there was a huge flood of sorrow.

She looked different after crying like that. It was as though she was more alive.

When a newly sober Celeste first began to tell her stories about the acts she had engaged in with the soldiers, Sofia felt sick to her stomach. She felt the way she did when she had dreams where she was naked. Vulnerable. And horrified. She was too young to hear about these things. Even though she was now well acquainted with mass murder, she should still be sheltered from such stories.

It seemed impossible that she would ever have to engage in sex. Or at least it was so far ahead in the future, it was inconceivable to even worry about it.

She and Celeste got under the covers together. Celeste liked to wrap her arms around Sofia when she was talking. She whispered the stories into Sofia's ear. She became very tactile whenever she was talking about sex. She held Sofia's hand up in front of her face. She pulled on each finger as though it were a petal on a flower. Another time they were lying next to each other and Celeste took a strand of her own hair and began moving it over Sofia's face as though it were a paintbrush.

"What's nice about being a girl is you really don't have to do anything in sex. You can just lie there. Just like you're having the most wonderful nap. Sometimes you can make a little cooing noise, and they like that. But really you can't go wrong. Sometimes they ask you to do the most peculiar things. And then you can get shy. But you shouldn't worry. They always like your performance."

"You can't believe the men are on your side," Sofia said, feeling distraught because of Celeste's misinformation. "They are never on your side. Not really. Not any of them! No men can be trusted during the war. I got kicked out of my grandmother's house by two boys. They were from our country too. They weren't even enemies."

"You say that about men, Sofia. But that is because you still act like a little girl. You haven't started liking men yet. When you do, you'll see. You can't turn back from it. It makes you feel so warm inside. Once you feel it, you can't go back to being satiated by any other type of affection. No other kind of love can work for you. You feel like there is stardust all over your skin. They make you laugh in a different way. There's nothing quite like a handsome man making you laugh. It's funnier than puppet shows and movies and the circus. And they do it just for you. I once laughed for almost six hours straight. Everything else is so boring.

"You can taste their words when they talk. They taste like warm tea with a little bit of milk. Some boys' breath tastes like there is honey on it. And they are so much stronger and heavier than us. When they sleep next to you, their arms and legs wrap around you. It's like you took a nap underneath a tree in the park, and when you woke up, all the roots were wrapped around you, holding you. And you feel powerless, but in a good way."

Sofia realized how dangerous a woman's psyche could be. The ability to romanticize and find things pretty could become perverted. It could lead a woman to value abuse and structure her whole life around it. She needed to rescue Celeste from this hospital and her own impulse. She had to fight against the villainy of heterosexual love.

Celeste made her index finger and middle finger tiptoe over Sofia's arms. She must have run these same fingers over the soldiers. What did they do to deserve such a wonderful tiny dancer all over their bodies? That was how they knew they had won the war. It was nothing the politicians said. It was nothing the bombs exploded. It was not the bodies lying in graves. It was these two pretty fingers. They had stolen them from Sofia's house. They had brought them here.

"We will go to the Black Market together. I will buy you everything the soldiers would have, I promise. I will treat you better. I won't expect anything from you in return."

"They make me feel special, Sofia. Please don't take this away from me. Please don't ask me to go with you. It will feel as though I am disappointing you."

She had managed to curb her addiction for drugs. But she had not been able to escape the deep, irrational addiction she had developed for being abused by men. Women who were addicted to men were always addicted to the wrong kind of men.

• • •

Her mother had always said that sexual desire was important in women. Celeste was talking about sexual desire. And it seemed a terrible thing. It seemed like something rotten. It was something girls caught, like a terrible cold. Or they pretended it was pleasant. But it was dark and dirty. She didn't understand why her mother would promote this. Why was this a feeling that could empower a young girl?

Sofia went scavenging through the town again one morning, this time looking for objects to trade on the Black Market. She found a decorated pink tin box with roses painted on it. There was a small gold-plated crank on the side. She turned the crank around gently, round and round until she felt resistance and it came to a stop. She opened the lid of the box, and the music began to play.

She knew this tune. It was one that was too mysterious and complex to play on her clarinet.

It was as though she were in the concert hall in the Capital. Many couples went there on their first dates. It was built by an architect who was known for being one of the few men who was happily married to the same woman for his entire life.

There was a ring in the music box, an expensive-looking ring covered in tiny diamonds. Her heart beat so quickly. With this ring, she would be able to get anything she wanted from the Black Market. Her mother's book could now be rescued. She would be able to buy it and hold it and protect it, and never lose it again. Oh, certainly this ring would cover the cost of the book she wanted most in the world. And there would be change! She would get a warm fur coat and eat food that was not in a can. And for Celeste, luxuries! She would be able to buy her a dress and chocolates and ribbons for her hair. She would buy her tins of flower-flavoured tea and lipstick and new high-heeled shoes. And she would be able to have her mother's book. She felt like dancing around. She held the ring in front of her and said, "I do, I do, I do!" She could buy herself Celeste's love, and have her mother's as well. The world was hers for the taking.

Sofia walked through what appeared to have been the town square, with a destroyed fountain in the middle. She stepped over the smiling green head of a bronze angel that had once adorned the fountain. She walked to the edge of town and found herself staring at a man hanged from a tree along the roadside. She wondered what he had done to receive this dishonour.

She was used to the bulging features of hanged people. Three members of the resistance had been hanged in the square by the bombed concert hall, and they were left there for a week. She imagined what this hanging man's face must have looked like when he was still alive. She suspected he might have been handsome. But that might also have been because he was wearing a dignified suit. Because of the tailoring, she was surprised it had not been taken. But without the suit, she supposed, no one would know it was a person of dignity who had been hanged.

Sofia circled around the body, looking up at the rope and the height of the branch. She felt nothing towards the body. It was as if seeing him there had turned a switch in her head, and she saw other humans and animals as abstractions now. His shoes were at the height of her forehead, and she could not stop looking at them. She felt entirely strange and full of desperation.

She examined the tree. The trunk was thick with low-growing branches. It was clear the soldiers had not climbed the tree in order to hang the man. They must have had a ladder of some sort.

She walked around, scanning the ground, and found an overturned kitchen table next to a pile of rubble. It was made out of metal, which, no doubt, had enabled it to withstand the explosion. She pulled it over by the leg. It made a screeching noise as she dragged it. She felt like a kid who was dragging a dog against its will home from the park.

The table let out such a loud creak when she flipped it over that she stood back and looked up. In order to see whether that noise had woken the man from the dead. He hung there with the exact same absurd expression on his face. As incapable of change as an oil painting portrait. Since that wasn't going to wake him up, nothing would. She climbed on the table, which wobbled slightly, as though a tank were passing nearby.

She was now standing face to face with him. And she was quite surprised to realize he was quite short, almost the same height as her. She took his jacket off first and laid it on the table. Then she unbuttoned his shirt and placed it on top. She pulled his suspender straps off his shoulders. She unbuttoned his pants. She then jumped off the table. She unlaced his shoes and pulled them off and dropped them on the ground. She pulled his pants off.

Well, he was naked now. Except for his underwear and his undershirt. She knew she ought to have some sort of empathy for this man, but she didn't. Instead she felt glee as she stuffed his clothes in her backpack and hurried back to the hospital.

• • •

She hung the suit from the window so it would air out. To someone who was not in the middle of a war, it would have smelled like rot and death. But these were smells that suffused the air and so didn't bother her. She spritzed the suit with a bottle of rose water the soldiers had given Celeste and put it on. She lit all the candles from the church. She wound up the music box. She opened the box and waited for it to summon Celeste. As soon as Celeste walked into the room with her mouth agape, Sofia swooped her up in her arms. Celeste smiled, and they danced to the tune together.

Sofia put her nose into Celeste's hair. And even though it was filthy, it smelled good.

"You are the prettiest girl in the entire country."

She waited for a second to see whether Celeste would play along or find it insulting. She listened for a response. And then Celeste sighed a little happy sigh of such contentment, Sofia would say anything to cause her to make it again.

"I shall do anything for you. I will murder anyone who tries to harm you."

"But I am so frightened all the time."

"You don't need to be. I will do all the worrying for you."

"Shall I make you dinner every night? And make your home the prettiest place you can imagine?"

"No, my love. I will hire maids to do all this for you."

"And what will I do with my time?"

"You will focus on being yourself. You will listen to the music on the gramophone I will buy for you. You will spend time in luxurious bubble baths I will draw for you. I will take you to a hairdresser and they will fix your hair. They will put products in it that make it so it will never get tangled. I will buy you tickets to a million different shows."

She wanted to win her over from men. She wanted Celeste to value and trust her as much as she did the officer whose return she had put so much faith in. She began to make promises to her.

Perhaps none of these things made sense to Celeste because they presupposed the end of the war and everything returning to normal. Celeste had given up hope of that ever happening. It wasn't even possible for the war to end. The precious things that made up her country had already disappeared. Her mother could never be returned to her, so that life was completely over.

"I have already given up, Sofia. I was captured. I am a captive. I don't have any rights or desires. Everyone is a captive now. All we can do is beg for kindness from the soldiers when they come. The best we can hope for is that they marry us. Then we can have babies. And they will be so cute and sweet. And they won't speak the same language as us. But they will be safe. Everyone in the country will love them. No one will try to kill them."

And the way Celeste put her hands on her belly, Sofia knew immediately that she was pregnant. She wasn't sure why she hadn't noticed before that her belly was slightly risen like dough. But she would never have imagined that Celeste, who was unmarried and so young, could be pregnant.

"I don't think babies like being born. That's why they cry all the time. It takes a few years for you to convince them that it is worthwhile to be alive and tie their own shoes."

Celeste bit the side of her thumb as she said this.

Sofia had always found the act of being pregnant to be humiliating. It was so strange. Whenever she thought about it, she found it made her uncomfortable. It defied all logic. What could be more embarrassing than walking around with a baby in your belly? Everyone would know it was there. It made her think of ogres who would swallow babies whole. And have them rolling around inside them. On top of that, everywhere you went, everyone knew you had had sex.

She hated to think about it. She could not believe her mother had let her live inside her body. She was not physically demonstrative. Sofia watched other mothers doting over their children, gathering them up in their arms, squishing them up against their chests, and smothering them with kisses.

Her mother did not think babies were interesting at all. She never stopped to gaze admiringly into perambulators when they rolled past her on the sidewalk.

Clara had told Sofia that one of the conditions she had when her father asked her to marry him was that she didn't want children. They went on a cruise to celebrate Clara's having won an award. She was thirty-one at the time. It was on this cruise that Clara became pregnant. Mistaking her symptoms for seasickness, Clara was too far along by the time she found out she was pregnant.

Her mother had told her that she used to adore caramel sundaes. But when she fell pregnant, they nauseated her. And she would sit at the café and order one and stare at it and just weep, with tears falling on the ice cream. She was sad because it represented everything that was being taken away from her. She was sad because she was a non-fiction writer and she didn't like metaphors.

Sofia preferred the stories of the origins of magical babies that she read about in her book of folk tales. There was one about a woman who gives birth to a turnip. The turnip has all these eyes that are always watching her. In the end she can't stand it anymore. So she boils the turnip and eats it for dinner. Then she gets pregnant and gives birth to a little girl with six eyes all over her face. The little six-eyed girl has to go through all sorts of adventures. In the end she meets a prince with six eyes.

These babies never belonged to their mothers. They were completely independent of their bodies. Even if their mothers loved them, they inevitably felt the call of their true natures and returned to proper landscapes and people.

But now that Celeste was standing before her pregnant, Sofia realized there might not be anything magical about pregnancy at all.

THEY CAME FOR THE POETS

When the Enemy took over the Capital, a quiet nervousness descended upon the streets. The orders they began to receive were very clear, and everyone tried to follow them to a T. But it was not long after people in the Capital had registered their identities and occupations at the new courthouse that the arrests began. They had all expected the wealthy to be arrested. Soldiers went through their houses seizing goods that they would use for their war effort. It was harder for the citizens to have empathy for the extremely wealthy.

But then cultural figures began to be arrested too.

An eighty-six-year-old actor was arrested on charges of pedophilia and corruption of minors. His extended family, filled with young children, followed him out onto the street.

Perhaps if there had been only a handful of arrests of cultural figures under absurd trumped-up charges, the citizens might have been able to turn a blind eye to them. But they became more and more frequent. And it became clear that people were being arrested only because they were cultural figures.

There was a professor of literature who in twenty years had not paid attention to a single event that occurred after 1876. He was particularly dumbfounded by the accusations. When he was accused of espionage, it was said by some that it was the first time he had properly understood the country was at war.

There was a popular cabaret singer who couldn't carry a tune but would belt out songs at the top of her lungs and with an infectious confidence. She was beloved, and everyone thought her voice was charming and endearing because she couldn't sing well. And it made them listen more carefully to the words she was singing.

She hadn't a violent bone in her bouncy, overweight body. So it was remarkable that she was arrested and disappeared on the charge of acts of terrorism. She had apparently served a tray of poisoned pastries to a group of senior citizens. This was hard to believe, as all those close to her swore she would never bring harm to a cupcake.

Then it was announced that all the universities would be closed. "The entire faculty of Freedom University has disap-peared," Clara yelled in the kitchen.

"I thought you said that university was second-rate," Sofia said, biting into a piece of toast.

"Don't be ridiculous, Sofia. Those are thoughts a person has during peacetime. It is a luxury to be able to tear apart your friends and colleagues. Now we are all united against the Enemy."

Then high schools and grammar schools were closed too. Sofia knew this was a shocking injustice. But she was happy she no longer had to go to school. She had created an idea and impres-sion of herself at school that was almost certain never to change.

She would be regarded as awkward and shy and unlikeable for years. Once your classmates considered you a loser, it was almost impossible for you to rectify this notion.

She believed she could become a different kind of girl now. She felt she had been given a blank slate. She would reinvent herself. She had this secret image inside her head of the girl she wanted to be.

"My books are being burned in the square tonight," her mother announced one day. "Anyone who has a copy of one of my books faces a fine and possibly imprisonment. They are mad. They can't erase me."

The list of banned books had grown to cover not only her own titles but almost the entirety of Clara's library. Many residents of the Capital elected to dispose of their collections all at once. Sofia would stroke her folktale book when she was out of her mother's sight. The Enemy seemed unconcerned with children's books.

"I think people, women especially, will never burn my books," Clara said. "They'll hide them in their walls. Women are very good at hiding things. They are always trying to hide that they are aging. Why do I bother risking my life writing these books if people are not going to do me the courtesy of risking their lives to own them? Why should I assume all the risk?"

"They have already read them so many times that the words are in their heads," Celeste suggested.

Her mother was delighted by this answer. She put her index finger out and waved it at the maid. Sofia wished she had come up with this answer herself.

"Of course I only want to write more now. I have been slowly working on my memoir. There was never any urgency before. But I will finish it now. It was always going to be my most popular work. It would have been a national bestseller in our country. It will only be available to read in other languages. Some of the intricacies will be lost, of course. But the ideas will come through. They will see we were enlightened people."

Clara began pacing excitedly around the living room as she spoke. A lock of dark hair escaped her kerchief and fell on her forehead like a question mark.

"This is what the West is like. They believe in Great Men. That is how they remember history. There was no French Revolution without Robespierre. The men of their age embody their country. Without a great orator, a people will not have a voice."

Sofia watched as her mother began rearranging her desk and papers, as though she intended to start writing immediately.

"Then I will get it out of the country. This manuscript in itself will have a great story. It will have been written under the Occupation. More than anything, the West adores a writer who was murdered. They will weep over every page, regretting they never knew of our existence. They cannot let our culture be erased like this. It will be way too hard on their conscience. They think we are ignorant and there is no reason to come rescue us now. If my books had a wider readership outside the borders, our allies would already be here. Through my fascinating and outrageous life, they will see in me all the qualities and aspirations of the country."

Finally, Clara sat down at her desk, and she held her pen up like a sword. "This will be a life, an Elysian life, from birth to death!"

"How can you describe your own birth?" Sofia asked. "Even if you can describe your own birth, how do you go about describing your own death?"

"Poetry, Sofia! Poetry!"

Sofia had no idea why her mother wasn't more terrified. If they were killing writers, it stood to reason that her mother should crawl underneath the bed and hide there for the duration of the war. But instead of making her numb and slow, the way it might a beautiful animal, terror made her spring into action. Before, she would take one or even two naps a day, and fully wake up only at night, when everyone else was asleep. But now she was awake all day. She was restless and alert. She would leave the house in a hurry.

Her mother felt alive with the possibility of danger.

Her mother began working furiously on her new book. She wrote through the day and night. Her mother sometimes got sick writing. She wrote for three days. And then wept in bed with a migraine, vomiting violently on the floor.

She muttered in the darkness. She begged for someone to help her. She was covered in sweat. She demanded a cold rag for her forehead. The sight of a glass of water made her weep. Perhaps because she wanted it so badly but couldn't drink it. She lay on the tiles of the bathroom floor so she would be cold.

Sofia ran as quickly as she could to the pharmacist, whose shop windows had been cracked and were now held together with brown tape. He opened a cabinet behind the cash register with a miniature key and took out a small blue jar of pills. He would never give her mother more than four pills. He said they were addictive. And no one would forgive him for turning the country's greatest writer into a drug addict. When she was recovering and the pills made her stoned, she was very content. She became very baby-like.

This time, the doctor gave Sofia an entire jar. He held her hand. "Tell your mother she is very brave."

Sofia was irritated by her mother's memoir. Because her mother, when she was exhausted from writing, would put her feet up and recount some of the events she had transcribed in the book. Her mother had a look of bliss on her face as she narrated, through the rose-coloured lens of nostalgia, her favourite life adventures.

She spoke about everything, from when she had the top marks on her college exit exams, to a time she climbed on the roof of her dorm to save a cat, to awards she had won and men who had fallen head over heels in love with her.

Sofia didn't want to interrupt her mother's respite from the war outside the door of their apartment. A war that, in all likelihood, would erase every trace that Clara Bottom had been on this earth. Perhaps she considered herself close to death. And her life was passing in front of her eyes. And she was writing it down. But what got under Sofia's skin was that there seemed to be no anecdotes about her. Which led her to wonder whether she was in her mother's memoir at all.

Sofia felt she could tell when her mother was writing about a college tryst. Sofia was observing her one night and she stopped writing to put on a record and danced to it with her eyes closed. She knew her mother had travelled in her head to a time before Sofia was born. And was at a dance hall with young men admiring her.

Sofia was angry at her mother for slipping away from her. While she was there in the room, dancing with men other than her father. It was as though one of them might whisk her away, to have another, more suitable child.

It made snarky comments leap out of her mouth. There was nothing she could do to stop herself from saying them. They were already out of her mouth. She was like cupid, firing arrows at her mother's heart. But none seemed to quite hit the mark.

"You look as though you are drunk," Sofia said. "You look seasick."

Clara, seeming not to have registered her daughter's comment, continued swaying around the living room.

"I would be embarrassed about writing about past lovers if I were you."

"And why is that, Sofia?" Clara answered with her eyes still closed.

"Because they were such ridiculous men. They were bad dancers. And told stupid jokes. And puked on their shoes. They thought they were so intelligent, but they only repeated things they read in books."

Clara stopped dancing and looked steadfastly at her daughter. "How did you know?" And then her face broke into a smile and she started to laugh.

"Well, then, why do you seem so happy writing about them?"

"Oh, it's not the men. It's the writing itself that pleases me. There is no language as beautiful as Elysian. It is poetic by nature. It is an incantatory language. It is like a magic spell. Sometimes I feel the temperature around me change while I am writing."

"Perhaps we are a race of fairies, making crazy poems in a language only the trees understand," Sofia said, sighing.

"Oh, what a beautiful way of putting it, Sofia." And to her delight, her mother added, "I shall put that in the book." She turned back to her desk and proceeded to scribble down what Sofia had said.

Sofia was pleased. She was somewhere in the memoir. Hidden somewhere in its pages, wound up in her mother's words, like a climbing rose.

And then, making Sofia feel even more involved in the memoir, Clara handed her a pile of notebooks one afternoon, saying, "Let's type some of this out."

The notebooks were wonderful. Look what she had been entrusted with. The pages crinkled when she turned them. It was as though her mother's words had set them on fire. Her cursive spread across the page like vines that were out of control. When Sofia typed, she was alarmed by the sound of machine-gun fire that emanated from the words.

Clara stopped and peered over Sofia's shoulder. She felt her mother's hair settling on her shoulder. She smelled her skin, which was a mixture of cold air and tobacco and a hint of a rose perfume she would wear sometimes before the war. But now that seemed to emanate from her naturally.

Sofia did wonder whether it was strange to be in love with your mother. She felt towards her mother the way you would feel towards someone who was unobtainable. Someone who had always held something back. Someone who would never commit.

It was said that mothers loved their children more than

children loved their mothers. But Sofia loved her mother monstrously, ferociously. Sofia was madly in love with her mother. And like any obsessive lover, she wanted to take her mother's freedom away. She wanted her mother to be beholden to her.

She had always held back on allowing herself to be in love with her mother. Because she thought it would only lead to further rejection. Because she did not want to love someone who didn't love her back. She wouldn't even admit that to herself. But now, she had let her guard down and was basking in her mother's new attention. How could she resist?

HANDCUFFS MADE OF SMOKE

S ofia woke up to Celeste's face in her own. As though Celeste were peering at her reflection in the mirror for imperfections. "Good news! The soldiers have returned."

Sofia found that her wrists and ankles had been secured to the bed. One hand was fastened with a man's tie, the other with a dress sock.

"Why have you tied me up?"

"Because I was worried you were going to leave. And I don't want to be alone."

"Then untie me."

"You have to promise to stay at least until the soldiers come."

"Untie me!"

"Fine. Fine. Fine. Fine. Fine. No need to get crazy about it. You're not my boss, you know. You're just my friend now."

As soon as her shackles were undone, Sofia heard a trembling noise coming from her bag. She always kept it next to her bed. So she would be ready to pack it at a moment's notice. The tinkling noise was audible. It began to speed up more and more. She opened the bag. She reached in and took out the teacup and its spoon and put them on the table. The spoon began rattling so much in the cup that it might as well have been on a table on a train.

"The soldiers are coming!" Sofia cried out.

She ran up the hospital stairs to get to the roof. She had to try to see them with her own eyes. For a moment, she thought they might be Elysian soldiers, arriving to liberate the hospital. But when she recognized the Enemy uniforms, she realized that had been madness. Celeste and the Goose were in such a trance of inertia, she did not think it would be possible to get them to move, based on the testimony of the teacup on its own.

She hurried to pack her bag. She crammed in all the treasures she had found in the obliterated town, all the while crying out, "Soldiers! Soldiers! Soldiers!"

Celeste stared at her dreamily. "Oh, you mustn't leave, Sofia. I demand that you stay with me. You aren't my prisoner. But I want you to stay. I need you to stay. I have to have someone who remembers the Capital stay with me. Otherwise, I have no past or no childhood. I am only this. I will become whoever people want me to be. I won't have a country. I won't have anyone to speak to me in my own language."

It occurred to Sofia that Celeste was demanding of her exactly what her mother had. Her mother had wanted her to stay. She had wanted her to safeguard the memory of life in the Capital. She had also needed her to sacrifice her own safety in order to preserve it. And then she had sent Sofia with a one-way ticket directly towards the danger so that the knowledge of life in the Capital would survive.

Looking at Celeste in all her grief touched Sofia. It was the most beautiful thing she had ever seen. She reminded her of statues of grieving angels in cemeteries.

Sofia turned to leave the room. Celeste reached both her arms forward, lunged off the bed, fell to the floor, and grabbed Sofia by the ankles. She suddenly no longer seemed like a girl. There were tales in her book of fables about the roots of large trees that were known to trip girls as they were walking through the forest, then grab them by the ankles and pull them underground. She realized Celeste had become a forest creature, someone who was half-dead and half-alive. Perhaps she was dehumanizing her because she knew she would save herself and leave Celeste behind.

She bent over to try to remove Celeste's hands, which were like shackles around her ankles. But Celeste rose up and grabbed Sofia's legs, knocking her onto the ground. Celeste then climbed on top of her. She pinned her down and began kissing her all over.

Sofia was afraid of the kisses. They seemed to have an intoxicating effect. They were like darts from a tranquilizer gun. She felt sleepy. Every kiss seemed to weigh five pounds. They were so heavy, she had to get out from under them. Sofia felt herself turn wild, grabbing Celeste's hair and kicking her in the stomach. The instant Celeste recoiled in pain, Sofia lurched out from underneath her to get away.

"Don't leave, Sofia! It's dangerous out there. You say you are looking for the Black Market, but you won't be able to get there on your own. The roads are too dangerous."

The Goose appeared in the room and began squawking furiously. Celeste ignored him entirely. Sofia had to grab the Goose and carry him away. She had to keep running away from the noise of the Goose squawking. Even though he was in her arms.

She wanted to get far away enough that he would settle down. And when they were far away enough from the hospital, he did become quiet.

They came to a crossroads. Sofia took out the teacup and put it on the ground. Then she placed the spoon in it. The cup began shaking and the spoon turned, as though it were a needle on a compass, and pointed towards one of the roads. "The army is coming from that way, so we will go the other."

The Goose didn't object or acquiesce; he just stayed silent in her arms. She wondered whether the Goose had wanted to stay with Celeste. He had very much been enjoying staying in the hospital, but she had taken away his choice and left Celeste behind.

What kind of survival was she choosing? Living right now required a certain ugliness. It was a rejection of all things that were considered fanciful and frivolous. Who was she now? Maybe this action had changed something irrevocably in her. Maybe she would always be cold and wicked afterwards. Maybe she would no longer have access to anything imaginative. She cut off a piece of her black skirt. She cut the edge off her sleeve. She cut two round holes in the strip. She sat in front of the Goose and tied it around his head. His eyes blinked from the holes.

"Am I meant to be a bandit?"

"No, you are meant to be a swan."

"Oh."

And they sat, staring at each other.

Later as they were walking, Sofia suddenly stopped and exclaimed, "Are you sorry you are stuck with me? I am such a pathetic example of a girl. I don't have any of the attributes girls are famous for."

"Well, girlhood is a temporary state. It is a brief transitory stage. If you truly excel, perhaps you don't make it through at all."

"That is probably true in some ways. But I can't help but be envious of girls like Celeste was before the war. I can't help but feel other girls have access to this feeling of lightness. I feel so earthbound."

"She went to all those ballet lessons. Why? Just so she could dance prettily for men who were going to abuse her. Is that the only thing you can do as a girl? Offer up your body?"

"Maybe I would like it. Maybe I would like being passed from one man to another. Each one would see me naked. And each night I would be married to a different man. And in the mornings at breakfast, they would all laugh at me. And I would sleep all day long. At night the Enemy would come, and he would be so gentle with me I wouldn't even know I was dead."

"Snap out of it! You know absolutely that you're not that kind of girl. You're too stubborn. You're too self-aware. You're too odd. You're maladroit. You don't know things you don't know until you know them. You don't fill in the blanks. You don't let others fill in the blanks for you. And that, Sofia, is a good thing."

"I wonder if you only think I have gravitas because you have not met my mother. If you were to meet my mother, you would be so impressed by her, you would find me ridiculous. You would say, How could such an impressive, accomplished woman give birth to such a plain and unremarkable girl? That is what people used to think when they met me. I seem like an idiot standing next to her."

"Perhaps the reason Celeste is so unmoored from reality is that she witnessed her mother's death. She is too young to be separated from her mother. You act like a girl whose mother is still alive. Even if she did die physically in the Uprising, she is still alive to you. You are completing the task she assigned to you."

Sofia reflected on what the Goose had said. It was true. She still felt as though she was obligated to act in a way that would make her mother proud, even if she had sent her out of the Capital.

"Maybe Celeste will make it to the end of the war."

"She won't. She can't. There is no place in society for a seventeen-year-old girl and her Enemy baby. Now it is dangerous to be walking down the street because it is wartime. But it was always dangerous to be a girl, walking anywhere in the world. Strange things happened to you. And once they happened to you, you were no longer even able to talk about them. They became great sources of shame. You were not supposed to even admit these types of things happened. They seemed fictional and make-believe. So once something horrible happened to you, you became a creature no one believed in. She won't belong in society after the war. Nobody will let her back in."

And then they were quiet, as they knew they had to let this motherless child go.

THE PRICE OF TEARS

DURING WARTIME

On the day Sofia and the Goose fled Abeu Ivor, there was a huge rainstorm. Sofia knew she could probably get out of the rain by going into the forest and finding shelter. But at the same time, she could not tolerate the trees in the rain. They turned into monsters. They became mad dogs. They lost all sense of human civilization. They acted as though they were at war with the clouds. They flung their sticks around like swords. They rattled their arms and legs. They acted like outraged male lions, furiously shaking their hair. They were like bears dancing about in the water. They shook the water off their heads. They encouraged the rain to come down and be destructive. They yelled out, We can take it!

There were trees that became so wild and the rain made them feel so young that they ripped their roots out of the ground and fell right over. They discarded their branches on the ground as though they were limbs lost on the battle-field. It made her wary of the trees. They were too used to death. So Sofia stayed on the road and got wet.

At one point, they came across large pieces of wood that had fallen from a tree in the middle of the road. They looked as though they could be put together to form a grey Elysian horse. She put her finger under the bark. It felt like the surface of a horse. She had the sudden electric memory of having touched a horse with a fingertip when she was little.

They walked for days. Occasionally Sofia and the Goose would come across solitary wandering citizens from their country. They also chose out-of-the-way routes. They also chose to walk down roads that were too small to accommodate the vehicles and numbers the army moved in. When they came across another person, they tried to pass with as little interaction as possible. There were collaborators everywhere. In fact, if you were a citizen of the country and you were still walking around, not confined to an internment camp or a town, there was a large chance you had traded something for that freedom. That was why they avoided eye contact with others.

There was a man who was bent under the weight of an enormous cloth sack over this shoulder. The bag was so large, it overwhelmed his form. He looked like a heap of garbage that was slowly moving. She did not greet it. She did not want to cause him to act like a human being. She did not want to awaken whatever was under that large pile because she might wake up his rage or heartbreak. Which would be akin to waking a bear from its slumber.

She wondered whether she was going to grow up to look like that. She wondered whether that was what growing up in this country now meant.

• • •

They came upon an old woman on the side of the road. She was wearing so many layers of clothing. The layers at the hem looked like strips of wallpaper that had been torn off. It was as though she had put on a different dress for every year of her life. It would take her an hour to get undressed. With each dress she removed, she would become younger. Eventually she would get to her wedding dress. And then a slip she put on as a young girl. And she would be as young and fragile and vulnerable as Sofia herself.

Sofia was always relieved by the sight of an old woman. She knew immediately and from afar that she was a citizen of the country. There was no way the Enemy would have brought along old women. They would shoot the elderly. But occasionally they thought they were not worth the bullets and let them wander around to their deaths. That was what the old woman seemed to be doing.

"Perhaps I am already dead. Who can say?" the Old Woman mused to Sofia and the Goose. "I only hope someone will tell me when I'm dead. Otherwise, how will I know?"

She invited them to have dinner around a fire with her. She roasted a hare. It had been so long since Sofia had had fresh meat that she let the juices run down the side of her mouth and chin. She knew she would have a hankering for hare now. She wondered whether Abelard and Balthazar were still at her grandmother's house. And whether they had developed a taste for eating cats. Or were still eating the cookies her grandmother had stocked up on in the pantry.

The Old Woman asked them questions about where they were going and where Sofia's parents were. "You can move to one of those cities in the north. Those weren't evacuated in the same way. You'll be around your own people, if that's what you're looking for. For me, I don't care what country I'm in. I was sold like cattle when I was a young girl. I suppose it would have been the same in any country."

The Goose spoke softly into Sofia's ear. "I don't feel safe around her. I think she is a witch. She'll kill us both. She looks like she eats the fingers of young girls as a special treat."

"Ah," said the Old Woman, "a talking goose. I haven't seen one since I was a very little girl. I thought they were all gone. I never missed them either. They never do anything but complain and criticize." And she laughed from the bottom of her belly. And it made the sound of gravel churning.

The Goose was so outraged and offended by the Old Woman's comments, he insisted they be on their way first thing in the morning. When Sofia showed the Old Woman her map and said they would be heading in the direction of the Black Market, the Old Woman said she could give them a ride to where the road crossed a river. Sofia was wary of driving on the road, as the chances of encountering Enemy soldiers seemed very high. But she was tempted by the idea of covering a distance. They walked with the Old Woman to a barn. She opened the door. There was a rusted truck inside. The front of the truck was missing a cover. The engine was exposed to the air. She banged the engine with a stick. A family of outraged rats skittered from it.

Her hands looked incredibly strong. They looked as though they had slapped dozens of children and then hundreds of grand-children. And after all that love, she had been abandoned.

It seemed to Sofia as though it was the nature of women to be abandoned at a certain age. Her mother had told her that society tried to orchestrate the paths of women so that they would inevitably become more and more irrelevant in society until they were eventually invisible.

The truck made a horrible hacking noise, sputtering like a bitter smoker, until the engine finally wheezed one last death rattle and then began to purr. The Old Woman drove them down an empty back road. The drive was bumpy and nauseating. But they were so glad not to be walking. To be covering all these miles without any effort.

They reached a fork in the road as the sun was beginning to set. It was the magic hour. This was a time when creatures that lived only in the dark began planning their night out. All the eyes that could see in the dark began opening one by one. You could feel the electricity in the air. They could see you, but you could not see them. But you could feel them looking at you. It made you feel like an actor onstage, with a spotlight on you. And everyone was watching.

The audience knew more about your possible fate than you could. They knew what act you were in. They knew it was time for tragedy to befall you.

The Old Woman reached into her layers and pulled out a knife. "You may go. But hand over the goose."

At that, the Goose lunged at the woman and began pecking at her face. She wailed a throaty cry. Sofia opened the door and clambered out clumsily, throwing herself along with her bag out of the vehicle. She turned and the Goose leapt into her arms, like a pile of laundry tossed out a window. Sofia dropped the Goose to the earth, and they began running together. The Old Woman didn't even make an attempt to follow. Old women could not run.

"Your countrymen are truly pieces of work," was the first thing the Goose said once they found themselves tucked in a culvert for safety, and gasping for breath.

"It's not their fault they are acting this way. It is because of the Enemy."

"You talk about the Enemy. But I have not had any negative encounters with the Enemy. All I know is that I have had repeated meetings with people of your country, and they are, without exception, quite duplicitous and nasty."

"Without exception! You mean to say I am duplicitous and nasty! You sound like the Enemy. I should hand you over to them since you seem to share the same worldview."

They slept in a cave two nights. They slept in a barn another.

They walked along the river. She developed a facility for catching fish. Afterwards, she would build a small fire and fry her catch. And then eat it with her fingers, unable to wait until it cooled off.

Never in her wildest dreams had she imagined she would be capable of feeding herself in the wild. But they needed shelter because winter was coming.

They spent another two nights in the woods with no sign of other life. Until they came upon a suitcase, lying abandoned in a gulley. Sofia staggered down the muddy incline to get to it immediately. She was desperate to see what signs of civilization awaited her. But as soon as she grasped the handle, the lightness disappointed her. She brought the empty suitcase with her into a clearing in the woods.

She opened it. Inside she found only a spool of red ribbon, which she took out and put in her pocket, as she was always in need of rope. Although the suitcase now had no contents whatsoever, it was not truly empty. It was filled with a smell. It smelled like mothballs and laundry and coffee and soup. It had absorbed all the smells of a comfortable home. The smell had wanted to stay in the suitcase. Which was normal. It was not the kind of smell that could exist in the woods. It needed four walls and a ceiling.

Sofia climbed into the suitcase and wrapped her arms and legs together. She closed her eyes and imagined she was in someone's house. Not her own. But the home of someone else in the Capital. Sometimes her mother stayed too late at a dinner party and started drinking and didn't want to go home. So Sofia had to climb onto the pile of strangers' coats on the bed. And she had been ensconced in a mixture of perfumes and colognes. And all the products adults put on themselves to smell more inviting and welcoming to other people.

The lining inside the suitcase was covered in flowers, was dark green with patterns of dark orange tiger lilies. If you stood away from the pattern, it seemed entirely dark green. But as you looked closer, the colours appeared. Like goldfish appearing in the murky green water of an aquarium.

She thought she could stay there forever. Trapped in a memory. A memory is protected. You can't change it. But you can always find it when you need it.

"Are we moving in, then?" The Goose stuck his head under the suitcase cover and peered around. Sofia laughed.

"One day I would like you to smell what women smell like in the city. We can buy a little perfume when we get to the Black Market. I'll put some on the collar of my coat. And we can close our eyes and imagine we are at the florist's to pick up our bouquet of flowers. I should like to smell like I am periwinkle bluebells."

"I might like to smell like dying roses in September."

"Then you shall! I would like to get a perfume that smells like the air outside the bakery on a winter day."

"What about the smell of wood burning in a stove, chamomile tea, and a bloody nose?"

"That would indeed be a pleasurable smell. I would like a perfume that smells like old books. I always liked smelling the books when I got home from the Central Library. My mother would say, You don't know who smelled that book before you. And I would find a little spot, away from everybody. In my closet or my bedroom, or behind the couch, and I would sit with my face down in the book and breathe in the smell."

"And what do books smell like?"

"Like dry roses, lead pencil shavings, horses passing by on the street, and earthworms from the ground."

"How I would like ink to write my own!"

"There will be ink at the Black Market. Rows and rows of small bottles. Like a row of whores, each desperate for you to dip your pen tip inside. And there will be enough ink to record all your gobbling. There will be enough ink to paint the sky black."

Sofia took a large stick and used it to prop up the lid of the suitcase. She tied a piece of the red ribbon to the stick. She placed a handful of acorns and bark at the bottom of the suitcase. She went to sit inside a bush. She had to be as still as possible.

The hares were very odd in the forest. Hares were a very mysterious element in her country's folklore. They were shape-shifters.

In her country it was said that the most wretched individuals were reincarnated as hares. If you were hanged, you had to spend your next life as a hare. Before you were returned to a human form in the life after that.

The hares appeared only to those who were pure of heart. She did not think she was pure of heart at all. She had not done anything that was noble. In fact, she was the opposite of noble. She thought she was the worst little girl in the whole world.

She decided to try to see if she could remember the hare poem that had caused her such humiliation at school. Then at least she would know there was one poem no one could destroy. She could keep it hidden safely in her head. That was where she had previously kept everything. She stored so many of her ideas in her head when she was young. She didn't even know what she was going to do with them. Why did she keep her ideas as though they had any value or pertinence? It was as though she believed there would be a time in her life when she was grown. And she would feel confident to say all the things she was thinking. And she would express her thoughts, and people would think they were of great value.

She fantasized about being an adult. She imagined herself sitting at a café, wearing a fabulous coat. She would say so many fascinating things. Everyone around the table would either laugh or be amazed at what she said. And she was sure some of her observations might be considered, if not revolutionary, then at least worth listening to. She thought there would be a time when she wasn't afraid to speak.

She closed her eyes and opened her mouth. She recited the poem perfectly. When she opened her eyes, there was a hare standing near her. Then another one appeared out of nowhere.

Like a splotch of ink that fell from the tip of a pen onto a page. Then three others appeared.

They moved in such tiny increments. They looked like chess pieces that were being moved in strange directions. That seemed to make no sense. But they were carefully orchestrated to check-mate you. An enormous one was so close, she was terrified.

The eyes looked so dead. They were like brown buttons sewn onto the coat of a child.

The hare closed its eyes. And Sofia felt an instant reprieve. From having to stare into those black holes. But when they opened again, she found herself staring at grey human eyes that bore an uncanny resemblance to her mother's.

It hopped over to the suitcase. It smelled it. And then it leapt inside. Sofia jerked the ribbon hard, and the suitcase lid shut fast. She snapped the latches on the suitcase. She sat cross-legged, star-ing at it. And wept. The hare kept beating wildly inside the suit-case until Sofia could bear it no more. She unlatched the suitcase, and the small beast lurched out drunkenly for a moment, before turning and darting off, back into the woods.

"Why don't we leave for the South?" the Goose asked, as he stared into their small fire.

"They have allied with the Enemy. In any case, they've never liked us."

"I don't have any idea how you managed to alienate the coun-tries all around you. It's troubling. Do you ever consider that you might have made an effort to be cordial?"

"Could you not blame the entire war on me now? It isn't helpful."

"Don't you have any table manners?"

Sofia shrugged. She was sucking the flesh off a few scrawny fish they had managed to trap. She wiped her filthy hands on her coat and stockings. Clara was so fastidious about clothes and deportment. She was always annoyed at Sofia's appearance. She would stop her at the door and tell the maid to fix her hair. "We are Bottoms, after all. People expect more from us, Sofia. They expect us to be regal."

The extreme shock she imagined on her mother's face if she saw her now, with her ragged clothes, men's shoes, and filthy fingers, suddenly made her laugh. She threw her head back and began to hoot. It was a different kind of laugh. It was deeper. It was louder. It came from her whole body.

She kept laughing. She couldn't control it. Her body began shaking. Tears started squeezing out of her eyes. She felt herself peeing a little. She was like a dog that became hysterical when there was a knock at the door and couldn't simmer down again. She had never laughed out loud like that before. This was a different type of laugh. There was something powerful and rude about it.

She had seen teenage girls laugh like this. Everyone turned and looked at them with disapproving glances as though they were swearing. Men's voices changed when they reached puberty. They became lower and gruffer. But with teenage girls, their laughs transformed. They grew louder and more aggressive.

She realized now why people were afraid of women laughing. Why men spent so much time trying to covet and control and curtail laughter and humour so they were the only ones who had access to this powerful force.

As though if she laughed long and hard enough, the soldiers would all break down. They would be too humiliated.

"Do you hope to meet your mother after the war?" said the Goose calmly, appraising her.

"No. I don't believe I will see my mother after the war. I think she is dead." Sofia wiped at the corners of her eyes.

"You can never know that. You are here and I am here. So it is true that people survive."

"My mother would not have survived. She is an intellectual. They were murdering them all."

"She could have disguised herself."

"She did. But I think she was found out. She is dead. I know it in my bones."

"It's strange. You seem more frightened by the idea of her being alive than dead."

Sofia was alarmed by this statement. She turned and saw the Goose looking at her. And he had seen just how vulnerable it made her. He would capitalize on that.

"So why do you want your own mother dead? What monstrous ideas do you have in your head? Possibly the one virtue humans have over animals is that they are affectionate towards their mothers."

"Why do I have to have a bird tell me I'm inhumane?"

"It's just an observation. That you are a peculiar example of your species. The Goose Girl frequently talked about her mother and always missed her. If that isn't the truth, then tell me why you are hoping your mother is dead."

"Not dead!"

"Sorry, not alive."

Sofia considered this carefully.

"It's not that I hope she is dead. I just hope never to see her again. What would she say if she saw me now. She would be appalled. She would make me feel so much dirtier and dumber. I don't want to see myself through her eyes. It terrifies me. The idea of seeing her again. When I imagine it happening, I get upset for days. It gives me a particular feeling of dread I can't get rid of for days."

"I'm sure she looks a little worse for wear herself. War is never easy on a woman's appearance."

"Yes, but I don't have her manuscript! I can't explain that to her. She would never look at me the same."

What she did not want to say was that her mother would want to know what she had done with her book. She also was aware that had she followed her mother's instructions, she would not be alive at all. She would have climbed onto the trucks, as she was instructed. She would have been driven to wherever the other children were going.

"I want to be able to cry," the Goose said abruptly.

"You shouldn't wish that. Why would anyone want that? It makes your face look so ugly."

"I watched the Goose Girl cry. I did not find it ugly at all. I found it rather impressive. And I quite relished what it did to her eyes. They looked like the ocean. And I swore I could see all sorts of things circulating in her irises. I could see small waves moving around. And ships sinking and albatrosses in her eyes. And after she wept, she always acted differently. As though she had forgotten all her problems. She would lie on the grass in a fit of exhausted ecstasy."

"I feel that I don't weep enough. I feel as though there is something wrong with me. If I were a normal girl, I would have been crying every day as we walked along the road. I would have been weeping at least because I'd lost my mother. I would have been weeping because everyone I know is dead. Because the country has been turned to rubble. I haven't cried in so long. I don't think I have any tears left."

"Perhaps I can buy a small bottle of tears. Then I can apply them to my eyes. Do you think they will have tears at the Black Market?"

"Perhaps."

"Where do the tears come from?"

"During peacetime these types of bottles can be quite hard to find. They get them from poor little girls and prostitutes. When normal girls cry, their mothers dab their tears with a handkerchief, or with their fingers, or with their kisses. But during the war everyone is hard up, so many little girls sell their tears. You might have the tears of a wealthy doctor running down your cheeks."

"Will you buy some too?"

"Perhaps on the chance I see my mother again. I will be so shocked, I may not be able to cry. And I wouldn't want to be impolite."

EVERY SENTENCE IS A MAGIC SPELL

During the Occupation, there were gatherings that began to take place underground, institutions that began to form. Cellars became a locus of activity. Everyone set up their cellars as shelters. Then more and more people began gathering in clandestine basements. They enjoyed them—because it made them feel as though they had their own universe, and they were the centre of it.

Her mother had told her that people had no idea how they would behave during wartime until there was an actual war. And everyone was to a certain degree surprised. People who believed themselves to be brave and courageous often found they were neither. But other people who hadn't been especially remarkable during peacetime discovered they had an ability to thrive during wartime and found secret powers everyone depended on.

Clara and Sofia went into the basement of a building and down a hallway dug into stone that led to a strange green door. Clara knocked three times. Then she waited and knocked another three times. The door opened, and she immediately walked in, followed by Sofia.

There was a rather large basement room. The walls were covered in green wallpaper with pink roses on it. There were kitchen chairs and armchairs crowded together in the room. Each had a student seated in it.

There were some seated on the floor. Sofia was surprised there was enough air for everyone to breathe. They also risked being buried alive if a bomb should fall. The buildings were still unstable since the bombing. And you could never be sure when one might topple.

They didn't care. They sat with their spectacles and frayed sweaters and leather loafers. And they stared at Clara Bottom as though she were about to convey the meaning of life.

Sofia was surprised they were so desperate to learn. She was delighted not to have to go to school anymore. She hated herself at school. She would try to encourage herself to learn what they were teaching. But she could never coax her brain into believing any of it was important or relevant.

But these students insisted on learning. Even though their futures were up in the air. They had such dim prospects for a future. It was not a given that any of them would even get to grow old. And anyone attending this class would in all probability, if they were caught, be lined up and shot. But they did not care. They wanted to learn. They wanted to learn everything there was to know, today.

It was important for the whole country that they get the lessons in their heads. Each idea was a contraband item. Every insight was something to be sold on the Black Market.

"What can I tell you? When I began my studies, I was told it was ridiculous to want to be a philosopher. I was a woman, after all. I should not be taking myself seriously. How could I? Never underestimate your worth. You are going to need to be arrogant to survive this. You must be outraged by every single injustice you face. It will be exhausting to be filled with rage. But you must think of your rage as your guiding force now. You must be educated by your rage because it is telling you the difference between right and wrong.

"What is inside your mind is contagious. If you keep a fire in your heart, it will set other hearts on fire. But you are scholars. You are bearers of the torch. You are the most important army we have right now. And unlike our other army, you have not yet been defeated."

The students erupted into an applause that sounded to Sofia like a crackling, snapping fire. Clara suddenly felt a million miles away from her. It was unbearable. It felt as though she belonged to everybody in the room more than she did to her. They knew and appreciated Clara in a manner Sofia never could.

Afterwards, they walked together down the street back to their apartment. Clara sighed and said, "We'll be eating porridge tonight."

Sofia did not understand who she was walking down the street next to. She only knew it was not the woman who had been speaking to the students. Sofia was beset by a feeling of unease. She wondered whether her mother reserved her true self for students and other intellectuals and thought of Sofia as a little dog that followed her around, needing only a pat on the head or a bone to be happy.

I HEARD THE ICICLES SINGING

Winter in their country made its first impressions through sensations and mood, rather than through temperature. People found themselves suddenly worried about money. You might abruptly feel guilty about friends you had neglected or betrayed. These things would give you a chill. A shiver of loss would quake through your body.

Sofia and the Goose were on a road that cut through an empty field. She felt that it might begin to snow soon.

It was always mysterious when it snowed in her country. It never seemed to actually be cold enough during their winters for it to snow. People chose to attribute the snow to things other than the weather. They thought it had to do with church bells ringing. If a woman called out too loudly for her child in the street, it might start to snow. The silence after a parade sometimes caused it to snow. It was said that hares turning white caused it to snow and not the other way around. Poets were blamed for causing the snow. It was said that when a poet wrote something destined to be immortal, it would start to snow.

A girl appeared out of nowhere, dressed in a pretty black tailored wool coat and patent leather shoes. Her clothes were quite well preserved. Her shoes weren't even scuffed at all. Her hair was tied to the side and held up with a barrette. And a curl dangled down the side of her face. Sofia had seen girls and women in different places all over the country in the days she spent wandering. None of them had done up their hair. They did not have the time or the inclination to do their hair up prettily. No, this was a hairdo that had been attended to by a mother's fingers.

The girl looked as though her eyes were permanently dilated. She had witnessed something so horrific, it had caused her to go into shock. But she had not recovered. She was in a permanent state of shock.

Her breath was so heavy that the puffs of air coming out of her mouth were as large as a small cloud. And for a moment, her face was temporarily obscured. She was nothing but a little body with a cloud for a head. They waited a moment for her to stop panting and the cloud to disperse.

"My name is Ewa. I am so cold. I can't do anything to keep myself warm. Even though I keep moving. I feel so cold. Like ice. I can't even feel the tips of my fingers. Can I have just a little bit of your heat?"

Of course, Sofia and the Goose were cold too. But she had made the argument that she was more cold than they were. They suddenly felt ashamed of not feeling colder. And they felt they had no right to complain about being cold. She asked Sofia if she could put her hands under her coat. So Sofia undid her buttons and opened her coat. Ewa quickly thrust her arms into Sofia's coat.

Her hands were freezing to the touch. It was as though her hands were drawing in all the warmth from Sofia's body. Sofia felt what it was like to be a corpse. She looked out at the world with frozen eyes. They were eyes that could witness the world but couldn't make any emotional assessments about it. She was left with a much simpler palette of emotions with which to experience the world. This was how the dead saw the world. It was as though her heart had turned from a glowing piece of lava into a hard rock. Her mouth tasted like ashes.

Ewa's cheeks began to flush. Her lips turned red, as though a coat of lipstick had been put on them. Sweat appeared on her forehead, dampening her hair. It was as though she were a teapot and had been filled with boiling water. Ewa looked delighted and pulled her arms out. Sofia felt her body revive.

"I need to find my mother," Ewa said. "We were separated only five minutes ago. I was holding her hand and then she was gone. We were leaving our apartment. She told me to wait for her. Then there was a crowd of people, and we got mixed up with them. And I don't know where my mother went. I'm trying to catch up with her, but I don't know where she is. But she can't be far."

Sofia and the Goose turned their heads, looking all around them. There was emptiness in all directions as far as the eye could see. Wherever her mother was, she was most certainly far away.

"What evidence do you have that she is close?" Sofia asked.

"I heard her."

"Was she calling out to you?"

"No, she was singing. My mother loves to sing. Everybody hears her singing when she takes a bath. She even knows how to sing opera. My mother has the most beautiful voice. It is more beautiful than an opera singer's."

Sofia doubted this very much. She had actually been to the opera. She knew that opera singers needed years of training. You couldn't simply be an opera singer while you washed the dishes. "How can you possibly hear her singing from here?"

"I can hear her singing when it snows."

Sofia was not sure this was her mother singing. It was not exclusively in Elysia that people claimed they could hear singing in the snow. It was a common experience. In other countries, they had scientists who were able to explain these auditory hallucinations. But it was impossible to dismiss the sounds people heard in the Elysian snowstorm as figments of the imagination. A person would not say, I heard a vague sort of singing. Instead, they described it as such: There were two baritone horns playing while a xylophone tinkled out a tune and a chorus of maybe five or six sang.

"Let's quiet down," Ewa said. "And if we are absolutely quiet, it will begin to snow."

She made a little *O* out of her lips and placed her index finger over it. They all quieted down to listen. Everything quieted down around them too. As though everything in the country suddenly heard Ewa's request that they needed to be quiet. It was as though her tiny finger over her tiny mouth had as much power as a great magic wand.

And there was a silence. For snow to come, everyone has to listen for it. Everyone is listening so hard that there is no sound left to listen to. It is the sound of a blank page. It is the sound of time standing still. It is the sound of death. It is the sound of grace. It is the sound of silence. The only sound that existed in the whole world was Sofia's breathing.

And then the snow began to fall. Sofia was amazed. Ewa could do anything she wanted with her finger. She could point to a hare and turn it into a man who wouldn't know where he was from.

"Do you hear it! It's coming from that direction," Ewa declared, pointing in a direction they could not really discern. Neither Sofia nor the Goose heard anything. "I'm going to follow it. You must come with me! Follow my mother's voice with me! And we will walk to school together with our books in our hands. And we can go skating together. And skate figure eights and all sorts of other moves that make us look so silly and pretty. And when we're done skating, we will sit and drink hot cocoa."

The Goose leaned against Sofia's leg, as if warning her to stay put. The girl ran off. They watched her hurry off until all that was left of her were footprints in the thin layer of snow.

They stopped talking because the snow had suddenly begun to fall more heavily. And Sofia tried to hear what it was that Ewa heard in the snowfalls. She strained to concentrate and pick apart all the noises the wind was making. Then she thought she heard singing. There was the sound of a children's choir coming from the branches. The trees were known to play tunes from different times. These could be a choir of her contemporaries. Or children from three hundred years ago.

"Do you hear the singing coming from the trees?"

"I hear nothing at all."

"It's too pretty to bear."

"You're hearing nothing but a memory."

Even when there were no bombardments, Clara and Sofia slept curled up in each other's arms. When the heat shut off, her mother's large bedroom became too cold to sleep in. It became her habit to sleep in Sofia's bedroom, which had been her bedroom when she was young too. Every time Clara entered the room, she acted as though she hadn't been inside it for decades. "Oh, hello!"

she said to a small wooden lamb on one of the shelves. "Long time no see."

It made Sofia tremendously excited when her mother came into her room to sleep in the evening. She never took it for granted. But each night she trembled with anticipation, waiting for her to come.

"I can't sleep," Sofia said in the dark one night.

"I could never get to sleep when I was a girl. I think it was because I was afraid of going to sleep and missing out on something. I don't know what. But I was always chasing things in life. Something that was just out of my grasp. My mother would sing me lullabies. She knew a hundred of them. I thought they were ridiculous later on. But there was a time when I must have truly loved them. Because I asked for them."

"They calmed you down, like warm milk," Sofia suggested tentatively.

"Yes."

"Can you sing one of the songs to me now?"

"I won't get the words right. And I can't sing them the way your grandmother did. She sang as though she had written the songs herself, and they were about her. Fascinating, really."

I planted my heart outside your house. And an apple tree grew there. And you bit into my heart every day. And your lover, your sweet pretty lover, came and bit into my heart. And your children bit into my heart, my one heart, and all my hearts.

Sofia sat in the dark silence. The echo of her mother's words hung in the air. She had heard her mother humming to songs on the radio or in the bath. She seemed to catch jovial jingles in her throat. Her mother was the type of person who sang when she was happy.

But this song was dark. Each word dropped like a tea bag into hot water. Then it would steep, and darkness continued to spread out of it.

She felt so content, it was troubling. She felt as though she might die from pleasure.

TIPTOE THROUGH THE LANDMINES

The trees were very vain in the winter. They didn't care that the world had grown cold and everyone's life had become more difficult. Covered in white fur, they looked elegant. The snow highlighted the wild, beautiful shapes of their branches. As though they were wearing skimpy nightgowns on their wedding nights. They had changed the colour of their fur like certain foxes do.

At times, the trees were encased in ice. They were beautiful this way, too, but they were deadly. They were ready to drop knives on people without warning if there was the slightest noise or disturbance. If she was to call out, if the Goose was to quack or make a great ruffling noise, as he was wont to do, it would upset the trees, and they would try to kill them. She put her hands over her own mouth. It wasn't just her either. It was incredibly quiet. The entire forest was still. There was not the sound of a footstep or a stick breaking underfoot.

• • •

They didn't see another real flesh-and-blood person until they came across a girl cooking at a small fire by the road. When they approached, they realized it was not a girl at all. The boy was wearing lipstick and a white dress with holes in it over a pair of grey stockings. He was scrubbing all the dishes in one pot. And he was cooking in the other. There was a long leash attached to a stake on the side of the road and tied to a manacle on his ankle.

"Abelard!" Sofia whispered harshly. He turned and looked confused, and then a great smile of recognition broke across his face.

"Look who it is! Sofia and her remarkable goose!"

"What are you doing here?"

"The soldiers stopped by the house on the way to the Capital. There were so many, there was nowhere to hide. There were planes overhead that were able to see the house too. They captured Balthazar and me. Come have something to eat!"

He reached out with a baked potato that was slathered in butter. Sofia could not resist. She hurried over, grabbed the potato, and began eating it ravenously.

"This butter is magnificent," Sofia cried, forgetting everything else in the world for a minute. "I had forgotten just how delicious butter is. I want to have butter on everything. When this war is over, I will have butter on my toast, on my fruit, on my meat, on my eggs. I will keep a small saucepan of butter heated up on the stove at all times so I can pour it over everything I eat. I have half a mind to pour it into a teacup and sip it just like that."

"They were about to put me onto a train," Abelard said, continuing his story. "But I told them I could do magical things if they would settle down for a moment and let me perform a trick."

"Do you know any magic tricks?"

"I transformed into a horse in front of their very eyes. They believed I was the most funny actor they had ever encountered. I didn't realize how humorous I was until I began performing for the soldiers. I knew my talent would be what saved my life. When I lived at the orphanage, they told me my clowning around would be the death of me. They said it was a terrible habit. But here I am!"

This impressed Sofia because Abelard had managed to barter for his life with art.

This seemed like a chink in the soldiers' armour. It was said that people who related to art were more sensitive. If the soldiers appreciated Abelard's art, perhaps they would be smitten with other aspects of the country's culture and would rethink destroying all of it. Or perhaps the Enemy soldiers had spent so much time in the country now that they had absorbed some Elysian values. And had begun to have a penchant for the arts. It was the first time she thought she might have something in common with the Enemy. She also really admired Abelard's theatrics. If she was apprehended by the Enemy, perhaps she could play the clarinet or recite a monologue from a play.

But the Goose, who had not said much, tugged on Sofia's skirt. She bent down to listen.

"Ask him why exactly he has the chain on his ankle if the soldiers admired him so much."

"I am going to be liberated if I manage to survive the walk to the western border," Abelard said.

"Why wouldn't you survive?" Sofia asked. "It isn't that far."

"Well, the walk there is very different for me than it is for others. It is more of a meander than a walk. I have to tiptoe over the ground to show people where to step. There are landmines everywhere. I must walk ahead of the others. I have been walk-ing for months, but I have not been blown up. I have a special skill."

"How on earth is that a skill!" the Goose exclaimed. "If he walks down a road and doesn't blow up, it is because there was no mine there. It has nothing to do with talent. It's not as though he is making the mines disappear by avoiding them."

"It does take talent. A certain focus and patience. I learned that from Balthazar."

"Balthazar!"

"Yes. At first we both were meant to walk. We walked together. They ordered us to hold hands. I quite liked that. It made me feel very secure to have my friend's hand in mine. Especially in such dangerous circumstances. And even if I died, I could do it while holding the hand of somebody I loved. And isn't that what everybody wants more than anything in life?

"But Balthazar didn't like it. He said it made him seem like a child. He said that after a certain age, two boys should not be seen holding hands in public. It made him so uncomfortable. We were holding hands one day, and he pulled his from mine and started to run ahead as fast as he could. He was hurtling himself into the future. Then he exploded. It was ghastly. I thought I would never be able to walk another step. I was certain I would be terrified to walk forward. But now I am sure I can't be killed."

"Why on earth not?"

"My father was a thief, so it's in my nature to be able to sneak around at night. I imagine that I am in a nursery and I am walk-ing through a row of cribs. And in each crib is a baby. And the slightest noise will wake all the babies up. Why don't you send the goose up ahead? If he blows up, it won't be so tragic and we will have something to eat for dinner."

"I would think it very tragic if my goose were to be blown up."

"Well, I don't imagine he would weigh enough to set off a landmine anyway. So perhaps he would only give us a false sense of confidence."

"Can you tell us which roads are safe to walk on?" Sofia unrolled her map on the ground.

"A map! Look at that. You could be hanged for being in possession of such a thing. Anyone might betray you. There would be a handsome reward in it." He bent over it. He began tracing the road he had already been on with his finger. "You ought to walk along this little road."

She and Abelard moved the tips of their fingers along the map, discussing possible routes for her. He showed her a secret road that he had seen leading into the forest. "There's a church through there if you want some shelter. The soldiers were too afraid to go that deep into the woods. So if you are running from them, go into the woods. They won't follow you. They will have to sit and wait for you to come back out."

"Isn't it amazing," said the Goose, "how the Enemy believes in your old religion more than you do?"

"If you aren't one of the ones they want to kill, they are kind of lovely," said Abelard.

"Ah," said Sofia, "but we are. Shall we help you get unchained? I could bash it with a rock."

"No," said Abelard. "I want them to free me from this chain themselves. They will need actors in the Capital after the war. I would like to fit in. I know their language, after all. It's a great gift. I don't want to run around in the woods anymore. I want to be on the winning side. I don't care what it takes."

They walked away from Abelard, who believed that remaining attached to a manacle would somehow lead to his freedom. They were terrified of the road they were walking on.

"I'm frightened about being on the road right now," Sofia said.

The Goose froze next to her.

"Can't you feel it? I feel like there is another group of soldiers coming. I feel like the earth is shaking. Do you feel that? Thousands of footsteps."

"Are you certain it's not your heartbeat?" the Goose asked.

Sofia took the teacup out of her pocket. She put it on a stone and then placed the spoon inside. The spoon began to spin as though the soldiers were coming from all directions.

Sofia and the Goose ran deep into the great forest without any sense of where they were going.

So often her mother had dragged her to the theatre when she was far too young. She would frequently be the only child in the theatre. She milled around all the legs as though she were in a tall pine forest. She was terrified of being lost in the legs. There was no path or fixed direction among them. And just when she saw a possible path through them, they would shift and move. Closing off whatever direction she might have perceived in them before.

The dead leaves were like playbills scattered all over the sidewalk after a show.

Sofia stopped running and considered the trees. She took out her map and then pulled the spool of red ribbon from her pocket.

She tied bows onto branches here and there so she would be able to find her way out. Sofia did not like to use her red ribbon. She liked to take it out of her pocket and unravel it, and then watch it dance in the air as though it were pouring blood.

The ground was all bumpy. She had to step over all the roots on the ground. They were like the arms of great sea creatures that might suddenly reach above the surface of the water and drag you a thousand feet below. But she stepped forward and remembered what Abelard had told her.

She knew the snow was coming again. They were looking for sanctuary. And when she saw the church among the trees, she knew that was going to be it. They were going to enter and stay a very long while. Opening the door was like opening the cover of a large Russian novel. One that was going to last for months and months and was filled with snowflakes.

There was a small chapel. Some of the older people in the country still believed in God. There wasn't anything anyone could do or say to stop them. They still carried prayer cards inside their breast pockets as though they were the identity papers they would use when they got to heaven. Or at least that's what they believed.

There was a framed painting of the Virgin Mary surrounded by flowers. It was like being at a funeral for the Virgin Mary. The flowers were made of cloth so no one had to water them.

There were three rows of pews. And the walls had been painted with flowers and songbirds. And a very small naked boy holding a lamb. He was being followed by a flock of sheep. They all seemed eager to be held by him.

Behind the chapel they opened a back door to find a small house where the minister once lived. They went inside it and dropped their bags.

Noticing the way that vines had crept into the house, through the windowsill and right through the wall, Sofia saw that it had begun to merge with nature. Nature was always ready to sneak back in and reclaim its stolen land. It happened surprisingly fast. And it did make her wonder whether a similar thing was happening to her. And whether she was turning into a woodland creature. Something she might have read about in her fable book.

She yanked opened a large wooden drawer that was sticky coming out. The furniture in the house was old, and it all had arthritis. Things stuck. It was difficult to open any door. It was as though each door was convinced it was a part of the wall. And then when it was finally ripped open, it no longer wanted to go back in.

The house was so cold. She turned on the faucet only to have a swirl of snowflakes fly out of it. When she turned off the faucet, there were still snowflakes floating around in the darkness.

Now that it was winter, Sofia would need some way to acquire meat for herself. She knew she only needed to capture two hares, male and female, and they would be able to mate. And she would soon be able to breed them. Again, she made a trap with a box and a cord attached to it. She captured three male hares and put them in a large bird cage that was in a back room of the house. There would be no question this time of letting any of them go.

Sofia took one out of the cage. She brought it into the kitchen. She put it on her lap. She petted it gently over and over again. She could feel the hare's heart beating. It ticked wildly as though it were some sort of fast-moving timepiece. It seemed to be beating too quickly. It was wondrous that it did not have a heart attack. Then, as soon as she sensed the heartbeat was slowing down, she grabbed the hare by the ears, stood up, took her silver knife, and slit its throat over a metal bucket on the table.

She felt the hares's heartbeat leave its body and enter her own. Her whole body shook with the force of it. She laid the dead hare on the table and felt herself shake so hard, her teeth knocked against one another. She shook violently, as though she had climbed out of a freezing lake.

"How gruesome," said the Goose, who had walked into the kitchen and was standing in the doorway.

The Goose had no blood on his hands, or feet, so he was free to judge.

"When I see you kill that hare and not look at all regretful or perturbed by it, it makes me realize just how much of a psychopath you are. I realize the war brings out different sides to a person. Sides you might not have previously believed existed. But the war doesn't lie, does it? We met at the beginning of the war, and now it appears only one of us is a murderer.

"It makes me nervous, of course. Because I know you are the type to sacrifice another for yourself. All I can say is that if only one of us survives the war, I think it's safe to say it will be you. I'm always so concerned about other people and creatures killing me. And I am always putting my fate in your hands. But the irony of it all is that you are the one who is most likely to kill me. I don't even find it terrifying. I only blame myself for being so foolish to think anything otherwise."

He turned around and waddled out the door.

It was at that point that Sofia's shivering toned down. She regained not so much her composure but her drive. And her drive was fuelled predominantly by hunger. She began to remove the hare's skin. She was surprised she knew how to do such a thing. But her hunger made it so she knew exactly what to do. She had the instincts of a predator. So perhaps, in fact, everything the Goose had said about her was true.

She took a frying pan and put it on the stove. The hare's meat began popping with smells and savours.

She had thought she might put some hare aside to eat later, so she could postpone killing another animal soon. But she could do nothing to stop herself from devouring the entire hare. She ate so fast that at first she had a stomach ache. It was as though the hare had formed and was kicking against her belly. She had cured hunger.

The red meat made her body feel different. She felt more awake than she had in a long time. She no longer had a headache. She began to see colours. Whereas before things had turned a sort of white, now their bright colours returned. As though the world had been newly dipped in dye.

She felt the way vampires did in folklore. Every molecule in her body was changing. The molecules were stronger. They lit up one by one the way the fairy lights came on during Christmas in the town square.

She cleaned up the table. She threw the bones of the hare away and mopped up all the blood.

She went to the cage. She looked at the remaining hares. One hare kept shifting its body in slightly different positions. As though it were the dial of a radio someone was trying to get to a station on. As though it were a planchette on a Ouija board that was having trouble communicating with the dead.

She looked into the eyes of one of the remaining hares. They were black and blank, framed with the eyelashes of a movie star. And the more she stared into them, the less she was able to understand. It was neither friend nor foe. And she realized this meant she was the hare's enemy.

"The Goose Girl would never be able to kill the way you are," the Goose said, interrupting her meditation.

Sofia swerved around towards the Goose, realizing she was feeling vicious.

"You always bring up that stupid girl when you want to irritate me. It's ridiculous that you think you can make me jealous by describing a girl who works on a farm. A farmer! What did you even talk about? She couldn't have had a very large vocabulary. Did you discuss the smell of hay? Why would I ever be intimidated by a farm girl? I was educated at the very best girls' school in the Capital. I lived in a luxurious apartment. I went to see plays and ballets and operas all the time. I would not have been allowed to be friends with this Goose Girl. My mother would have considered it beneath me. She would have imagined the girl would bring me down. And that I would start acting like her."

At that, the Goose froze. The only way to win an argument with the Goose—and by win, she meant make him stop his rant—was to humiliate him. Humiliation always made him suddenly stock-still. He would become completely immobile and stare at her, his eyes a more intense shade of blue. As though he had been hypnotized. He would be uncharacteristically quiet, incapable of saying a word.

She felt for the first time that she had a right to be angry. She had the right to express her anger. Her anger was like a dog she had let off the leash. And when she was angry, she let it govern her body, as though in a dance. She threw her hands up in the air. And let out a moan.

"Do you think my preferred companion is a goose? Why would I choose a goose to go through the war with? You make me more vulnerable. I could have had a Great Dane. Any dog, really. But have you seen Great Danes? They look like horses. It would make sense."

He waddled off to a corner of the house and refused to look at Sofia. After this fight, they did not speak for two days. And afterwards, he never brought up the Goose Girl again.

"Sense!" he cried, but said no more.

She was wary about spending the whole winter in the house. But she had no choice. She couldn't risk going out in the cold and having to sleep in the woods. And waking up to discover she was a frozen corpse.

They lit a fire in the hearth. They sat in front of it and immediately they became entranced.

Between the warmth emanating from the fire and the small theatre taking place in the flames, they became addicted. There was a strange play that took place in the fireplace every night. There were tiny players with unkempt red hair.

She made a lantern out of a large rusted tin can. She fashioned holes in the sides of it, near the top. She put it on the side of the bed, and she built a little fire in it. When the light from the fire glowed through the holes, it made a group of stars on the ceiling. She held her hands in front of the light. She made the shadow of a billy goat dancing around. It was so pretty. Sofia forgot that she had created it. And that it was not its own little being dancing for them. Having the time of its life, absolutely carefree.

The Goose raised his wings and cast an enormous shadow of an angel. It looked like an angel of death. And they both cowered when they saw it. They crept under the covers, closed their eyes, and went to sleep.

She drew a chessboard on a flat piece of wood. She took stones and drew the images of which pieces they were supposed to be on top of them. She drew a fat, wide crown for the king and a tall pointed one for the queen. She sat and played against the Goose. It was during these games that they conversed about intellectual topics.

The Goose always made inscrutable moves. But if she beat him at the game easily, he would become infuriated and would squawk angrily, accuse her of cheating, and knock all the pieces off the board with his spread wing.

And then he would shut his beak firmly, like a clasp on a purse. There was an armchair by the fire. The upholstery had an image of trees and a stream. He would climb into the chair and sit there as though he had discovered a little piece of Eden. The heat from the fire would cause him turn his head around 180 degrees, tuck it into his wings, and go to sleep.

• • •

Sofia looked at her reflection in the mirror. She was surprised at how grown-up she looked. It was as though a magical curse had been lifted and she was released from the body of a child. And could now return to her natural one.

Sofia found she did not want to bathe with the Goose anymore. This would mean they had to have two separate baths of water heated over the fire, which was wasteful. But she couldn't bear for the Goose to see the changes her body was going through. She wasn't sure why. She wasn't sure whether she was humiliated by it, or she wanted to keep it a secret. But she didn't want the Goose to see.

If they had met when she had already gone through puberty, she probably wouldn't have minded. Celeste had had no problem bathing with the Goose.

But now that he had seen her body when it was that of a child, she couldn't let him see it any other way. She felt as though he would accuse her body of being a lie. Or say that she was pretending to be something she was not. How strange it was to have the body of a woman. Didn't a woman have more authority than a child?

The Goose would be angry because her new body would naturally demand a sort of deference. He would no longer be able to speak to her in a condescending way. She didn't know why she felt guilty about taking this away from the Goose. She knew how much bullying her meant to the Goose.

Sometimes she had peculiar dreams. She was back at home in the Capital and she heard a voice she could not place singing in the bathroom. It was the voice of a male, but it was not her father's.

She opened the bathroom door to find Balthazar standing in front of the sink shaving. The bath had already been drawn. And she found herself taking her clothes off, as though in a trance, and climbing naked into the tub. And then she said, "Will you join me?" The shock of her own words awoke her from her sleep.

When she woke up from one of these dreams, she did not appreciate having the Goose there, wrapped up in her arms. She wanted to lie in that puddle of strangeness all by herself for a bit.

For a few moments after waking up, she still believed the events of her dream were at least plausible.

Sofia had never had a boyfriend.

In her school, it was customary to have a date to the Spring Ball. All the girls thought and planned and worried about the Spring Ball for months and months. Once you had gone to the Spring Ball, you were allowed to start dating boys and going out to movies and dances with them. It was at the Spring Ball that everyone broke the ice.

Whenever children asked their parents whether they could get romantically involved, they were told to wait at least until after the Spring Ball. But Sofia had never gone to the Spring Ball.

She had never shared an ice cream float with a boy at a diner. She had never let a boy hold her books on the way home. She had never waved her hat at a boy coming down the street on his bicycle.

She was small for her age. There were girls in her class who had begun to have more developed bodies. They were transforming into women right before her eyes. But nothing happened to Sofia's body. The metamorphosis seemed too extraordinary to Sofia. And she was convinced it would never happen to her. She would be trapped in the body of a little girl forever. She would never be a sexual being, and Elysia celebrated being open about liking sex.

There were many aspects of Elysian culture that were reactionary. Where it might seem they had gone a little mad by overcorrecting. The Enemy was known for having severe anti-sex laws. Homosexuality, cross-dressing, prostitution, and all-night dancing were all illegal. So when Elysians had their own country, they collectively decided everyone should have complete sexual freedom.

There had been an entire museum show based on the gamines who were prostitutes in the Luminous Park neighbourhood. The pictures were drawn with pieces of charcoal on brown paper and then taped to the walls. There were so many prostitutes in the area that you felt as though you had walked into their personal space. They were not dressed in the manner of people who had left the house. Instead, many of them were in various states of disrobe. They slept ten to a room in hotels. They all lost weight because they could barely afford to eat. So their clothes began to hang off them in revealing ways. Sometimes they would slip out of a shoe and a stocking on the train.

There were groups of young boys who also sold their bodies. They always hung together. They tended to wear the most fanciful clothes. They dressed in top hats and wore old decorative army coats over soiled undershirts. Whenever Sofia saw these young men on the Luminous Park subway platform, she wondered what and who they were. And what did they mean to her.

Sofia grew to know the forest quickly. The Goose had a knack for finding bodies of water and found a lake that was icy to the touch, but he seemed not to mind. She sometimes swore there were figures following her when she walked in the woods, gathering mushrooms from under the snow. But when she turned, she found it was only ever a tree. Younger trees were more likely to pull up their roots and begin assuming the shapes of young women.

One day she saw a woman with her hair standing in dreadlocks up above her head. Sofia's attention was drawn to the woman's knees. They were red as though they had been dragged across the dirt. They had dark circular rings on them. She was naked and seemed unaffected by the cold. She did not have skin colours humans normally had. She had a greyish-bluish-brownish hue, the colour of bark and stones. Sofia was so terrified.

She tried to remind herself over and over again that they were not real. But her body froze when she saw them. She felt like a deer whose body had become completely immobile when she became aware of them. It was as though her blood had stopped flowing. And she had to wait for her heart to begin pumping warm blood through her veins so she knew she was alive.

She saw a very skinny woman running through the trees. It was as though she was trying to sneak back to her bedroom after having an affair with the son of the house. The trees were all mocking her with their sexuality. She had forgotten how, in such an old forest, there were still so many young trees.

There was a young man sitting on the edge of a cliff. His feet were dangling over the side while he looked straight ahead. He had a desolate stare on his face. He was considering jumping off. Sofia was about to call out to him, but then he turned back into a tree.

She was desperate for company, but she did not want to talk to the people in the trees at all. Her grandmother had told her to avoid tree people. She said once you started talking to them, you could never return to human discourse.

In many of the folktales she read, terrible things befell girls who spoke to strangers in the woods. There was almost always a villainous suitor in the tale. One whom the girl would be too friendly with. One who was out to rob the girl of everything she knew. One whom she was a fool to talk to. But why did she talk to him? Sofia could never understand why the girls in the fables always had such complicated conversations with ogres and giants and wolves.

If there was one word to describe these suitors, it was unpredictable. Their personality traits did not add up. They could be excessively kind and then commit the most heinous act. They might be effusive and caring, and then eat your dog when you went off to the washroom.

Sofia did not understand them, nor did she want to.

SONGS FOR CITY BIRDS

ON CLARINET

Her phosphorescent mushrooms had grown expo-
nentially. They now filled buckets and jars and
pots she had found. They were placed around
the house on every little ledge and surface. Even
though they made peculiar-looking plants during the day,
at night they illuminated the house in such a pretty way. It
made it seem like their house was an old-fashioned home.
It seemed cozy and pretty. And like its own country, one
that was at peace.

She put the teacup and spoon on the table. And for the
whole of the winter it was always quiet. It was so quiet
that if the teacup had made the slightest tingling sound,
it would have startled them with the same vigour as a
church bell. The church was quiet and still, because it is in
the nature of a church to be quiet and still. But the forest
all around the church was quiet as well. It was as though
the forest had made itself into an arbour, a vaulted ceiling
above and all around the church. As though it was perhaps
the forest itself providing the sanctuary the girl and the

Goose were able to live in. At one point in the winter, she had wondered if she and the Goose might stay in this house for the rest of their lives.

When she was evicted from her grandmother's house, Abelard had let her pack the clarinet in her bag. Now Sofia spent a great many evenings playing clarinet to the Goose. She only knew a few tunes that were popular in the country. And these tunes had become illegal. The Enemy might have assumed they had eradicated the songs forever. But she still knew them. And maybe she was the last person in the world who was playing these lullabies. Even if she played them in a broken way. The notes she mixed up and got wrong would be a part of the song now forever.

She played so often that she became much more proficient. It was true what the teachers had said about practising. She had never really believed them that there was a possibility she might become good at something if she tried. Or maybe she only thought she had become good because there were no other students to compare herself to. She was the last child alive who could play the clarinet.

The Goose was her audience. He was her sole audience, and her main audience. She now noticed that an attentive audience changed the way she played. It made her feel as though her playing had purpose. It made her focus. It made her want to be better. She was thrilled when he was enraptured by her playing.

"It was once said by a great French poet that there is no beauty that does not contain a hint of melancholy," the Goose said one time after she put down her clarinet. "And I did not understand it until I heard the sadness in your playing. I cannot rightly say if you are rendering sadness beautiful, or if you are making beauty sad. Either way, your playing affects me profoundly."

And now that she received compliments, she realized how much she had been missing them. She realized there was a hole in her heart. It was where praise and outpourings of love were meant to go. Because after the Goose celebrated her playing, she would feel so full. As full as she felt after eating an enormous piece of pie after a meal.

One night in the apartment after curfew, Sofia and her mother were sitting in the living room. The light of a small candle made her mother, lying on the couch, seem like an oil painting.

"I miss listening to music. I miss the way it makes you feel so much emotion. All of a sudden, you will be feeling a sadness that seems so real it brings tears to your eyes. But it isn't even your own sadness. It is someone else's sadness. Pure sadness. It's so good to feel, isn't it? I don't know how they do it. I never had any musical ability myself. Sofia, take out your clarinet. Play us a tune, just a quick one. Oh, the Wlinken you play so sweetly. I love it when you play that one. It's more fragile than I've ever heard it played before."

Sofia was surprised. She had no idea her mother could care at all for her mediocre playing. She immediately went to fetch her clarinet and then brought it into the living room. She sat on a small wine-coloured ottoman and began to play the song her mother had requested. Her mother listened with her eyes closed, and Sofia had no idea what she was thinking. When she finished the melody, she laid the clarinet across her lap.

"There's something touching about your playing, Sofia. You aren't a perfect player now because you are coming at it in a different way. If you keep at it, you'll see you'll go much further than the people who are ahead of you now."

Sofia was perfectly silent because she was happy.

Sofia had proven herself resourceful. She had proven she was a good thinker. She had learned to tell jokes. She had figured out how to lie to soldiers and had mastered how to dart in and out of alleys and keep to shadows. She had taken on all the household chores. And she had learned how to speak to adults.

Now, unlike all the other little girls in the world, she had earned her mother's love.

She felt her days were rich. She had her mother's individual attention. She had always felt she was missing something from her mother. She felt everyone had access to her mother that was her right to have, but she did not have at all.

"We have to stay together," her mother said. "If two people get separated during the war, they may never find each other again."

And at that moment, Sofia wished the war would never end. She wished there would always be bombs falling from the sky, as regular as thunderstorms. She wished even more soldiers would enter the city, as boisterous as a sports team returning with a trophy.

What was more important? The lives of all the citizens of the Capital. Or one girl feeling loved.

THE TOY SOLDIER

Sofia had always thought her father was much kinder than her mother. Her father came from a wealthy family that had made its fortune in silver. Her father seemed to know a lot. But he had no desire to impress his knowledge on anyone else. You were reminded only when he had an answer to a random question. Someone might ask at dinner what the population of France was. And he would suddenly answer with an undeniable assurance: Forty-one million.

His home office was tidy and accommodated a shelf of business awards. He listened to the radio for hours, preferring radio plays most of all. Ones that you could listen to with your eyes closed to forget where you were. He never missed the murder mystery show. Sofia liked to sit on her father's lap and listen to the show with him. Although she much preferred the children's hour. And no matter how closely she listened to the murder mystery, she was never able to guess who the killer was. This gave her a sense of happy dependency and ineptitude.

Her father would take her out to the Centre Park on Sundays when they were together. He liked to sit in front of a huge four-hundred-year-old tree in the park. He said it calmed him and let him think his deepest thoughts. Clara scoffed that it was the Elysian in him. She said his family came from deeper in the woods then hers did. "He is still bonkers about trees." And she said it sometimes took a few generations to wash the tree fetishism out of a person's blood.

Sofia liked him because he did not ask her questions about why she had no friends at school. He did not ask about her grades and then look at her as though he could not quite comprehend how she could be his child. Unlike her mother, he didn't expect her to be anything other than an ordinary maladroit child. And the expectation, or lack thereof, made her feel relaxed and lazy and content.

Right before her father left, she had run up to him and said, "Take me with you. I want to be safe and away from the war too. I don't have to stay with Maman!" He had put his hand on her shoulder. And she realized he was gripping it firmly in order to hold her back if she came any closer. "A girl should stay with her mother."

And her mother had said one word from her boudoir. "Idiot."

And Sofia had felt ashamed because she believed her mother was calling her an idiot for asking to leave. She blamed her mother for their being left behind in the Capital when the war came.

But now she realized it was her father she was calling an idiot. Because he would not take their daughter to a safe place while she stayed behind to fight the war.

He said it as though he were doing her a kindness. But in truth, he wanted to be free. Sometimes war can set a man free.

Her father was alive and well. But he was dead to her. He could never be her father again. It was that she and her mother had lived through something. And had fought through something that was so life-changing.

Her mother, with a bullet in her head and buried in a mass grave, was more alive to her than her father, who was sitting somewhere comfortable in the United States.

One evening in the tiny house in the woods, Sofia fell into the topic of her father. Since there was no beginning or end to the winter, she would allow herself to wax poetic for as long as she wanted on any given subject. She was slumped in the armchair, holding a stick that she was waving around like a wand.

"My father is a stranger to me now. He would not even recognize me. He would be ashamed to call me his daughter. He is dining in New York City tonight. And sleeping in his comfortable bed. He is going to get remarried. How wonderful it will be for him to start over again. He won't marry anyone like my mother again. He will be the centre of attention in any room. He will be the God of his family. And he will have other children. And they will be very clean and tidy. His new children will have perfect teeth. And perfect hair. And they will do well in school. They will write essays about the past and not the present. They will have impeccable manners. They will have no memories of the war."

"It is impossible to be a child who has lived through a war your parent has not," the Goose agreed. "You will spoil the dinner party with your tales of degradation. Your existence will be a sort of affront. It will definitely be rude. You will be an accusation to everyone around you."

• • •

They both knew from the power of the knock that a man was at the door. They froze like animals that were so frightened by danger it made them incapable of movement. They were just a goose and a very skinny girl. For all the power plays they had engaged in during the winter, they could not defend themselves now. They did not have a gun. They might have very well used something in the kitchen to defend themselves. But they knew they didn't possibly stand a chance with their clay pots and wooden spoons.

They could only beg for mercy.

"What if it's a soldier?" the Goose whispered.

"What if it isn't?" Sofia whispered back.

And the Goose looked at her completely startled, having no idea what she could possibly be thinking about. Because he was under the assumption that nothing could be quite as bad as an Enemy soldier at your door.

The man was wearing his long khaki army coat. And his large bag was the kind she had seen soldiers carrying on their backs as they went off to war. But when he took it off, he had on a knitted yellow sweater underneath a large suit jacket that had cigarette burn holes in the sleeves and stains on the lapels. He was wearing a pair of blue pants held up with suspenders.

He had a pin of a small flower he wore on his lapel. They gave those pins out for free on Constantina Day. It was the national flower, a lyridina. She thought it was charming that he had a flower on his lapel, as it was more traditional for a woman to wear such a pin on hers. She thought he wasn't afraid of being feminine. She liked that about him immediately.

He took off his fur hat and long coat and slouched onto a kitchen chair. His limbs were so long he didn't seem to fit onto it properly. If the world were the same as it had once been, she imagined he would have had trouble being seated on a bus. His limbs would trip other passengers going to and from the doors. He introduced himself as Tobias.

The water from the lake was probably poisonous to anyone who had not become accustomed to drinking it. It would certainly give you diarrhea. She poured him a glass from a pitcher that had a broken handle—but a pretty painting of a scenic village on its side. His glass was transparent, which she regretted and was self-conscious about. The water was the colour of rain and not the colour of water from a tap. It was filled with tiny bits of debris and mud. They floated around like small sea creatures.

She waited to see if Tobias would say something. But he raised the glass to his lips and drank it with a great look of satisfaction. She was pleased.

She did not know why she felt the need to entertain this man in a manner that would have been suitable at a dinner party before the war. Except that she suddenly wanted, more than anything, for him to like her. She didn't know him at all, but for some reason his opinion was more important to her than anyone else's.

The more she looked at him, the younger she realized he was. And the more the difference between their ages diminished, the more pleased Sofia was. She didn't dare ask him his age because he would then ask for hers. And she was hoping she could pass herself off as more than fourteen.

"Why would he just knock on a door like that? If he really is fleeing captivity? He would be terrified of soldiers being in the house," the Goose demanded.

"Why would you just knock on the door like that?" Sofia asked the man. "What if there were soldiers inside?"

"I saw the mushrooms glowing from the window. I knew it was someone who had been raised in the same country as me. The first thing I thought when I saw all those mushrooms was that the girl from the Elysian children's story about mushrooms must be in that cabin. And now that I have come in, I am so delighted to find that I was right."

"My name is Sofia."

"Of course it is."

Tobias was so familiar with her. He acted as though she had been expecting him. His familiarity was so off-putting, it made Sofia doubt her sanity for a moment. It made her wonder whether she did know this man. Whether he had always lived there with them.

He also had the mark of someone who had survived the winter. But he was more alive and humorous than she was. He seemed to have found a way to exist in this war without being transformed by fear.

Tobias wasn't beautiful. His eyes seemed slightly too large for his head. When he looked askance, it seemed as though his eyes might roll out of his head for a brief moment. But just as quickly, his face went back to looking normal. His eyes quickly realized they had gone too far and settled back into his head.

Tobias's lower teeth were stained black along the bottoms. It gave his grin a distinct resemblance to that of a wolf. He had grime in the pores on his nose and around his eyes. He might have had beautiful hands if the thumbs had not looked as though they were hit with a hammer and flattened as though made out of clay. His hair was so dirty it stuck up over his head and kept the marks of his fingers having run through it.

He appeared older than he actually was, at first. From his clothes and bearing he seemed to be in his late twenties. But when he came in, it became more apparent he was around eighteen or nineteen years old. She noticed he had dog tags around his neck.

"Is this dinner tonight?" Tobias said, sitting down and pointing to the Goose.

"No. He is my companion."

"Well, forgive me for such an affront. Truly."

He had a smirk on his face that seemed practically permanent. As though he considered everything around him perpetually hilarious. But he was the only one in on the joke. In his old age, all the wrinkles in his face would surely form to accommodate that smirk.

Tobias tried to act as though he were completely in control. But when Sofia put the hare down on the table, he couldn't help himself, and he went at it like an animal. He ate with his head and body over the plate because he had been starving for the whole war. And he now had an animal's attitude towards meat. She could tell he was trying to talk and be social, but his passionate gorging of the meat got in the way.

When he was done, he pounded his fists on the table. "My God. It feels so good to eat another's flesh."

He reached deep into his enormous backpack and began rooting around in it. His backpack was so large, it could pass for a magic sack from a fairy tale. It was the type of bag that was given to you by a troll. Whatever you wanted, you only had to picture it, then you would reach into the bag and find it there, at your fingertips. She wondered what the price to pay for such a gift was. Very often in these stories, it ended up being your first-born child. Tobias pulled out a green bottle with no label on it.

He looked around and then spied the teacup on the shelf. Both Sofia and the Goose cried out so abruptly that he froze in his tracks and then turned towards them.

"Sorry," said Sofia. "We never, ever touch that cup. It's very important it stay still. You're welcome to use the other glass for as long as you want."

"As long as I want?" He smirked slightly as he said it.

He poured himself half a glass of the booze from his bag and knocked it back.

"Drinking always makes me feel like dancing." He started jumping up and down and kicking his legs out and clapping his hands. It was a dance that was popular in the very north of the country. They had an annual New Year's concert in a large performance hall in the city, and people were known to accidentally kick each other in the head. It was conjectured in the Capital that this was the origin of their slower ways.

"Where are you from?" Sofia asked.

"Where am I from? That's a fascinating question. Is anyone from anywhere?"

"Well, yes, I think. Maybe not. Never mind the question."

"Where are you from? You don't have to tell me. You're from the Capital. Ah, yes! A fine and spectacular place to be from. The jewel of the country. Or I imagine it was the jewel of the country. I hear it's in ruins and infested with soldiers. It's suicide to go visit it."

"You have never been?"

"No, I have not. And I suppose now I never will. I know it was once considered very gauche never to have been to the Capital. It always shows. Those from the Capital are polished and cultured in a way people not from the city could never be."

"Are you from the north?"

"What was it that gave it away? Was it my table manners? My speech?"

"Nothing. I was simply asking."

"No, please do let me know. I'm dying of curiosity."

"It was the dancing."

He sat down and leaned back in his chair, his eyes gleaming. His face cracked into an enormous grin. His face more or less remained fixed like that as he continued to stare at her. She had never had anyone stare at her like that. She could not make sense of it. It was equally intimate and cold. He filled his glass and leaned forward, handing it to her.

"Here. Have a drink. I don't want to drink alone. You've been a great host. The most wonderful host. Both of you are. I have to be an equally amenable guest, do I not?"

She swallowed, and the liquid went down her throat as though she had swallowed a goldfish. There was a burning in her chest. And then her head was a light bulb that had just been turned on. Her heart was beaming the way Jesus's was in statues and paintings in the church. It was wonderful. She laughed. But the laugh didn't seem to come from her mouth. It seemed to come from some place farther away. As though it were passing through a wall, or as though the laugh were coming from a bedroom upstairs.

Why did she like him? Of course she would be predisposed to like anyone who walked through the door because she had been alone all winter. It was as though her veins were vines, and small leaves began to grow on them. Small little flowers blooming, popping open, stretching their petals. She wondered whether he felt it too.

• • •

"How did you end up here, so far south?" Sofia asked.

"I'm a deserter. Or I was. I enlisted in the army because I was looking for adventure. I lived in a tiny town, and I felt trapped there. All anyone ever spoke about was the weather and their aches and pains."

As he was speaking, he took a coin out of his pocket. He made it dance back and forth across his knuckles. He watched the coin dancing over his knuckles as though he were a nurse monitoring a heart machine, waiting to see if it would skip a beat. It was like he was hypnotizing himself.

"It was more horrible than anything you could imagine. It wasn't heroic at all. They tell you that fighting for your country is dignified. You think the worst thing that can happen to you is that you will die. You believe there are two options for you. And they are coming out alive or being killed. But what you don't know is that dying isn't at all the worst thing that can happen to you.

"You don't understand what it means to be sent to your slaughter until you are sent to your slaughter."

He smiled, and it was impossible to know whether he was satisfied by his tale or by the smooth motion of the quarter. The coin was like a ship dancing on the waves.

"There's plenty of room here," Sofia found herself saying. "You can stay here with us if you would like. And you're the first person who has come by in months. I mean, I would offer that to anyone from our country who stopped by. I think it's a duty."

"A duty? Peculiar. Are we even still citizens of the same country if that country no longer exists?"

"Yes. Aren't we still nicer to one another than the Enemy is?"

"I've been shot at by both. Once I was shot at so many times, I took off all my clothes and stared at my body in wonder. I couldn't believe there weren't any bullet holes."

"How do you miss the bullets?"

"I run back and forth. I've observed terrified animals. The trick is to never look back."

"And run for the woods," they both said at the same time.

"What's your trick?" Tobias suddenly asked.

"What do you mean?"

"What wicked thing have you done to survive? What trick do you have up your sleeve? You know what? Forget about it. I really have no right to ask."

That night, Sofia was awakened by Tobias calling out in his sleep from the other room. "No, don't do it. I'm so afraid. I want to go. Please don't hurt me anymore. I can't bear it. Please, I want to see my mommy. Please, where is my mommy? Take me to her. She wants to see me. I want her to hold me. I want to go home."

THE SABOTEUR WEARS

PATENT LEATHER SHOES

Clara Bottom was a talker, and conversation was her favourite activity. Sofia was now the only person around for her to share her ideas with. And so, for the first time in their lives, they found themselves engaged in discussions all day long. Sofia realized that her tongue was loosened during the war.

Children and old people were suddenly listened to. When Sofia spoke, adults paid heed attentively. It could very well be a six-year-old who knew an arrest had happened in their building the night before.

It was in a basement—a small one, beneath a pharmacy—that Sofia first heard talk about an uprising. She was seated on a wobbly chair against a musty wall in the corner. Nobody was concerned she was listening. While she was with her mother, people ceased to treat her as though she was a child. There was a sense that there was no room for childhood now. Is there such a thing as childhood anyway? There were six people in the basement. But it seemed as though it were an army.

The Capital was not the same as the rest of the country. The people who lived there were not going to let themselves be defeated the way the rest of the country had. Perhaps the country had accepted occupation and annihilation, but the Capital had always been different from the rest of the country. People there were wilder and more nationalistic. They would refuse to be under anyone's thumb. They needed to be free. The Uprising might mean a quick death, but the alternative was a slow one.

They had drawn a map on a chalkboard that was nailed to the wall. This way, if they were raided, all they needed to do was to throw a glass of water at it, and the evidence would be washed away.

They believed the noise created by the Uprising would signal to the rest of the world how unhappy and miserable they were with the Occupation. It might also convey to the West that they were not taking the Occupation lying down. They were actively resisting and fighting.

The messengers of other resistance cells would bring information to the pharmacist, and he passed it along to their group. Clara agreed she would, on their cell's behalf, go deliver their plans to a certain baker the next afternoon.

The soldiers would do random checks of apartments. They were looking for hidden artists. But Clara said it was more of a pretext to leave the apartments with arms filled with valuable objects they loaded into a truck.

They had come earlier that week and looked through their home. Clara followed them around, acting as though she had nothing to hide, as though she were not the most contraband object in the apartment. Sofia kept staring at her mother, who she knew was acting in an odd, solicitous manner, and praying she would not break and give herself away. There was some discussion of the paintings on the wall before the soldiers began removing them one by one. They were very good at locating objects of great value, which surprised Sofia since the one unequivocal thing she had heard about the Enemy was that they had no taste or cultural sensibility. But they knew which paintings, in all their avant-garde splendour, were worth money. There was a soldier who climbed up and took down the chandelier in the living room. There was one who removed a particularly beautiful chair that had been put in the apartment by her grandfather. They took all the utensils, and they rolled up the rug from the living room floor.

There were some serious discussions about the piano in the living room, but in the end, they left it be.

Sofia had gone to sit on the balcony and noticed it was not only their apartment but all those on the block that were being raided. She knew immediately because of the books. Any book the Enemy found was tossed out the window. The books burst into flight as soon as they hit the air. It was like watching birds in motion. Sofia found it quite beautiful. It was a testament to how many books the inhabitants on that block read. They had been warned to destroy their books. But they hadn't taken it seriously, and now the sky was filled with birds.

Books weren't the only things tossed out of windows. It began raining clothes. It was windy, and the dresses tossed out the windows opened up like they were parachutes. They were like ephemeral ballet dancers who twisted this way and that. They were like the husks of insects that had been shed upon their metamorphosis.

They were dresses that were used to dancing. One filled with air like a pregnant woman. It was as though the *Titanic* had capsized and all the girls in their fancy dresses were floating around in the water. Drowning.

She remembered once seeing a tank of jellyfish in a travelling exhibit. That was what the dresses reminded her of. She held her hand out as though to catch one. She held her hand out to a scarf that was floating high in the air, as though it were a butterfly she wanted to land on her finger.

One morning when Sofia and her mother were getting ready to go to the bakery, there was a heavy knock at the door. What could be more terrifying than a knock at your door during wartime? It was more disruptive than the sound of a bomb. It was as though the war itself were knocking at your door. Wanting to enter your home, which, until that moment, you had still seen as your own, which you had regarded as a safe space.

She could still feel the effect of the knock in her body. She had felt the knock as though it were up against her chest. And it made it feel as though her heart were hollow. Her mother stiffened, and her eyes looked frightened.

Her mother then reanimated and went to open the door. Sofia followed behind her at a distance in the hall. There was a solitary soldier standing in the entranceway. He said something in the Enemy language and stepped over the threshold. The soldier said the word "piano." They both knew what he meant. He walked into the living room with her mother following behind.

Clara Bottom owned a famous piano. Or it had been played by a well-known pianist. Her father had purchased it for her.

Clara did not play. She had perhaps had lessons when she was little. But clearly had had no desire whatsoever to run her fingers across the keys since.

It was played often, nonetheless, by guests at dinner parties. It was surprising to Sofia which of the visitors were able to play piano. If a guest was a musician, certainly it was normal for that person to play. There were pianists who asked to play almost as soon as they entered. They had come expressly to play the piano, and would sit at it and play all night. There was a playwright whose face was preternaturally wrinkled. He sat down and played a short, pretty tune on the high keys. Then stood up and walked away from the piano as though it had never happened. Once an accountant had sat down, and an explosion of notes came out of the piano, which surprised Sofia, as she did not know accountants could be touched by the mad mathematics of music.

When the soldier walked in, Sofia did not understand. How did he think he was going to remove the piano by himself? Perhaps he was going to take out his machine gun and fire at it, enabling them to then throw the piano in pieces out the window. Instead, he sat down and began to play with obvious proficiency. The tune was odd and different from any Sofia had ever heard. He didn't even acknowledge anyone in the apartment once he began. He acted as though he were somewhere far away playing the piano.

Her mother went over to Sofia and lowered her head. "You must go to the pharmacy for me. Here is the prescription." She shoved a piece of paper into Sofia's palm.

Sofia saw a skinny black dog hurry across the street and disappear into the alley. As though it were on a clandestine resistance mission just like her. There were more stray cats and dogs than before the war. When people disappeared, it was as though the only creatures prepared to speak out about their being missing were their pets.

The dogs acted ashamed. They had guilty consciences. They wondered over and over again what they had done to find themselves in this predicament. And how, in this context, they could be good boys.

The cats had no integrity. They meowed and wailed. They were like women at the death of a child. They were deeply in mourning. Not for their owners but for themselves. They were indignant, abused. They demanded their former status. The cats didn't care if they were shot at this point. They even seemed to be offering an ultimatum. They demanded they be returned to their previous life of luxury. Or be murdered right there on the street.

Children were supposed to be wary of drawing attention to themselves now. They couldn't do things like skip rope in the street.

As Sofia made her way to the pharmacy, she saw there were children on all the balconies. It was like being in a prison where all the cells were filled with children. They whistled down at Sofia. They were doing it to catch her attention. They wanted her to look up and acknowledge they were flesh-and-blood human beings and not just angels haunting their previous lives.

But she looked down on them all. They were pitiful. They were pathetic. They were in their parents' way. They were a burden, and they made their mothers sick with worry. She, on the other hand, had the freedoms of an adult. She was so proud to have been given this responsibility of delivering a message for the resistance.

On the way back from the pharmacy, after delivering her mother's note, Sofia heard her name called. She wasn't sure who had called her name. Then she realized the voice was coming from the building next to her. It was a tall, white stone building with a flight of stairs up the front. She saw some girls sitting underneath the stairs.

She looked between the slats and saw two twins from her class there. They were popular because they were the only twins in school. One was slightly more popular than the other. They were easy to tell apart because the favoured girl had a unibrow, while the other one didn't.

If it hadn't been wartime, Sofia would never have stopped to greet them. And they would never have acknowledged her. They did not have the hierarchy of school anymore. The distinctions between being popular and unpopular no longer existed. But they were curious about one another. They were people they knew from before the war. They came from a time that was worry-free. Sofia went around to the side of the stairs and went underneath to see the twins.

The stripes of light cast them in an odd way. One twin's face was bathed in light, while the other's was in shadow. As though they were a two-headed demon that represented good and evil.

One of the twins raised her hand as she was speaking to Sofia. It was bright and lit up—as though her hand had been turned on like a light. It looked like a dove had suddenly been let loose.

"We are being sent to the country in a week. We are going to live with our grand-uncle."

"We went to stay with him two summers ago."

"It was so much fun. He has a house on a lake. We went around in a speedboat."

"He lets us do whatever we want."

"We ate ice cream for breakfast once. The boys are so good-looking in that town too."

"They are so much better-looking than they are here."

"It's hard for some children who are being sent away. But not us."

"For us, it will just be like we get to go on summer vacation so early."

Sofia knew there was a train called the Children's Train. It would be taking children out of the Capital. They would be safer in the country. Everyone expected the allies to come soon to liberate the Capital. And who could say what further retributions would be meted out on the city. It was best to send the children away.

"I can't leave the Capital. I have too much work to do. My mother needs me here."

"What for?"

"She will miss you too much?"

"My mother and I are witnessing everything that is going on in the city. So that she can write about it all. She needs me to witness things too. And remember them. There are things I see that she missed out on. When I tell them to her, she is always so impressed. I am like a journalist."

She knew she was provoking them. They were staring directly at her and were very quiet. They were getting angry. Sofia knew exactly why they were upset. She was telling them that her mother needed her and loved her more than their mother loved them. Their mother cared for them only out of duty, because they were loved unconditionally. But her mother valued her. She liked her objectively. Her mother loved her as an equal.

Sofia reached into her inner pocket and pulled out a notebook. She took out a pen from between the pages.

"What are you writing?"

"That two young girls are going to be sent away from their homes. Away from their mother. Where they might not ever see her again."

"That's not what we said."

"Don't write that about us!"

At that, Sofia closed her notebook, stuck it back into the inside pocket of her coat, turned on her heel, and walked off with her chin in the air. When she was far enough from the girls, she began skipping with delight. She had bested the girls. They had always made her feel inferior. But she had turned the tables on them. The war had turned everything on its head.

Those girls were going to be sent into hiding. But she was a member of the resistance. Sofia lollygagged happily, observing her city, on her way back to the apartment.

She was surprised to see her mother standing outside their building. She ran up to Sofia. She grabbed her by the wrist and pulled her inside. As soon as they were at the top of the stairs, her mother slapped her hard across the face.

Her mother had never been physical with her before. She had watched mothers in the parks and on the sidewalks losing their patience with their children. She had watched a mother chase her son around a baby carriage, lunging at him with a baguette as though it were a sword. She had found it so strange. She was almost envious of the violence.

The slap changed everything in her body. She did not feel like the same person. It was a gift her mother had given her. It was a taste of pain. It was so real. The blood coursing through all her veins was black. The slap made her know she was wicked. The slap made her know she could survive anything. The slap made her know she was a person who was designed to survive a war. She hadn't known who she was beforehand.

She was grotesque; she was pathetic. She had pathetic motives and ill intent. She liked losing the war. She wanted to see her classmates lined up against a fence and shot. Did she have any right to feel this way? The slap told her that she did. The world was a violent and treacherous place.

Her mother dragged her to the apartment. She opened the door with one hand and pushed Sofia in aggressively with the other. As soon as the door slammed shut behind her, Clara fell down on her knees and wrapped her arms around Sofia and began to weep.

"I didn't know where you were. I thought the soldiers had apprehended you."

"But I would never have given you up!"

Clara laughed. She wiped her tears from her eyes. "You ridiculous child!" she said.

PUT A RED ROSE

IN MY BUTTONHOLE

In the morning, Tobias had no memory of any of his dreams. So she was afraid to let him know she had heard him talking in his sleep.

He came out of the bedroom. He had on a pair of long johns that seemed to have stains from piss on them. He stretched his arms all over the place. As though his arms had been folded up for days or months. The sleep had allowed him to finally unpack and stretch his body. As though he were a plant that had just been placed in the sunlight and was now unfurling.

He stood on his hands upside down. He had a pure and perfect whistle. He seemed as though he had not suffered during the war. Although there was no way this could be true, there was something marvellously attractive about the fact that he seemed to be in good spirits.

He had been there for only a day, but he already seemed more comfortable and at ease there than Sofia. She wondered whether that was how men felt in their bodies as well. They felt they had a right to be wherever they were.

They had a right to have their desires met. They weren't pre-occupied by a feeling of embarrassment.

There was something so masculine about his gestures and presence, she couldn't help but find it somehow attractive. Dis-arming. Perhaps men had a confidence women could never have. Perhaps to be a woman was to be in a perpetual state of unease.

He suddenly let his body relax and drop, as though he were a puppet whose strings had been cut.

And he smiled. He had a different kind of smile.

His face looked almost wildly different when he smiled this smile. He looked more handsome. It was a practised smile. Or it was as though he was aware of just how potent it was. He was somehow smiling at his smile while he smiled. Which made it a strangely self-aware smile. He was weaponizing his smile, whether he was prepared to admit it or not.

When Tobias stood close to her, it made all her movements stifled and awkward. As though he were standing on her shadow, and it felt like he was standing on the hem of her dress. She couldn't express exactly how it made her feel trapped, except it did.

The more she looked at Tobias, the more handsome he seemed. There were two types of beautiful people. Some you looked at and they were immediately stunning. And then you couldn't help but start to notice flaws in their looks. It was almost as if the brain set out to find these flaws. And then there were people whose beauty began to emerge and improve the more you looked at them.

He looked at her occasionally as though he was waiting for her to give up the act. As though he was waiting for her to mentally catch up. He was waiting for her to realize what a creep he was.

He looked at her for a moment as though to ask, Are you seriously falling for the nonsense I am selling?

• • •

There was a legend that bears sometimes took off their large fur skins, and underneath they were handsome men. They would seduce young women. And the women would give birth to children who were half bear. They were human, but they had bear hearts. These were so heavy that they often had heart attacks. They were strange beings.

Sofia's mother scoffed at these associations. She would say they were repulsive nonsense about bestiality. Her mother did not have the same affection towards animals that the rest of the country did.

Sofia wondered about Tobias. He had a sneaky way about him. He seemed to be reacting to some internal discomfort or battling with his conscience. She watched him wrap his arms around his body. As though he was trying to get himself warm or comfort himself. It was as though he had had a magical curse lifted and his bearskin had fallen off, and he was not used to having returned to his naked human form.

Tobias was outside in his underwear and jacket and bare feet. He was smoking, and she was able to see his cigarette shaking, ever so gently. Like the antennae of an insect that is so vulnerable, it is in a state of constant alertness. When he smiled his eyes were sad. He reminded her of a dog then. This mood made him venture to say the most peculiar thing to Sofia.

"When I was in the woods, I noticed the stars were providing maps to the Enemy. They were like collaborators. Imagine. The moon isn't on our side either. The light of it was always shining on me. Everywhere I moved,' it followed me. As though I were the protagonist in a play under a spotlight."

He spoke in a distant, melancholic way. He was quiet for several moments before speaking again. It gave the impression that he wasn't saying the first thing that came into his mind. But was articulating a thought he had long pondered.

"I hate seeing my reflection. I went into an empty house not long ago and I looked at the mirror inside. My eyes had turned blue. But not a regular blue. Not the normal blue you sometimes see in people's eyes. But a terrible light blue. The blue of glaciers when they crack in half. It was then I realized the most terrifying thing was my own face. They were the eyes of a monster."

Sofia looked at his eyes. They were still blue, but she didn't know whether to advise him of this or not. He spoke in metaphors. Sofia, having grown up around writers, was accustomed to people who spoke in metaphors. But this was different. She liked the way he talked about trauma. It was as though there was a new sort of literature—a new language had emerged now that the war had happened.

It seemed as if Tobias had brought the spring with him. She could not tell whether it was Tobias or the spring that made her feel alive. It was like her whole body had come out of hibernation.

Small buds began to appear on all the branches. Sofia went up to a low-hanging branch and had an urge to place her tongue on one of the tightly whirled buds. To her surprise, it suddenly unfurled into a pink blossom. The trees were no longer naked human beings. They were too busy with their foliage. Everything in the forest began to smell so much different. There was the smell of flowers and leaves. The air smelled colourful. It smelled of animals. It smelled of mud.

When the trees were bare of leaves, she would peer into the forest and look at the different trees for miles. But now the foliage made the forest impenetrable. She only saw the trees that were around her. And they created a nook around the house. It was as though they were protecting her house.

She was afraid to do anything to her appearance to look pretty. She was afraid it would not make her look pretty. Then he would see that she had tried to be pretty but had not succeeded. She went to the lake to take a bath. There was filth all over her body. It had become a sort of second skin for her. She thought the dirt kept her cozy. It kept her thoughts inside her body. The pores of her skin were all clogged. It made her skin feel tougher. It was as though nothing could get in.

She went to wash her clothes in the lake, with the Goose waddling behind her. It hadn't occurred to her previously that she might smell. But now she became very conscious of it. Before it had been too cold to put her hands in the water. It was still cold. The Goose slipped into the water, unconcerned by its temperature.

She hung her underwear and clothing from the branches of overhanging trees. She was standing in a stained undershirt and a slip that was torn at the hem when she saw Tobias walking towards them. The Goose had swum way off to the other side of the lake. He was dunking his head obsessively in the water.

Tobias handed her a cup of tea that he had carried carefully as he stepped over the rocks so as not to spill it. She was so grateful for it. No one had done anything for her in so long—even something small. She sipped the tea. He had made it from sprigs of peppermint he must have had in his bag or had found while wandering around the property. It was a delicious taste. It tasted different than it would have if she had made it. It seemed stronger and sweeter. Or perhaps she was just imagining it.

She had been responsible for people's well-being, and running around cleaning up after people, since the war began. Taking care of other people and not yourself does not leave you with a glowing, happy feeling. What it does, instead, is make you feel anxious and guilty all the time. All the things they teach young girls about being good people turn them into nervous wrecks.

He sat down on a rock. She sat down on one opposite him. She felt self-conscious and wanted to put her clothes back on. But how could she when all her clothes were soaking wet. Dripping from the branches.

And then part of her, a strange part whose feelings seemed as new and tender as a plant that had just emerged from the soil, was delighted she had an excuse not to put her clothes on and to just sit there.

He reached into his pocket and pulled out an egg-shaped treat wrapped in tinfoil. "I have a chocolate."

"Impossible! I mean, wonderful! Oh, I can't believe it. I haven't had a dessert in so long. Before, I would have them every single night."

"You might think the first thing the Enemy did when it came to the country was to raid our pantries and bakeries and eat everything good."

They both giggled at this image.

Then Sofia put her hands on her stomach because she wanted to eat the chocolate so badly. She suddenly had the appetite of a hundred uniformed men for that chocolate. Her body began to anticipate the pleasure she would feel once the chocolate was in her mouth. She became conscious of her lips. She licked her lips. She was certain they had become fuller.

"I've been thinking about this chocolate in my pocket for days," Tobias said. "I kept waiting for a special occasion to eat it. I've been holding out. I was waiting until I was all by myself and

I was sure no one could bother me. But now I really, really, really want to eat the chocolate with you. Is that okay?"

"Yes," she said, and her voice cracked as she spoke. She wanted to say more. But she was too shy about the way her words would sound. So she nodded. She nodded until she figured she had nodded too long, then she stopped. She felt her nipples become erect under her shirt. She felt her privates begin to throb.

Tobias bit into the egg, just hard enough to crack off a side of chocolate. Syrup began to spill out over his lips and onto his chin. He sucked on the syrup so it would stop dripping. He held up the egg. There was a cherry inside of this chocolate.

"Suck out the cherry," he said.

She sucked out the cherry. It tasted like liquor. It tasted like cake soaked in brandy at Christmastime. It tasted like her favourite uncle's breath. He would come over and hold her in his arms and dance with her roughly. And everyone would yell at him that he was going too far.

Tobias bit off another piece of chocolate and handed her the rest. They looked at each other, smiling, as they ate the chocolate. She laughed. It was the first time she had ever laughed without finding anything funny. It made her blush.

"So the chocolate did the trick. Did you like that?"

"Yes, very much. I very much did. Where did you get it?"

"Black Market. I almost got murdered by an Enemy soldier who was there."

"Did they shut the Black Market down?" Sofia said in a panic.

"Why would they do that? The Enemy uses the Black Market more than anyone else."

"I thought the Black Market was filled with things the Enemy had forbidden."

"Right. The Enemy soldiers aren't supposed to like our bourgeois sensibilities. They are supposed to condemn us for our affection for luxurious objects. We are decadent. They talk about how expensive the women's coats and shoes are. How can one person justify dressing like that when there are people in rags? They go on and on about it on their radio. And the reason they keep harping on it is because as soon as the soldiers and officers come here, they fall in love with all our crap.

"I don't hate the soldiers because they are different from us. I hate them because they are exactly the same. It's so boring. So disappointing."

"Where is the Black Market, please? Will you tell me?"

"It was down on the Southern Road bend when I was there. If you walk along there, you'll probably find it. What is that goose doing?"

"Eating."

"I have never spent any time with a goose. It's not the type of animal I would even think about owning as a pet. We once had a dog. It was so horny all the time. We were terrified of it. It would try to rape everything. The priest came to check in on my mother. The dog came up behind him and started humping the priest's leg. We were all mortified. My grandmother started screaming that we were all going to hell."

She laughed so unexpectedly. He made her laugh in a way she had never laughed before. It was as though he'd thrown a baited hook into her and pulled out a live squirming fish from her throat.

"Did anyone ever tell you that you are beautiful?"

Sofia felt her cheeks turn a pretty shade of pink. She shook her head. She didn't believe it was possible. There was no way such a claim could be true. So she shook her head, but she did it lightly and not emphatically. Because she wanted him to continue saying and thinking what he was saying. She wanted him to undo everything she had ever thought about herself. He was the only person in the whole world who could make her feel beautiful. And if he could do that, she would never abandon him. She would set fire to her map and would have no interest in going anywhere, only in following him.

"I don't know if I should say this," Tobias said, clearly registering his effect, "but when you were laughing, I had a sudden impulse to kiss you."

Sofia immediately felt her face turn a red the shade of roses at night.

"But I would never do that to you," he continued.

"Why not?"

"Because I like you too much."

"But isn't that exactly why you should kiss me?"

"You're not the kind of girl a guy just kisses. You're the type of girl a guy wants to marry. You're so smart and nice, and you know how to do so many things. I wish I had given that to you." He pointed to the ring on her finger. "Where did you get that?"

"It belonged to my grandmother," Sofia lied.

"Ah, yes, a very wealthy family."

With a little effort, he pulled the ring off Sofia's middle finger and then slid it onto her ring finger, where it sat loosely.

He stood up on a rock. "Isn't life perfect sometimes? Like if you live in the moment, is there anything to complain about most of the time? I would rather live like this than have a job. This is better. It's better to live on your own and not have people tell you what is right and wrong."

He quickly removed all his clothes and dove into the water. His arc was flawless in Sofia's eyes. She did not know why.

Especially since his legs flew up awkwardly behind him and he landed with a bellyflop. His head popped back out of the water, and he shook it and screamed, "Holy shit it's cold!"

When she saw him emerging from the water, shivering, she held up a blanket in her arms. They ran back to the house. She was aware of the Goose waddling hopelessly to catch up with them. But she didn't slow down to wait for him; in fact, they quickened their speed. They went into Tobias's bedroom and crawled under the blankets. They shut and locked the door of the bedroom so the Goose could not get in.

She felt her body fall into a sea of pantyhose. Each one smelling of a different day at school. Each one smelling of a different grocery store, a different gasoline pedal, a different city bus, a different park, a different pet, a different husband, different little children everywhere, and yet all coming together in one perfume.

It felt as though her intestines were moving around in her body like the roots of a great tree. As though they were moving in the direction of a deep body of water inside her. The roots were going to find the well and descend slowly down and down, and then fill up with that strange underground source.

It was as though there was a secret part of her that was composed of electric filaments. A current of electricity was running through them now. She almost looked down to see whether her privates were glowing. It was nice to feel that warm down there. Then the shock of a light bulb blowing out in a sudden poof. And then she found herself lying in an open grave. La Petite Mort.

• • •

The Enemy said Elysian women were like animals. They were worse than men. They were responsible for leading ordinary men astray. It was said that men could not be blamed when they slept with Elysian women. They were so wanton, no man could resist them. They were strange nymphomaniacs. She knew her mother had affairs. She recalled the times she had heard her mother's laughter late at night mixing with that of a man who was over. And the way it was like birds warbling. And she would fall asleep to it.

Sofia always thought "nymphomaniac" sounded like a sort of fairy. She closed her eyes and imagined the Elysian nymphomaniacs who used to live in the Capital—who used to be out loose in the night to pursue virtuous men. She imagined them scaling the roofs of the Capital at night. Skinny like insects and fairies, and completely naked. They would be looking for open windows and balcony doors to slip into. She wondered whether she too might become a nymphomaniac.

Afterwards, they sat on his bed. "I'm going to go back to the Black Market and get some more treats."

Sofia was very worried. She didn't want another chocolate if it meant the man was going to go away. She had an urge to stick her finger down her throat and regurgitate the cherry. She wished she had swallowed the cherry and choked on it and died.

She hurried to the living room with only her socks on and came back with her rolled-up map. She unfurled it on the bed. "Do you think we might go to the Black Market together? I have been looking for it for the entirety of the war. I have been wanting to go since before I left the Capital. I made this map."

"A map! Very contraband. You know the penalty for having a map is instant death?"

"Someone has mentioned that. But isn't that the punishment for everything these days?"

"I suppose it is."

"Will you take me? I wouldn't care as much about anything that happened to me afterwards. I would feel as though I had reached my destination. I would feel as though I hadn't just wandered around aimlessly through this war and through life. But that I had looked for something and I had found it."

Tobias put his finger on the map. He pointed to the messy X's and arrows that Abelard had drawn onto it. Abelard had put little X's on roads that had not been scanned for mines yet. He put arrows on roads that he and the army had rolled over, where he knew for certain no mines existed.

"What are these marks?"

"This shows what roads the soldiers have already cleared for mines. So you can walk on them. This is where we went into the forest because the road hadn't been cleared yet. But when we come out, the soldiers will have passed, so we can walk along without worrying."

"Oh my! Well, this map is more beautiful than I thought it was going to be. Was it you who made it so colourful and pretty? Only the most loveliest of girls could have made such a thing."

For a moment, Sofia was inclined to say that she had added the colourful additions and details herself. This lie would serve her well in Tobias's eyes. If she was able to create this pretty thing, she would be able to create other pretty things.

"It was a girl named Celeste."

"And where is she now?"

Sofia hesitated. If Tobias went and found Celeste, he would fall madly in love with her. He would forget Sofia ever existed. And Celeste knew how to love a man. How to get a man to love her.

What did Sofia know about that? She wished she had listened more carefully to Celeste. She had never known what questions to ask. Or what of Celeste's strange stories to retain. She had believed the world of men to be so far away from her. She thought it was so far into the future that it couldn't even be considered real. She wasn't even sure it would happen to her.

"Can I come with you?" Sofia asked for the third time.

"I'm better off alone, I'm afraid. We would attract too much attention together. Especially with your wonderful goose. We'll be stopped immediately by people who want to hear your goose converse."

He smiled and closed his eyes and fell asleep. Sofia wasn't sure if he was using the Goose as an excuse not to let her travel with him. She thought she would leave the Goose to be with Tobias. She felt sick with guilt. It was at that moment she realized the Goose was more dependent on her than she was on the Goose. But that didn't change the fact that the Goose was in control. Controlling someone through guilt was one of the most powerful ways of dominating a person.

The saddest thing she could imagine was the Goose sitting on the spot where he was now. And not knowing she wasn't coming back. And just waiting and waiting and waiting. And perhaps he would find another child. She knew he would be cruel and impetuous to another child, the way he was with her. But the other child wouldn't be able to stand the way he treated them. And they would hang him by the neck with a wire or a rope or a shoelace or a ribbon until he was dead. And then eat him for dinner.

She fell asleep not knowing what to do.

• • •

Sofia walked down to the lake to bathe the next morning. She found the Goose already there. She knew he was going to say something to reprimand her, but she did not know what.

"Why don't you ever play the clarinet in the evening?"

She didn't know what to say. She had no desire to play anymore. She didn't want Tobias to hear her playing the clarinet badly like a child. She wanted Tobias to think she was a girl who had given up the clarinet long, long before.

"Oh, who cares about the clarinet. I was only ever sixth in my class."

"I feel as though you might need a mother right at this moment, to warn you about this soldier."

"I don't care about anything my mother says. She didn't love me enough to keep me with her."

"I see. So to make up for the lack of love your mother gave you, you are going to throw yourself at the mercy of a complete idiot?"

"What do I care whether he actually cares for me? He makes me feel as though he does. He makes me feel like I am normal. And I am worthy. I don't care whether he is pretending to love me. What is the difference between pretending to love someone and actually loving them? I prefer it. At least I know I can count on it. When someone tells a lie, they commit to it. If they are being nice to me out of a sort of contempt, or to get me to do whatever they want, what do I care? Love is fickle. Love doesn't last. It's better they feel nothing for you right from the start. At least he acts as though I should be treated like a lovable girl. At least he assumes I ought to be treated as though I am wanted and cherished. At least he imagines I know what that feels like and am expecting it."

"How horrible it must be to be a girl. No matter how low I thought a person's self-esteem could go, you surprise me, Sofia! You are making no sense. You were afflicted by cabin fever during the winter.

Your mind is your own worst enemy now. Remember the plans we made before your madness? We were going to the Black Market. It is having this purpose that has kept us alive. We kept moving."

"Ah! My mother's manifesto. Your manifesto. Other people have decided their manifestos are so important."

"No! I do not think that, Sofia. You are just a young girl. It is not your business to have a manifesto. You are still in the process of becoming. You have not come up with your great ideas as of yet."

"Aha! Well, I am tired of being seen as a little girl who has only half-baked notions of the world. Who can have only a half-baked identity. I want to be regarded as a woman."

"A woman! Sofia, no. You are not one. And to behave as one is to put us in grave danger."

"Women can't survive on their own. They need protectors."

"You are going to depend on men the way Celeste did? How is her situation one you should aspire to?"

"She was dating one of the Enemy. We are at war with them. They were raised for their entire lives to hate Elysia. That's why they behaved in that way. Tobias is one of us."

"One of us! He is certainly no goose. I do not care what side he is on. A soldier is simply a soldier during wartime. And a girl is just a girl. The dynamics are always the same."

"I am tired of sense. I am tired of logic. I am sick of being rational. I am tired of considering all sides of a thing."

"You are surrendering. Don't do it now. Not yet. Not before we get to the Black Market."

"He will take us there. He knows the way. We have been trying to find it, but we never do. Our map is useless. He knows how to get there."

"No, Sofia. He will never take you to the Black Market."

"How do you know?"

"He has nothing to trade. We are the ones who have been accumulating trinkets to exchange. We have a map."

Sofia and the Goose came back from the lake to find Tobias dressed in his army clothes, with his large bag on his back. And the map tied to the top. The bag, which had been emptied over the course of his stay, was now full. The Goose ran off into the woods. Sofia made her way into the house. She looked for the bag of treasures she had intended to trade at the Black Market. It had been taken. She ran back out to Tobias.

"Are we leaving?" she said breathlessly.

"I'm leaving. Not you. I'm taking the goose as well. He'll be a meal for the soldiers when I need to bribe them."

"You can't have my goose. He hates your guts!"

He smacked Sofia. She was certain later that his hand had struck her in the exact same spot her mother's had. She fell to the ground, dazed. Before she knew what was happening, he had put a noose around her neck. He picked up a chair under one arm and pulled her along to a large tree. He made her stand on the chair and tied the rope to a branch. He then tied her wrists behind her with twine. She stood there. She could not believe it. She had managed to survive the winter. But now this was happening.

Tobias stood looking at her. Startled, as though he had stumbled across her in the woods and had no idea how she had come to be standing on a chair under a tree branch with a noose around her neck.

"Call the goose back or I will hang you."

"Why would he come back? He knows you are going to kill him."

"Tell him the coast is clear."

"He's too intelligent."

"Were you really trying to get me to love you? I saw the way you were looking at me. You were trying to trap me. Did you think you would trick me into staying with you? I don't give a damn about any woman. I never have. I hate you. Are you too stupid to realize that? I don't care what happens to this country. I hope everything burns to the ground. I hope they shoot every person. I don't feel anything. I wish I were one of the Enemy. I'm not in mourning for anyone. But why should I be? I don't care about this country. They had already put me in prison before the war started. Everyone talks about freedoms and liberty. As if those characterize this country. But I didn't have any of those. I was a dirty criminal. Anyone back then would have said I was dangerous to be around."

He walked up to her. "Don't say a single word, or I will kick that chair out from under you." She was so worried about his threat that she didn't dare breathe a word. He walked around behind her. She felt him take her finger and slide her valuable ring off it.

"That's mine!" she whispered harshly. But then, she clamped her lips shut and she tasted the tears running into her mouth.

He left her standing on the stool with her hands tied behind her back and the noose around her neck. She waited for the Goose to arrive. She stood with her back perfectly straight, as though she were a soldier of sorts. Any type of slip would cause her to hang herself. She wondered whether the Goose had flown off for good. And just how long she would be able to stand there without slipping and hanging herself. But she was quite sure the Goose would return. And she wasn't going to entertain the notion of his departure quite yet.

And then she saw him tentatively waddling towards her, craning his neck to make sure Tobias was gone. She knew it would take everything in the Goose's entire being to not tell her he had warned her about this man.

"I suppose standing up there must put you in quite the quandary, allowing you to rethink your choices in life."

"Are you going to help me or not?"

"Now you know exactly how I feel every day—as though I am standing on a chair with a noose, waiting for someone to come along and kick it."

The Goose continued squawking these things. But at the same time, he went into the house in order to help her. She heard him rummaging around in the kitchen and the sound of him squawking and the sound of something metallic hitting the floor.

He came out with a knife in his beak, dragging along the ground. The screeching sound was similar to his squawking—a sort of high-pitched version of it. By the time he arrived, Sofia had managed to wiggle her arms out of the twine. Her wrists were bright red from chafing. She pulled the noose off her neck, and the instant it was loose, she leapt so quickly and so far from the chair that it toppled from underneath her.

She fell on the ground and found she could not get up. She was seized by a terrible chill, and her body began shaking uncontrollably. She wanted to throw up. She could barely stand. She hunched and hurried into her bed. She felt naked in a way she had never felt naked before. No, it didn't feel as though she was naked. But it felt as though she was exposed to all the elements. And her skin didn't offer her a defence against them.

She pulled all the covers over herself. She was inside a cave. Lonely and freezing. Then she felt a nudge of the blankets. The

THE CAPITAL OF DREAMS

Goose's white head poked inside. He looked at her and she looked at him. Then he scooted the rest of his body under the blankets with her. His body heat filled up the cave. It filled her with a sense of calm. It was like having warm chamomile tea.

She remembered one time when she had a fever. Whenever she was ill, it was one of the maids who would tend to her. Her mother would say that she couldn't afford to catch a cold because she had a deadline and her work was invaluable. But that night Sofia was lying in bed, lost in the darkness, feeling that she would never survive, feeling as though she were not a person but a sock that a body had cast off. She was suddenly made aware of a cup of tea floated in front of her. She turned to follow the arm holding the tea and was surprised to find it attached to her mother.

She took the tea and drank it. And it was as though the tea were magical. It filled her with happiness. It was as if the tea were an opiate. She wondered whether this was what Celeste had felt when she ingested opiates. Sofia felt the same way with her arms around the Goose.

"Nobody loves me," she whispered. "I am unlovable. My mother didn't love me. What was worse was that she didn't like me. And everywhere I go, people treat me the same way my mother did. It's a curse."

"Feeling sorry for oneself is the impetus behind all great movements in society, all art and invention. Those who feel sorry for themselves as children have a great advantage. Because they began feeling sorry for themselves at a young age. And the well of their self-loathing is so deep, they are able to draw from it whenever they want."

"I wonder if that's true. I think I've felt sorry for myself my whole life, and nothing has come from it."

"But you are young. You will find greatness there. Never be ashamed of your worst quality. Our weaknesses are what make us unique."

"Are you angry with me? You must be. From the moment we met, I promised I would take you to the Black Market. And now I don't know the way there. I have nothing to trade. I have ruined your life and your dreams. I have done to you what I did to my mother. And I have sacrificed the dreams of those closest to me. I wish I could have been the girl you thought I was when we first met on the road. I wish I was the girl who brought you back to the Capital right away."

"When I saw you outside the train station the first time, I knew you were different."

"I know. You told me. You said you were certain I was from the Capital because you could tell I had a conceited air about me."

"Is that how I communicated it then? I had just met you. I was defensive. I was perhaps worried about being rejected. I was operating on pride, I suppose. I knew right away I would value your opinion. I had believed so many things about myself when I was on the farm. And there was never anyone to contradict me. How could they? They could barely grasp what I was talking about, let alone contradict me. But then I saw you and I thought, Here is someone who will understand what I am saying. And she might very well change my highfalutin opinion of myself, which was all I had at the time."

"Why would you leave all that up to another person? Why would you leave all that up to me?"

"Because I trusted you. I trusted you as soon as I saw you. You looked so alone when I first saw you. You looked absolutely alone. You didn't belong to anyone around you. You were making your own decisions. I thought, Here is a girl who is relying entirely on herself. I knew you were going off on your own adventure.

"And I thought, I am in the same boat as her. There is a kindred spirit. And when you picked me up in your arms, I was so shocked. I had no idea what you wanted from me. I knew you did not intend to eat me. I was glad we were together. And the whole time I was on the back of the truck with you, I knew you were in disguise. I knew the coat you were wearing wasn't yours because it didn't smell like you. And you smelled as though you were from a place I had never been. And it smelled like home."

"You don't understand. You have much too high an opinion of me. You think this is out of character for me. But it isn't. It is who I am. I cannot be trusted. I have lost all our treasures. I sold us out. I could never be a member of the resistance. To be a member of the resistance, you have to be bold and selfless. You have to put your country and those you wish to save above yourself. But I am pathetic. I am a fool. I will surrender everything for my own stupid desire to be happy. To survive. I am the very worst kind of Elysian."

"Next you will be telling me that you are responsible for your country's having lost the war. You might as well say you caused a rainstorm by forgetting your umbrella at home."

"My mother was right about me before the war. I was a creepy disappointment. She was right to ignore me and scoff at me."

"You have too high an opinion of your mother.'

"You would too if you met her. She is exactly the type of person you would admire. She has a horror of small talk. She never laughs at jokes that aren't funny. And she does not suffer fools gladly."

"Good grief. How did you bear being her child? How insufferable."

She reached over and hugged the Goose so hard, he lifted his neck up towards the ceiling and squawked. She wasn't entirely sure whether she believed him. But she had very much liked that he had expressed it. She appreciated the Goose because he was the first being she had met who did not know her mother. And did not think highly of her.

"Sofia. These have been the most extraordinary days of my life. I joined you on your journey; you did not join me on mine. You have shown me the most incredible friendship. You have taken me seriously. You have treated me as an equal. You treated my life as though it was as valuable as yours. You respected my journey. You have shown me what the Capital is like. Even though it is no longer there."

"It is when you get to the Black Market. Then you will see that the Capital exists."

"Think about what it is you want from the Black Market. It might not be the manuscript. You are looking for a manuscript that describes life before the war," the Goose said. "And how is that of any use to those of us who have survived the war? It will be written in an obsolete vernacular."

"But that's precisely why I have to find it. Otherwise, the language will go extinct. And what about your own manifesto? What language do you intend to write it in?"

"I never believed I had to write it down anyhow. It is in my head, and changes daily."

"May I hear it?"

"My manifesto?"

"Yes."

"Well, yes, I suppose."

"One moment. This is a rather grand occasion. You will need some sort of stage or podium to stand on."

Sofia jumped out of bed and hurried to get an empty wooden crate. She dragged it to the centre of the living room and picked up the Goose and put him on it.

"I am looking forward to this. It has been so long since I saw any sort of public lecture. I went to so many of these lectures. I'm not sure why my mother always considered it necessary to bring me along. But I miss them now. Just listening to people get all worked up about subjects. People talking about the importance of literature and how it can save the world. I wonder how much they believed it. They seemed so insistent. And yet it didn't save any of them. Perhaps you will deliver the first post-war literary lecture."

"Well, you are starting to make me nervous. I don't know if my manifesto will measure up now. You have heard so many before."

"Every other critical manifesto has been burned. And all the critics have been shot. There is no one you have to compare yourself with. Consider the air before you as a blank page on which you will write your ideas with your voice. You will be the inventor of new literature. The old literature cannot encompass our experience. There is only silence and fear now. Yours will give a voice to the silence."

"Okay, okay. I don't know if you are helping. Each of your words terrified me instead of encouraging me."

"Well, it's really just me here."

The Goose closed his eyes for a moment, then raised his beak and began:

What use are old sentences to the young people who have survived this war—who will crawl out from the basements, and the rubble? They will be looking for a vocabulary and form of expression that they can use.

They will want a literature that reflects them. A literature for children who missed out on their schooling because of the war, or because they were interned, or because they were beggars.

They had two years when they didn't go to a traditional school but instead learned the punctuation of bullets. The pauses of bombs. The occupation of paragraphs. When the page turns, it should sound like fire. The margins will be protected as though by an electric fence.

The words will be taken not from dictionaries but from the sides of trucks, from headlines of newspapers. They will be taken from graffiti spray-painted on walls. They must have the clarity of coerced confessions.

No new words should be introduced to a child after the age of eight. These are not sophisticated words. They are words you will have to pronounce with a mouth filled with missing teeth. They are words that are easy to pronounce. No one will mistake your meaning, even if you speak with a split lip or are bawling your eyes out.

What are the words spoken in this silence? Where there are no nouns. Where there are no verbs. There are only approximations. There are only monsters. There are metaphors. There are birds for sadness. There are apples for bitterness. Everything is a hundred other things. And metaphors are by their nature beautiful. Because they are impressive and delightful if you can make them work. A magic trick.

Every sentence must be able to exist on its own. Each sentence must contain the entire meaning of the piece. You cannot expect your book to remain whole. If only one sentence survives, from it the rest of the text can grow.

The way that a cutting from a plant, when buried, can return to the whole thing.

This will be a style of literature for those who have lost a war. This is a literature by and for the occupied and destroyed.

PINK IS A STATE OF MIND

Sofia had tried to experience love from a man. During wartime! How ridiculous. Everyone was hell-bent on surviving. Love was only a currency now. And it was a currency you got nothing for in exchange. It left a woman broke. She did not like to acknowledge that her mother had been right about this.

How wonderful it was to be romantically rejected. It was quite possibly the most wonderful thing that could happen to a girl. What if he had loved her back? She would have lost her entire self. She would have done whatever he told her to do. She would have changed everything about herself to make him stay. What did it mean to live happily ever after? Couldn't a person assume it meant death? Since death was one of the few circumstances where you could feel truly freed from the vicissitudes of human emotions. And death seemed closer to happiness than it did to sadness.

She could no longer stay cooped up. She was living in limbo. She was going to leave the woods and their fables behind. She was no longer a child, after all.

"I will head to the Black Market, Mama. And I will find your book! And we will still have a country!" she yelled out, squeezing the Goose.

She closed her eyes and inhaled deeply. Her nostrils were filled with an aroma of chocolate. It filled up her head, the way smoke filled up a bowl or a hookah. It filled her with total delight. She held her palms to her face and inhaled. She was sure they smelled like chocolate. Her body was transforming into chocolate. She thought that if she were starving, she could break off her pinkies and eat them one by one.

Now the idea of the Black Market had a flavour and a smell. She had tasted the Black Market. She had taken a bite out of it.

She longed for the pleasures that came with engaging with the world. There were risks that were very much worth taking. She might be killed by soldiers. But she was going to accept the gamble, nonetheless. She wanted chocolates. She wanted a novel. She wanted a silk scarf. She wanted a cup of coffee with cream. She had been waiting to get to the Black Market since the war began. It was everything good in the Capital separated from the chaff.

She looked at the empty spot on her finger. She would go to the Black Market despite the ring's absence. She shuddered to think what they might ask from a young girl with no possessions. She reached into the inner pocket of her coat and stroked the piece of paper she had been carrying since her flight from the train. Might it be of value?

Tobias had stolen the clarinet, even. He was a scavenger. That was how he had managed to still be alive. He was like a dog that not only survived on leftovers but was thrilled by them. He coveted them. The Goose explained this to Sofia as they closed the door on the house behind the church and set out.

He went around looking for people who had things he needed. And he would take from them. Was this what it was now like to be a survivor in this country? Was there any way for them to actually create some sort of community where they cared for each other? Or would they always be wicked and conniving now? Would they always be at each other's throats? Would they treat each other the way the Enemy had? Would they be responsible for ferreting each other out of hiding and destroying each other?

Tobias imagined he was the one who had suffered the most during the war, said the Goose indignantly. He didn't think Sofia had suffered at all. He had come across a fourteen-year-old girl, starving and freezing in the woods, whose only company was a goose. And he thought she had no feelings. He had to judge her to be entitled. He thought she owed him something because he had suffered more than her. Women's suffering was trivial. Their tears were idiotic. They were ridiculous. They were nags with their demands.

"Good riddance to him! It is good to be back in the pursuit of our own fortunes," the Goose exclaimed. "You never know. You shall perhaps change the world as we know it."

"Oh, I am just a young girl," Sofia whined. "Have young girls ever done anything in any of the history books?"

"I don't get my history from books, so I am perhaps better informed. Birthday parties were invented by a little girl in Brussels in 1614. There was a little girl in China who invented ribbons. No one knew what to do with them for at least a hundred years. The first cartwheel was enacted by a Romanian girl.

No one could believe she survived. She proved to people that cartwheels did not equal a certain death. There was a girl who decided the moon showed up every night. And it caused all the waves and shipwrecks."

"Worth it to have a moon, though."

"They invented buttons. That's for certain. And before buttons, everyone went to the battlefield and their clothes fell right off."

"That would explain Vikings."

"That's correct. A wee British girl saw the Vikings arriving on their ships. And she quickly invented buttons. And before you knew it, they were all affluent bankers in suits."

"Anything else?"

"Oh, it was a girl in Kenya who invented the colour pink. That is why there are so many debates about whether pink is actually a colour."

"Well, of course pink is a colour. What else could it be?"

"A state of mind. A state of confusion and uncertainty and upheaval."

A SUITCASE THE SIZE OF A COUNTRY

Clara Bottom was hurrying around the apartment, packing Sofia's things. Sofia stood adamantly in front of her mother and did a rare thing—she raised her voice.

"I don't want to go."

"Sofia, this is a war. Everybody is doing something they don't want to do."

"I am part of the resistance too. You want to send me away so that you can take all the credit."

"Everyone is sending their children out of the Capital. You'll draw too much suspicion if you stay. Don't you want to be safe? Don't you want to go to bed and not worry about the building coming down on your head?"

"No, I do not. That is boring. I like the war!"

"You like the war. You like it. Only a child would think this is some kind of game. I suppose that's what happens to children during the war."

"Why don't you escape the Capital too, then?"

"Darling, I can't."

HEATHER O'NEILL

"Why do you think you love the Capital more than I do?"

"I am the Capital. I helped make it what it is, or what it was. I can't leave. I need to stay. I gave up my mother for the Capital."

"Oh, you are always mean to Grandmother. She is so nice, but you always try to make her feel bad about herself."

"Sofia! This is not up for discussion. You are leaving on the train."

"I hate you! You are bossy and snobby. You are mean to everybody. And you are mean to me," Sofia screamed. "You never wanted to have me. I'm here only because you got pregnant on a boat. Why didn't you just throw me overboard? All you care about is your stupid book!"

Clara ran and shut the window. "You know very well I am not supposed to be writing a book. Why would you scream it at the top of your lungs like that?"

Sofia felt so exasperated. She felt she had spent her whole life trying to get her mother to like her. She had accepted long ago that her mother didn't have a high opinion of her. But now she had lowered her guard. She had believed that her mother had actually changed, that her mother had come to respect her. And she had delighted in this reversal. Now she was outraged at all the things she had previously accepted.

"Your stupid book!" Sofia yelled again. Smashing her foot on the floor. "Your stupid book!" she yelled again.

She repeated this motion, which made her look almost as if she too were a soldier, advancing in military formation on the city. Perhaps she meant to express that her mother ought to fear her as much as she would any approaching army.

"Stop it, Sofia. I abhor masculine displays of force like this. We are both women; we need to be on each other's side."

308

Sofia ran to the window and flung it open and screamed, "Your stupid book!" Then she leapt onto the couch and ran across it as though her mother were on her heels. And she ran into her bedroom and slammed the door. She proceeded to throw every object that was immediately at her disposal at the door. Then she flung her body on her bed. Hot tears of rage escaped from her eyes.

Of course Sofia didn't believe her mother's book was stupid. She wished more than anything that she could. But her entire childhood had been based around the central mythology—religion, almost—that Clara Bottom's writing was important. She wished she could believe her own words.

AN ARMY OF LITTLE BEASTS

Sofia and the Goose had left the woods and were walking on a road. Tobias had mentioned this road when he arrived from the Black Market, so Sofia thought, in absence of any map, they might as well try it. There were white lyridina flowers sprouting in the grassy banks on the sides of the road. This was the flower Tobias had as a lapel pin. These flowers were alive, however, and their long white petals danced in the wind. They were like a group of people in the far distance, waving white flags in surrender.

It was time to return to their quest for the Black Market. In truth, Sofia had no idea what the Black Market would even look like. There was a flower market in the square near her building in the Capital. They had bins of incredible flowers ready for sale. The flowers had drops of water on them, as though they had just come out of the shower. She imagined the Black Market looking like that. Except it wouldn't be filled with flowers—it would be filled with stockings, and handguns, and foie gras, and notebooks.

"Maybe there will be a bottle of pop, and when you drink it your head will be filled with bubbles. And there will be coffee—it is so nice to drink. And books we can read in our own language. And wine so we can be tipsy. And shampoo! You will see how good your feathers feel after you have taken a bubble bath. And chocolate! And fancy outfits. There will be ties you can wear around your neck and look every bit like a gentleman."

The contents of the Black Market exploded in their brains like the fruits and flowers of spring.

She was making a list of her favourite things from when she was a little girl. And Sofia saw that the Goose was quietly staring at her. It seemed as though nothing in the world could distract him, and she was delighted. And continued her magical grocery list of items they would retrieve from the Black Market. She was truly more satisfied with the feeling his attention gave her than with any of the objects on her list. And she got it into her head that when they got to the Black Market and were able to stuff their pockets and suitcase with these extraordinary items, then she would reveal to the Goose the depth of her feelings towards him. Thus, she believed it was the Goose's love that she was going to buy on the Black Market.

"What will you buy all this with?" inquired the Goose. "You don't have your ring anymore."

"I happen to have, in my inner pocket, a very important document that will have to be worth something."

The Goose stopped as though he was going to say something about this, and then shrugged his wings and walked along next to Sofia.

Sofia felt she and the Goose were happy together for the first time in weeks. Even if they never found the Black Market, the idea that it was just up ahead would have lasted them at least several more wonderful days. They felt they were so close to the

Black Market. It might appear before them at any minute, the way grand cities surprisingly revealed themselves to travellers. The Goose moved his neck around happily, almost as though he were whistling.

The clouds looked like the bodies of overweight women floating on the surface of a lake. They were on holiday. If their children went and got themselves killed, they would not be able to be reached.

Sofia had to pass near a small village. She was surprised to see so many people on the road. They were milling about as though there was not a war going on. She wasn't at all sure what had been happening to the people in the towns. She expected they were all being massacred. They would have all been put on trains and sent off to the Enemy country to be murdered. But these people did not seem afraid. She had not realized going into the woods that when she came back out, her people would be entirely different. She thought she could just pass through this town easily. How could the Enemy possibly tell she was not one of the peasants?

But the peasants were regarding her with suspicion. As they passed, they gave her looks that communicated, in no uncertain terms, that they knew she wasn't one of them. They knew she was a stranger. Their eyes seemed to say, I know who you are—and I have power over you. I can turn you in at any second. Everybody is eventually betrayed by their own.

She was terrified of her own people. These were the survivors. These were the people who had not been killed by the Enemy. These were the turncoats. These were the traitors. They had done nothing at all while the cities were being viciously attacked.

They had let the soldiers ride into the cities. She was certain of it. Nothing belonged to her anymore. She was in a very strange country. It was not the country she had grown up in at all. It was all gone. She could tell that now.

Perhaps she would have been more trusting if she had not been tricked by Tobias. She had already had her eyes opened to the treachery of her fellow Elysians. She remembered all the meetings the resistance had had. It was perhaps better that they had all been shot in the head. Otherwise, they would have to know that the peasants and all the citizens outside the Capital had turned against them.

Maybe this was a victory of sorts for the peasants. After all, the Enemy really supported and revered the rural life and regarded the big cities as sites of decadence. And so did the peasants.

There were several little girls holding hands and hurrying down the path. They stopped in their tracks when they saw Sofia. They were frightened and wary of her. They began circling her as though she were prey and they were intending to eat her. They were looking for an opportunity to attack.

She saw it in their gestures and their mood. They had taken the contempt and hatred of the Enemy and had internalized it. They did not seem to have the expressions of girls. She recalled going to the zoo when she was little. And looking into the enclosure filled with wolves. These little girls all had the same suspicious and inscrutable eyes.

They began speaking to her all at once, not letting her answer any of their questions.

"Where are you from?"

"I've never seen you before."

"She's from the Capital. I can tell by her stupid look."

"You are from the Capital? You started all this trouble. It's because of you that my cousin was killed. And he was the most handsome one in our family."

"We were always having to turn away people from the Capital at the beginning of the war."

"It's been a while since one came. What do you think we should do with her?"

"We should set the dogs on her."

"We will tell on you, and they'll hang you from a tree."

"Do you have any coins?"

"You have to pay us something before we can let you pass."

"Or we will turn you in."

They stood in front of her with their hands linked, as though they were paper dolls.

The girls looked so small and pathetic to her. She realized they did not perceive her as one of them. Her arrival was a threat, the way an adult's might be. She had come out of the woods, and she was no longer a child. Nothing would ever make her a child again. And nothing could make her feel intimidated by other children again.

She had sometimes considered that life would have been easier had she climbed into the trucks with the other children. She would be buried now in a mass grave. But she was not a child even when she had boarded the train. She already had begun to be a woman. And it was that part of her that insisted she get out of the train and run. It was that part of her that wanted to survive. That insisted she survive.

Sofia opened her mouth and made the long honking noise of a goose. The girls all stepped back as though she were a monster.

A man yelled for them brusquely. Upon hearing his call, they forgot that Sofia and her Goose existed. They were like dogs that had been called to dinner. Dogs that were often whipped. Even though they were pretending to be wild and independent, they were subservient little beasts. That was why they were so brazen. That was why they were loud. Because they had no actual power. The way small dogs bark the loudest.

Sofia was no longer a child. She was a young woman. She belonged to no one in particular. Her life was unpredictable now that she was a young woman.

"You scared them all away," the Goose said. "With your astounding honk. You were magnificent. We showed them!"

"Thank you," Sofia whispered. "But I don't feel safe at all. Let's leave this place."

As they hurried out of the village, Sofia had an odd feeling. Soldiers had an aura that preceded them. It was like being able to sense the snow or feel the calm before a storm. She could not shake the presentiment that there were soldiers near. She and the Goose turned onto a road, and soldiers appeared in front of them. They turned around as if to flee and noticed soldiers behind them as well. They were surrounded.

There were too many of them to bother running. You could hide from the soldiers successfully, but once they found you, you were finished.

There were about fifty soldiers. Every time she turned around to look, more of them appeared. It was as though they multiplied every time she thought about them. There were always so many of them. They seemed to manifest as many as were needed to vanquish whoever they needed to.

She hadn't ever experienced the numbness of this kind of

fear before. She watched the Goose squabbling and honking. She couldn't make out anything he was saying. He was reacting so strongly. He was reacting for the two of them. That was the nature of having a travel companion. You could take turns occupying yourselves with certain tasks.

One of the soldiers pointed to the Goose. "We will eat this," he said with a thick accent in Sofia's language.

"No!" cried Sofia. "This isn't an ordinary goose. It is a talking goose!"

The soldiers looked at her and at each other. They weren't sure she was saying what she was saying. They did not speak her language well. They knew the children they had come across had all gone mad.

"It can talk! It can talk!" Sofia yelled again. The Goose pressed himself up against her, terrified and quiet.

A man who was older and clearly in charge pushed through the crowd. He wore a long black coat that went down to his feet. It was like the cloak of the Grim Reaper. He had a birthmark under his eye that looked like a tattoo of a tear. It made him look wicked.

"We arrested a thief," he said, speaking the girl's language clearly. "He said we were to go to the church to find a member of the resistance. He gave you up to get himself free, but we did not believe him. And sure enough, all we find is a little girl and a goose. But we will take your goose, as we are hungry. And you can be on your way. I am not going to harm a child today."

"The goose can talk. You would be foolish to kill him. He can make you a fortune at any opera house. He is miraculous. He is a once-in-a-lifetime creature. He will change you."

At least they should know exactly what they were killing.

Even if they could be blasé about killing him now, it might come to haunt them later on. If they ever tried to be good people in the future—and who knew, some people did—then this act would destroy them. For their whole lives, they would have to be the people who had killed a magical goose.

Sofia pulled the folded-up yellowed piece of paper from the inside pocket of her coat. "Here," she cried.

The officer took the paper and looked at it. "Well, this says to spare your life, but there is nothing about a goose, I'm afraid."

"Take me and kill me if you must, but let my goose live."

The officer turned to his men, ostensibly translating this, and they all burst out laughing.

But Sofia knew she meant it. The Goose's life was more valuable than hers. She was only an ordinary girl. She had no value. She had done nothing in her life. She probably wasn't going to do anything of note. What could be the point of ordinary people other than to protect the extraordinary ones? She would sacrifice herself for the Goose. He was all that was left of the magic in her country. If he was killed, perhaps the trees would stop walking from place to place.

"You must listen to him," Sofia said. "It is wonderful to hear an animal speak. He is more intelligent than anyone you know. The way he speaks, it seems as though he has been educated in the most important schools. As if he has made a twenty-year career of lecturing on human rights and important subjects like that. He has more lectures to give and books to write. Books to write!"

"If the goose can speak, we will let you both go."

He then turned and shouted something in his own language to the men, and they all burst out laughing.

"Of course," said the first soldier with the heavy accent. "If the goose can speak, we will let you both go, and I will shoot myself in the head." He repeated this to the men, and they again exploded with mirth.

"If the goose can speak, I will shoot all my men in the head," the officer said. The soldiers whispered this to one another in their own language but did not laugh.

"You all won't stop talking, but are you going to let my goose speak for himself?"

Sofia stepped one pace away from the Goose and nervously held out her hands as though she were performing a magic trick. They all moved closer in their circle to stare at the Goose. She wanted to see their faces when they realized she had something to teach them about the universe. She wanted them to be profoundly surprised and in awe.

She waited for the Goose to speak. She waited for the Goose to begin one of his intellectual discussions. He would impress them with only a few phrases.

But the Goose was silent. He looked at her with wide eyes. As though supplicating her to come to his rescue. He took a step towards Sofia. But a soldier put out an arm to hold Sofia back. The Goose stopped and stood quietly in place. The Goose didn't say anything. He opened his mouth and made a honking noise. It seemed as far from human speech as any animal sound could ever be.

Looking at the Goose, she realized he wasn't playing games at all. This was the manner in which he communicated. It was the only way he could speak. Whereas the other children had been willing to play along and pretend the Goose was speaking, the soldiers were not. The children had decided to see the Goose through her eyes. The soldiers were most certainly not going to stoop to seeing anything through a girl's eyes.

Sofia was staring incredulously at the Goose, and the Goose was staring incredulously at her. Then a soldier leaned forward, grabbed the neck of the Goose, and broke it.

Sofia screamed so loudly, it surprised the soldier and he dropped the Goose onto the ground. She wrenched her body away from the others. She fell on her knees and held the Goose in her arms. She began weeping hysterically while stroking the Goose's neck. She wanted him to come back to life. There was nothing that could make the Goose's neck stand up again. It was so limp, it now seemed impossible that it had ever been able to hold itself up. Being alive defied physics. Consciousness went against all the rules. It was a miracle. It was a miracle that had to perform itself every minute of the day.

The soldiers were mystified by the intensity of Sofia's reaction. Was she genuinely that upset the goose had been killed? Did she truly think of it as a pet, and was she now reacting as though her dog had been shot? Or did she want to eat it herself? Perhaps she had a starving family waiting for that goose.

She stood and she held the goose in her arms as though it were a body. She reminded them of sculptures they had seen of the Virgin Mary holding Jesus in her lap. And they did not know what to make of this. How could a filthy atheist enemy with a goose resemble the Virgin Mary and the Son of God?

THE BLACK MARKET WORE

RIBBONS IN HER HAIR

The death of the Goose made Sofia feel alone in a way she hadn't felt since the beginning of the war. It was a loneliness that knew no bounds. She had no idea how to situate herself in the universe. There was no one to make her feel small. There was no one to put her in her place, so she didn't know what or where her place was.

She had never been allowed to feel vulnerable because the Goose had made her feel he was more so. She hadn't even been allowed to have her own emotions. She would wait to see what the Goose was feeling. And it wasn't difficult to find out because he was so solicitous and articulate about his own state of mind.

She began to properly grieve her own life and all she had lost. She had lost her mother. She had lost her home. She had lost her city. Before, she had not even felt she had a right to weep for these things. Because she had not really felt they belonged to her. But the Capital and all its details and splendours had belonged to her. They belonged equally to every resident there. That was the thing about a city—no one could own it or call it their own. It was a collective voice. And there were no main characters. Because behind every door of every apartment was a completely different story in which the inhabitants were the central characters.

Her mother had duped Sofia into thinking she was the main character of the whole city. Now that the city and all its books had been destroyed, she realized her mother was not the main character. Sofia, as a survivor, was the main character because she was alone.

The soldiers left Sofia in the middle of the road in her misery, and she felt doubly abandoned. She realized there was nothing left to the world she had known and loved. She didn't even care about getting to the Black Market. She felt as though she had been rudely awakened from her delusional dream. Of course her mother's book was not there. For the first time since she had decided to run from the train, she felt as though she had no purpose whatsoever. Had any of this been worth it? She should have just listened to the soldiers. She should have gone off to her death then. She would have been shot while wearing her own shoes. She would have died with dignity, with a pretty coat and shiny shoes, a packed suitcase at her side.

She had been rejected by the little girls in the village because she was no longer one of them. She could never re-enter the world of girlhood after the things that had happened to her. And what had she done to the poor goose? She had dragged him along on this adventure with her. She had made him behave and act like a human, only in the end to be killed like a goose. She had given him an ignoble death.

She stood in the middle of the road with her arms stretched side to side. "I am from the Capital! Do not mistake me for a peasant. I am bourgeois. I am a bohemian." A military car swerved around her. It blared its horn. She waited, standing absolutely still, expecting that at any minute, the car would back up over her. Or that someone would come out of the car and shoot her. But the sound of the car faded into the distance.

Everybody walked past her quickly. She seemed to have become untouchable now that she no longer had the Goose. She thought they were slightly frightened of her. A small truck was approaching. She ran to it, shouting into its open window.

"The Capital is not destroyed. Not yet! There's one head you haven't put a bullet in. I escaped from the Children's Train. You were right to get rid of all the children. We may look skinny and weak, but our roots are deep. And we will each grow into an enormous tree, and there will be a new forest that grows. And we will believe in the absurd. And those branches will tangle with one another. And they will form a line you can never get through. You will go mad when confronted with our nonsense."

And then Sofia became quiet and just stood there.

A truck full of soldiers stopped in front of Sofia on the road. It was much too big to swerve around her. One of the soldiers got out of the passenger seat. He walked around the side of the truck and over to Sofia. "Is there anywhere you want to go?" he asked her in her language.

What could she answer, except "Can you take me to the Black Market?"

He looked one way down the road and then turned his head in the opposite direction, as though it were impossible to ascertain the difference between one way and the other. Perhaps she and the Goose had contemplated the Black Market so much, they had relegated it to the sphere of the imagination and it could no longer be obtained in the real world.

Then he bent down and picked her up. Sofia had not been picked up since she was a much younger child. She forgot how it made you feel weightless. It made you feel as though you had nothing to worry about. It made you feel as though there were people in the world who were so much stronger than you. And you could let them run the world. She allowed someone to make her feel like that. In that moment.

The back of the truck was lowered. The soldier lifted Sofia higher and passed her to one of the soldiers on the back. He seated her between himself and another soldier. She rode along in the truck. She felt nothing at all. She wasn't sure where they were taking her. She did not believe they could possibly be taking her to the Black Market because she no longer believed there was such a place as the Black Market.

She simply could not believe any magical site existed anymore. All magic had died with the Goose. Even if it had ever existed, which she could not from experience say it had, it had surely vanished into thin air.

Sofia knew she ought to be paying attention to the landscape. That was what she ordinarily did in order not to be lost. But she was already lost. There were no landmarks. The road looked the same all the way along as she was travelling. There were only odd spindly trees along the road. They were only cracks in the porcelain that was the sky.

She didn't react when the truck slowed and the soldier handed her down to the side of the road. Soon she was alone, but she still expected them to come back and hunt her down, like some sort of hare in the wild. She found she didn't have the will to run. She stood there for a while after the sound of the truck disappeared into the distance. She was coming to terms with the fact that she was still alive.

Sofia noticed a golden car on the side of the road. The car looked as though it had been in an accident. One of the doors on the right side had been smashed in. It was a fashionable make to drive. It was a sports car. A race car driver had gone up in flames in this same make. For that reason, it had become very popular. It was synonymous with living dangerously. Her mother had the exact same car. All the male intelligentsia loved her car. Sofia had heard one of them say it was a very masculine car, and for this very reason, he found it attractive when her mother drove it.

Sofia thought for a moment it was her mother's car. She was terrified. She thought her mother had survived the war. For the moment, she couldn't imagine anything more disconcerting. She wanted to turn and run. Sofia approached the car, hoping to dispel the illusion, hoping it would vanish, as it might in a nightmare. She peeked into the car. She knew immediately it wasn't her mother's at all. The seats were a dark red instead of black like her mother's. The back seat was filled almost to the roof with metallic cookie tins and boxes.

She noticed a woman squatting down in the trees while going to the bathroom. The woman pulled up her tights and walked over to her. She was tall, and her brown hair was tied in a bun over her head. She was wearing a man's blazer over a dark blue dress. She was wearing a holster with a gun under her jacket. It rocked up against her full breasts.

She had on a pair of boots that were made for a man. Sofia wondered whether there was a single person in the country who still wore women's shoes. And what they had done with the women's shoes. Maybe they had been tossed in a huge pile. They were being kept somewhere in a storage room for when the war was over.

The young woman smiled at Sofia. Sofia immediately relaxed. The smile she was offering was so friendly. She looked at Sofia as though she were recognizing a friend. It put Sofia at ease. It made her want to weep. She felt as if she was suddenly not completely alone in the world.

She wanted to speak to someone. She wanted to hear the sound of her own voice. Before the war she had always been so quiet. She hadn't realized just how much she had changed since the beginning of the war. The Goose had prevented her from getting to know this new self. The Goose had always spoken to her in a way that kept her shackled to the past.

The woman called out something, but Sofia did not know how to answer. "Hello," the woman said. Sofia was thrilled to hear her own language come out of the woman's mouth, even with a thick accent.

"Hello," she said.

"What in the world are you doing out here all by yourself?"

The woman pulled a string of sausages from the inside of her coat. There had been no previous indication her coat could contain such wealth. It was very much like watching a magician pull a never-ending rope of handkerchief out of his pocket. She ripped one sausage off for herself and one for Sofia. The woman ate hers slowly. But Sofia was ravenous and devoured hers. The spices delighted her mouth and taste buds. She felt the sausage fill her body with comfort.

"What is your name?" Sofia asked.

"Most people call me the Black Market now. But my name is Rosalie," the woman answered. And whereas Sofia had no previous affection for the name, she now would think of it as the most beautiful she had ever heard in her life.

Rosalie put the rest of the sausages back in her inner pocket.

Rosalie opened the trunk of the car. She pressed the latch, and it sprung open. Inside was the aroma of coffee. It was the same kind Sofia's mother liked and insisted she could never live without. There was quite the trove inside the trunk. There were piles of stockings and fur stoles and gloves and jewellery. There were jugs of vodka and jam and dried fruit. There were bricks of butter and cartons of cigarettes.

Sofia looked in the trunk. She was searching for her mother's manuscript. Would the book be there? There was part of her that felt if she was to see her mother's book there, she might drop to her knees as though shot. It would shock her to such an extent, she wouldn't be able to bear it. But of course, the manuscript, hidden between the covers of a folktale collection, was not there.

How can we ever be given proof that something does not exist? That absence, the unknowing. Is that what keeps us going in life? Looking for something that we lost, that we believe should be ours. Do we ever come across anything we are looking for?

She had needed to come to the Black Market in order to know that, truly, her mother's book was gone. It had been destroyed in the great bonfire of Elysian culture. She had to know that there was no such thing as magic. It was not at all possible for the limbs of the trees to pluck her mother's manuscript from the hands of the Enemy and drop it into this trunk of ordinary marvels.

She had believed in the survival of her mother's book because she still put stock in make-believe. And in a fable, an object as precious as her mother's manuscript could never disappear. It could only ever transform into a stream, or a wolf, or a tree, or a road, or a talking bird.

She had to come to the Black Market to stop believing such a thing was possible. To trade in her childhood desires for new ones.

"You thought the Black Market was a place," Rosalie said, interrupting Sofia's silence. "You thought it was like the strange garden of jewels that Aladdin was led to. But now you find it is only me, an ordinary girl in a stolen coat and a beat-up car. You must be very disappointed."

"Oh no," Sofia said, returning from her thoughts to reality. "This is much better than I expected."

"What do you like?"

"I only wanted to see the Black Market. I wanted to know it really existed. I have been imagining and picturing it for so long. I drew a map to be able to find it."

Rosalie again reached into her coat, and this time pulled out a map. It was an official map, printed on ordinary paper. It was not like the childish hand-drawn map filled with green trees and blue rivers that she had made herself. It was not at all like the map Tobias had stolen from her. But she did not hand it to Sofia.

"You needed a new map to be able to find me. There's no use for an old one. The names of all the cities have changed. The old maps are really more like traps than anything else. I will be your map. I will take you wherever you need to go."

Sofia watched the map disappear back inside the coat. "How can I pay you? I had a bag full of treasures just recently with things to trade. I lost it, along with my companion who was a goose."

"You were looking for me, but I was looking for you. I had heard a story about a girl who travelled around with a goose, and it infected my imagination."

Rosalie reached into her shirt and pulled out a necklace with Sofia's stolen ring on it. Sofia looked at it as though it were a miracle, and she smiled.

"Where to?" Rosalie said as she opened the passenger door wide for Sofia.

"Back to the Capital," Sofia answered.

"Excellent idea," said Rosalie. "I adore the Capital."

Sofia was wary for a moment. Who in their right mind would get into a car with a member of the Enemy? She liked her accent. For some reason, it seemed familiar to her. It reminded her of the scoop of molasses her mother often put into her milk, even though she would beg her not to.

It made her happy to see a young woman acting as any young man might. She did not like to think about Celeste, sitting in her wondrous, submissive glory, like a statue of a martyred saint. She was happy to see a woman war profiteer. She would make a choice to trust this woman.

And Sofia also knew she needed to go back to the apartment. Her mother had burned all the rough drafts of her memoir in the fire while she was writing, so as not to leave evidence. But surely she had ferreted away some sort of draft, some evidence of her great work. So she would see if her mother had left anything behind at all.

Sofia bent down and got into the passenger seat. She could see right away that Rosalie liked to add a flourish to all her actions. She made a wild swing with her hips and slammed the door of the car shut with her behind.

Rosalie climbed into the driver's seat. She pulled down the sun visor. Some papers and change fell out and landed on her lap. But she didn't notice at all. She fixed her hair in the mirror by grabbing her topknot with her fist and moving it one way and then the next. Then she took out a tube of lipstick. She spread it over her mouth. It became a sparkling shade of light pink.

As Sofia was adjusting herself into the passenger seat, Rosalie turned towards her and asked, "Did you eat the goose?"

Sofia immediately felt guilt. She was guilty that she was alive and he was not. She didn't know whether she was allowed to feel joy and pleasure and happiness. How could she when the Goose had undergone something so horrific? She thought the only thing she could do for the Goose was to contemplate his terrible tragedy all day long. She and the Goose had spoken so much about the Black Market. They had arrived now, and she was enjoying it all by herself. There were so many things that were going to happen to her. The Goose wasn't going to have anything. He would never get to see the wonders in this car.

"What are they being changed to?" Sofia asked, wishing to move on to a new subject.

"What?"

"You said the names of the cities were being changed. And I was wondering what they were being changed to."

"Famous people from our country."

This surprised Sofia as she did not know there were famous people in the Enemy country.

As the car began to pick up velocity along the road, Sofia noticed a body hanging from a tree. She looked away, but something in her own body recognized Tobias.

Rosalie's driving soon distracted her. It felt so free to be driving in a car. Rosalie sped when she drove, taking full advantage of being in a race car. The moving and bustling and jerking of the car made all the tins in the back rattle up against each other. It sounded as though they were in a funeral marching band.

Rosalie rolled down her window. The wind began to blow her hair wildly all over the place. The bun on her head fell down over her forehead. As though she were a unicorn. She didn't try to straighten or right her hair, even if it was going to blind her for a split second, which might cause her to crash. She didn't slow down when she came to a bend in the road.

Sofia didn't care about Rosalie's dangerous driving. There was some danger that led to a beautiful feeling. She was so used to peril leading to terrible, sad places. To discover now that it could be used to elicit joy felt good. It made her want more of it. That was what Rosalie was selling from the trunk of her golden sports car. It was the thrill of adventure, the wonder of risks, the pleasure of transgression, the delight of self-destruction.

All her limbs were alive. She felt ready to leap, as though she had the legs of a goat. She felt as though she were one of the forest trees that she had observed turn into lithe human-like forms. Trees stretched deep down into the ground, their roots twisting around one another like telephone wires singing messages through them in a rapturous, entangled choir. A tree could never be uprooted from a forest. That was why, for a moment in the spring, they took on the forms of young people. The thing about the metamorphosis out of girlhood is that there is a buoyancy to it. It is a moment in life, a brief flash when you must at least try to run. To see if you can run fast enough to catch up to that feeling of being yourself. And claim it as your own.

Rosalie drove the car along the coast. There was a small road on the cliff that went up and down.

Rosalie turned on the radio in the car. There was a scratching noise for a brief moment, and then a voice came on. Sofia was surprised. She was so used to radios having only static on them that she had not thought to try turning it on. It was a man speaking calmly and melodiously in the Enemy's language.

So another language was in the airwaves. New voices and songs were being broadcast all over the country. If she were to meet a talking goose at some point in the future, she was quite sure it would be speaking in the Enemy's tongue.

Sofia actually recognized the speaker. It was the voice of the Leader—a voice Sofia hadn't heard since the beginning of the war, inside a movie theatre with her mother. But Rosalie had no visceral reaction of fear. Instead, she listened to his smooth, authoritative voice as though he was relaying something obvious and mundane. And he might have been, as the war was now over.

"What is he saying?" Sofia asked.

"He is wishing everyone a happy St. Vasilia Day. Everyone loves this holiday."

"What is St. Vasilia Day?"

"St. Vasilia danced for thirteen days straight to prove she believed in God. So in my country, when you turn thirteen, you have to wear a long white dress that goes down past your feet and put a crown of candles on your head and walk through the town. Everyone lines up to throw flowers at you. It's totally crazy. You always forget just how many flowers there are until they arrive. They come in trucks. It takes three or four truckloads. We used to grow daisies in the backyard to make a little extra money on flower day. But everyone likes it because there is a big party afterwards. Everyone gets so drunk. There's a dance everyone likes, where you move in a spiral and wave flowers over your head. You don't have this?"

"No, but we have Porcelain Day. There was a porcelain factory that burned down once, and all the little girls working there were killed. So now we paint eggs every year to commemorate it."

"Well, we can celebrate both days. I have a cake. We should stop on the beach and eat it."

When they got to the beach, Rosalie jumped out of the car and began running towards the water. She ran like a deer being flushed out of the forest.

Rosalie took all her clothes off and flung herself into the water clumsily. The waves knocked her this way and that. She had trouble standing upright. She stood up for one second and was dragged violently under as though a shark had just bitten her. Then moments later, she righted herself with her hair in her face and her arms spread out wide.

Sofia undressed more slowly. She was self-conscious of how dirty her body was. There was black along the lines of her toenails and fingernails. Her feet were stained with black. As though they had gangrene. As though they had been run over by a truck. As though they had frostbite and needed to be amputated. She stepped with them into the water. The waves rushed up to them. Like the hands of a hundred pedicurists rushing to massage and clean the dead skin off her toes, and to polish her toenails. And when the waves pulled back, her feet were clean. As though by some sort of miracle.

She wanted her whole body in the water. She ran forward and dove into the waves. She heard the roar of the waves around her as though she had entered a portal to a new reality.

The two young women swam out in the water. They were just two happy heads floating on the top of the water like beach balls filled with dreams. They laughed and pushed each other under the water. Rosalie disappeared and grabbed Sofia by the feet. As though she were the mysterious Elysian mermaid. How wonderful to be murdered by a myth.

While hunched over and clasping her body, Rosalie ran to the trunk and brought out two blankets. They were both shivering violently. They spread their blankets on the sand. And lying down next to each other, they let the sun fill up their pores.

Then the hunger set in. It was as though a hole opened wide in Sofia's stomach. It was a well. The hole went right through her and deep into the ground. It seemed as though nothing could fill the hole in her stomach. She could have fed herself turkeys and hares and pigs and loaves of bread with pats of butter on them. She could have swallowed an entire couch. She could have swallowed an entire battalion of soldiers. There was room for them in her belly.

They ate together. Ripping off chunks of bread with their teeth. They ate the thickest, densest cake Sofia had ever encountered. The cake was almost black, and the dried fruit inside it lit up like windows in the night.

They grabbed at it with their hands. They didn't need forks or knives or napkins. They enjoyed instead eating like dogs. She no longer had any table manners. She was no longer civilized. Because she did not belong to any civilization. Her nation had been destroyed. They were just two girls on holiday in a foreign country.

"How did you come to be the Black Market?" Sofia asked.

Rosalie looked at Sofia carefully, then she looked out at the sea, as though her story were as long and wide as it was.

"When I was a little girl, I was so wild. I thought I was just like the boys. I could run around the way they did. I loved to climb trees. I loved playing soldier with my brothers. I would pretend everything was a gun. I loved the thrill of it. I was always getting myself dirty. I used to imagine being on ships and trains and driving cars. I imagined going to different countries. I imagined going to America. But when the extremists took over the country, it changed everything. My father told me I would have to marry a man I didn't even know.

"Everything was forbidden to me. There was a song that I loved by a singer who was executed. It was still stuck in my head. I was taking a shower, and I started singing the song out loud. My father came in and attacked me while I was naked. He beat me. And I couldn't see or defend myself.

"I went and I denounced my whole family two days later. I turned them in at the local office. All of them. I said they were enemies to the cause. They hated the Leader. They were spies who were giving information to the enemy. They were sympathizing with the resistance. I put all the ideas that were in my head in their mouths. I accused them of all my crimes.

"They loved that. They executed my whole family. They didn't care whether what I was saying was actually true. They wanted to make an example of a family who had been denounced by one of its own. I didn't feel anything when they were shot. How could I? When it meant freedom for me? My freedom was the most important thing. And there was no way I could be free with them alive."

Rosalie turned to Sofia, as if to see whether she was shocked.

"Can I hear the song?" Sofia asked.

"You want me to sing it?"

"Yes."

"I don't know if I can do it justice."

Rosalie put her forehead down on her knees, to indicate she was shy to perform. Then she lifted her head and began to sing. Although the song was in the Enemy language, Sofia knew exactly what it was saying. Or she thought she could make out the meaning, in any case. It was so kooky and sweet, and from Rosalie's expression, she could tell the song was funny.

And it was by listening to this girl sing a contraband song that she knew the Enemy had not won and would never truly win. There would always be artists. There is a need to create art. And the nature of good art is to express freedom. It finds a way to reject oppression. And some people might say that artists are silly. And that art is a frivolous and unessential part of life. And that artists are irrational and live ridiculous lives and never truly grow up. And that you cannot equate art with necessities like food and shelter.

But here was a song that had survived a war. And when Rosalie sang it, whenever she sang it, it would be a reminder that the Leader's vision had not penetrated the souls of everyone in their country. There was a dissident voice.

This song written by the executed singer was contagious. Rosalie might sing it around a group of soldiers, and they would then have the song in their heads. And it would cause them to think in an irreverent way.

That was why Sofia's mother's book was of such radical importance. If she could save anything from the artists, if she could take even a single clipping from the branches of their thoughts, it could be put in a glass on a windowsill by a child with an imagination and it would grow into a beanstalk.

"So what was it you did to survive?" Rosalie asked.

She didn't mind telling Rosalie any of her secrets or insecurities. She didn't feel judged. There was no one alive in the world who knew her story. She told Rosalie in case she did not make it across the border.

"I was supposed to take my mother's manuscript out of the country. You see, I wasn't supposed to go to the country for safe-keeping, like all the other children were doing. My mother would never have done that. She would rather I die in the city than be sent to the country. She used to say she hated what the country did to people's minds. That it made them lazy.

"She sent me to the country to be with cousins. But they weren't really my cousins. I had never met them. They might have been third cousins. But I didn't believe her. It was a house that was near the border. I was supposed to wait. Then I was supposed to establish a routine of gathering berries in a large bowl by the barbed-wire fence along the border. One day, I would find a hole cut in the barbed wire.

"I was supposed to get her manuscript out of the country. There were people on the other side of the border who were waiting to publish it. There was no way she could get to the border unnoticed. So she sent me with this very dangerous manuscript. She sent me, even though I'm not fully grown, to be a spy."

• • •

All those months ago, Sofia had left the train, with her suitcase, after being evacuated by the Enemy. She was running through the woods when she was suddenly cut off by a soldier. There was no way to escape him. He grabbed her hard by the arm and dragged her out of the woods. He brought her to a cabin at the train station that was being used as some sort of headquarters by the Enemy.

The soldiers all laughed when Sofia said she wanted to be a collaborator. But they sent for someone higher up. He looked thinner and harder than the others, and peered through round wire glasses. He introduced himself as the general. The others still had grimaces on their faces because they were not sure whether to take her seriously because she was a child. "But I could see he took me seriously. That was why he was in charge." The general knew that in wartime, things are not at all what they seem. The most innocent-seeming person or place carries the seeds of your destruction.

She sat across the table from the general. Another soldier came and put her suitcase on the table between them. She opened it for them to look at. There was nothing out of the ordinary in their eyes. They checked the lining of the suitcase. They had an enormous dog come and sniff it. But no one detected anything wrong.

"I know of information that is going to be taken out of the country."

"In what form?"

"A book. A very important book."

"What book is this? I don't think I could consider it important. I'm not afraid of any book written in this country."

"The book hasn't been published yet."

At this, the general raised his eyebrows.

"A manuscript?"

"Yes. It was written by a very famous intellectual. One of the most famous in Elysia. It is about everything marvellous in our country, and how you have destroyed it. Others will read it. They will think of you as villainous, even if they don't come to rescue us. They will use it to take the country from you in the future."

Everyone in the army had been told it was through the written word that Elysia was particularly vicious. No one had ever weaponized words the way Elysians had. That was why the order had gone out that all books in the country were to be burned.

There were no Elysian writers abroad. The language would quickly be forgotten. But this was a new book. This was a book written after the war broke out. It wasn't meant to be read by citizens of this country. It was specifically meant to be read by people on the outside. The Elysians were going to spread their hatred of the Enemy to the rest of the world through this book.

The Enemy had thought that the war was almost over, and that they would achieve a definitive victory. Their hard work had triumphed over the sophistication and bourgeois pretentions of the Elysians. Their fancy words had proved to be powerless. But this was the one thing they had not factored. This was the general's worst fear. This was why they had to be so brutal. There could be no words escaping from this country. There could be no witnesses. But people did not believe witnesses. Instead, they had an almost absurd faith in the written word.

"The book is to be brought immediately to a translator who will render it in English in order to make it accessible to everyone in Europe," Sofia said.

"Who is the writer of the manuscript?"

"Clara Bottom."

There was a noticeable shudder through the room as they recognized her mother's name. She thought her mother would have been delighted to know her name was recognized. And even better, it was associated with power.

Sofia knew then she had made a deal. She would be able to trade her mother for freedom. When she began the conversation—or negotiation, whatever you want to call it—she wasn't sure she really had anything to barter.

Perhaps she had fool's gold. Perhaps she was negotiating for her life with her mother's narcissism. But her mother had not exaggerated the importance of her book.

"I heard there are papers you give to collaborators to keep them alive. That you can show them to any soldier and they are not allowed to shoot you or imprison you. They have to let you live."

"You speak about this paper as though it gives you immortality. But yes, there is such a thing."

"Show it to me! Fill out the paper. I want to have it near."

"You don't trust us."

"No, of course not."

They all laughed.

"If you don't trust us, how can you believe we would respect what is on a piece of paper."

"You believe in words."

The general stared into Sofia's eyes, seeing his own truth there. He then nodded to a man in uniform who was seated at a small desk at the side of the room with a typewriter on it. The desk was surrounded by opened boxes filled with files. And there were stacks of folders surrounding the typewriter. It seemed quite impossible he would know where anything was in this disorder. But he quickly went to a pile of folders next to him, retrieved a navy blue one, delicately pulled a sheet of paper out of it, and put it in the typewriter.

"What is your first and last name?" the general asked.

"Sofia Bottom-Zier."

The general's eyes opened. The others who understood her language also stared at Sofia with a different intensity.

"Clara Bottom is my mother."

They all paused for what would normally have been an imperceptible moment, but to everyone in the room it seemed long and heavy. Sofia was careful not to allow any expression on her face. She did not have much pride left. She had revealed her weakness to every soldier crammed into the room. She would preserve whatever pride she could by not allowing them to see her feelings or her reaction. She would not let them know how it felt to betray your own mother. They could all go home and imagine it for themselves.

Perhaps her actions made them feel justified in their genocide. There must have been moments in their carnage when they wondered whether they were murdering people who were just like them. And their loved ones.

But she had shown them the Elysians were monsters. They would walk into an office and trade away their own mothers. They had no values and familial ties. They cared only for themselves. They were pathologically narcissistic. It didn't matter if you killed them.

They did not understand her. Sofia could tell they could not understand her. For the first time she felt like the most intelligent person in the room. This was an unusual feeling for a child to have in a room full of adults. But there you have it. She understood them, but they did not understand her. The general handed her the paper.

At the same moment, another clerk typed out an arrest warrant for Clara Bottom and a search warrant and placed them next to the general.

"You realize this is a search warrant to go through your mother's apartment looking for the book, and this is the warrant to shoot her?" said the general.

Sofia held her paper in her hand. It was thick the way important paper always was. She ran her fingers over the raised print of the insignia at the top of the page. It felt as though she were running her fingers over the numerals on a bill. Or the lines on the palm of an old woman. It felt like skin. Something that, if it were ripped in half or cut, would regenerate and heal itself. It was a living thing. She was going to survive the war because of this. She was the only one who was going to survive the war. She was safe.

And to be honest, she was happy to be freed from the burden of carrying the book around. Now she did not have to wander near a barbed-wire fence where at any minute enormous dogs might come to attack her. Or she might be murdered by soldiers. Also, there were landmines! No matter how hard she tried to imagine being blown to smithereens, she could not.

She wondered whether she would be in a hundred pieces in the air. And would then perceive the world simultaneously in a hundred different ways.

She was safe. She was safe. She was safe.

"Do you know where exactly she keeps the manuscript? Is it in your apartment?"

Sofia could tell from the blank and unresponsive faces of the other soldiers in the room that the general was the only one who spoke her language fluently.

Sofia then stood up and asked to see her suitcase. She put her arms out towards it so everyone in the room was quite aware of what she wanted. They looked to the general, and since he showed no objection, one of the soldiers placed the open suitcase in front of her. All the grown men in the room leaned forward to see what was in the shiny pink lining. They were all rather wary. They believed that they had searched the suitcase thoroughly. And were she to pull a weapon or something else contraband out of it, it would reflect very poorly on them.

She took out the book of folktales. Everyone looked once again at the cover. There could be no doubt it was a children's book. And a much-loved one because the sharp edges of the cover had become rounded and bent. There was an illustration of a goose on the cover. The goose had a debonair expression on its face, which was enhanced by the fact that it had on a bow tie.

There was an illustration of a girl standing next to the goose. Her hair and manner registered impeccable breeding. She had on a prim black coat and a matching black hair ribbon. Her black buckle shoes were shiny. She quite obviously lived in the city, which made her affinity for this farm animal even more absurd.

Sofia opened the book. She turned past the table of contents, which was a list of fables that were no longer in the book. And when she arrived at the first page, she turned the book for the general to read.

Everyone in the room was impatient for the general to stop reading and explain to them why he was poring over the pages of a children's book with such concern. But Sofia was in no hurry. She could watch him read for the rest of her life, if need be.

"You realize, of course, that this means the immediate execution of your mother."

She looked up from her paper. At that moment she saw the general pick up the warrant for her mother's arrest. He handed it to a soldier, who folded it, tucked it into his breast pocket, and headed out the door to put an end to Clara Bottom.

The soldiers motioned to Sofia that she was free to leave herself and return back to the war. The moment Sofia's feet touched the dirt outside, she began running again. As though she had never stopped running, as though she were still running from the train and the bullets, as though she had never been captured, as though she had never betrayed her mother. She spotted a peasant girl and asked to switch coats with her. But she was careful to take the certificate the soldiers had given her out of her pocket.

The small certificate moved in her hand, as though it were struggling to take flight. She whispered "Hush" to the paper and stored it safely in her new, tattered coat by her heart. She was surprised it was still beating. She was very much in shock that she was alive.

And then she was on the back of a truck, cradling a goose, wondering how she could reclaim her mother's manuscript. There was no logical way to do so. Except to head to a place filled with all the things children weren't allowed to yet understand: the Black Market.

A VALENTINE FROM THE CAPITAL

The Capital appeared like a mirage out of the ground. It wasn't there. And then suddenly, it was. Sofia pressed her face up against the window. When she used to ride into her city, she always hoped to be the first one to see it, and in that way, imagine it into being. It was dangerous for Sofia to go to the Capital. When she left the apartment, she had never properly said goodbye. She had never acted as though she was leaving and might never see her mother again. Sometimes one must embrace ignorance in order to go about one's day. How joyful it is to be stupid. How wonderful to be oblivious. To be able to trust that your parents are protecting you. But she needed to take another look through her apartment. She needed to see there was nothing left of her mother's writing.

Even if she'd wanted to turn back, Rosalie had to enter the Capital anyway, for gas and supplies. And the war was over. She would soon have to find a way to walk around in her dangerous new country.

"To be honest, I never went to the Capital before it was sacked," Rosalie said. "Maybe you'll say it was more beautiful before the Occupation, but I can't begin to imagine that. The Capital was this mythic place that we had been exiled from. Everyone always talked about it. But I'm the only person in my family who has been able to actually see the Capital. And I guess if I have children, they will be able to see it too."

Sofia found it strange that Rosalie talked about the Capital not as a place the Enemy had stolen but as a place the Enemy had recovered, as a place that had once been stolen from them.

"Wait here," Rosalie said. "They'll leave you alone if you're with me."

Rosalie got out of the car and went to the trunk and took out a small valise. She went into what was once a post office. When she came out, she no longer had the valise but was carrying a canister of gasoline. The smell filled the car as Rosalie poured the gasoline in the tank.

When Rosalie got back in, she turned and looked at Sofia. "Shall we go see your old house, to say goodbye?"

"Yes, please," Sofia answered.

Rosalie and Sofia drove down the back streets. Sofia was shocked to see how the city looked. It was known for its architecture, and this had effectively been ruined. It was difficult for Sofia to even situate where they were in the city, since all the landmarks she used to identify her location had been razed to the ground. Most of the narrow streets were impossible to navigate because huge piles of stones and debris had made them impassable.

There would never be any way to restore the city to its former glory, or to anything that vaguely resembled its former glory. All that could be done was to move the piles of stone out of the way. The entirety of the city needed to be thrown out.

They passed an apartment building that was partially standing. Sofia could see right into one apartment as though she were looking in a dollhouse. She could see a bed balanced on a remaining floor of the building. It made her cringe. She would hate if her old bedroom were exposed liked that. She loathed the idea of strangers looking up and seeing the bed she had dreamed in and masturbated in. She hated to think of them seeing the room she had walked around in her bare feet and changed her underwear in.

When they got closer to Sofia's apartment, the roads were too cluttered with debris to navigate. So Sofia and Rosalie got out to walk.

As they walked down the rubble-strewn street together, they heard whistling and cat calls. Sofia looked up and saw soldiers sitting on the edge of a building's roof with their legs hanging over the side. She looked across the street and saw some men leaning against the walls in an alley and smoking cigarettes together.

They were wearing soldier uniforms. They weren't on duty because they were wearing their uniforms in a dishevelled, unbuttoned way. One was wearing a large green sweater over his jacket. Another had his army coat unbuttoned and was wearing a white undershirt underneath.

"Don't even look at them," Rosalie said. But she didn't quicken her pace. She began to walk more jauntily, as though the attention of the men made her happy. Nothing in her body reacted to them as if they were threatening.

"Rosalie! Rosalie!" one of them called out. He said something else in their language. Sofia could not understand it. It caused Rosalie to roll her eyes up and laugh. She took Sofia by the elbow and sped up.

"There are so few women here. They are all in a good mood because their wives will be arriving soon."

Sofia realized that men acted a different way when women of their own country were watching them. When they were around women from an enemy country, they behaved as ugly as they pleased.

They treated the women like disposable objects—things bought to serve their purposes for one day, then tossed away.

Rosalie did what she pleased in this country. She was so at home here. She wasn't at all afraid of being shot in the head. The way she described it, it seemed as though she felt more at ease in this country than she did in her own. She was delighted by her new life, as if she couldn't believe she got to live here, and how much better she was suited to it.

When Sofia halted outside her building, Rosalie seemed unsure of why they were stopping. She then realized they were at her building and looked confounded by its grandeur.

Sofia gripped and squeezed Rosalie's hand to coax whatever affection she could out of her friend, in case she turned against her. "It's very decadent, isn't it? I know that now. God, it's so opulent."

"I'll let you go up there yourself. There's a possibility that building is going to come down on your head. A lot of buildings that seemed to have survived the bombing will collapse suddenly. I'll wait for you out here."

There was garbage and debris all over the stairwell. It had fallen there when the soldiers were looting the apartment. She saw an armchair that had once been inside lying upside down on the landing below. She walked past it and up the last flight of stairs that led to their penthouse. Sofia felt her heart beating so heavily as she stared at her front door.

She stood on her tiptoes to reach the ledge above the door, on which there was a key. She was about to open the door, but her body temperature suddenly dropped. She experienced a terrible chill. The terrifying thing about a chill is that the coldness comes from inside the body, not outside it.

She began trembling violently. She was helpless. There was no way she would be able to open the door. But when she touched the doorknob with the tip of her finger, the door opened, without any need of a key.

The apartment had always smelled of coffee and fresh pastries and her mother's perfume. Now it would smell no different than the hallway. She had always considered her house to be messy. But it was a wonderful accumulation of beautiful and colourful items. When the door swung silently open, she saw what the apartment actually looked like messy.

The furniture had been taken out. There were framed photographs that had fallen all over the ground, and they had been stepped on and broken.

It was rare to find the kitchen empty. It was the room her mother occupied the most. There was a table by the window. And she would sit at it drinking coffee, reading the newspapers that were placed there for her.

There was a large black telephone on a ledge near the table. It rang often during the day. Her mother would answer it herself. She loved talking on the phone. Her body language would change quite radically depending on who was on the other end. But more often than not, even if it was a casual acquaintance or a stranger, her mother spoke as though it were a lover. She would play with the long telephone cord, wrapping it around her fingers in a manner that could only be called erotic. It was as though she were playing with the curls of a lover whose head was resting on her chest after lovemaking.

There was a smell of rot in the kitchen and smashed plates all over the floor. She heard the squeaking of what might perhaps have been a rat. She hurried out.

She felt as though she were a ghost in her old apartment. Perhaps we all haunt our childhood homes, she thought. When children are afraid of the dark, what they are sensing is their future selves coming back, looking for them.

She passed by her mother's office, which had been ransacked. The giant piles of manuscripts her mother had begun but never finished were not on any ledges. Perhaps they had all been packed into boxes and taken to be examined and destroyed. There was a photograph of her mother in college on the floor. The frame had been cracked, so Sofia left it there.

The bookshelves that lined the living room had been emptied of books. This was the main difference of the apartment. Now that the books were gone, it was as though an audience had been ushered out of the theatre. And it made the apartment quiet and no longer alive.

There was a large bloodstain on the carpet in the living room. The carpet, which had once been light blue, was now a dark burgundy. She realized it was that way because it had been soaked in blood. It made her want to retch. They had shot her mother immediately, then. Sofia wondered what her mother had known. She wondered whether they told her she had been betrayed by her daughter.

The minute she had entered the apartment, Sofia already knew all the papers had been destroyed. She didn't hear them whispering to her. Paper is so vulnerable to any movement or breeze. And paper that has been written on is even more so. Paper loves nothing more than to be read. Because it was once a tree with a story that was layers upon layers upon layers. But there were no written words singing in cursive to her.

And then she heard a tiny whisper of her mother's voice from somewhere else in the apartment. She followed it down the hallway, past all the nails poking out of the walls. Only the square shadows of old paintings left on the walls. It was coming from inside Sofia's bedroom. She opened the door and stepped in.

Her bedroom was the room that had been the least touched. The window was broken, and everything near the window had been destroyed by rain, water, and snow. But her toys were surprisingly preserved. She heard the whisper coming from her desk. She went to the bottom drawer and carefully opened it. There she found her book of fables whose cover had been ripped off. The one her mother had used to house her manuscript, in order to conceal it.

The pages were still bound together by a spine made of rope and sticky, clumpy glue. The first page was curled at the edges. As though someone were peeking out from under a sheet to see what had woken them up.

Her mother's handwriting was on the title page. It surprised Sofia to see it. She had long forgotten that her mother had written a dedication to her inside the book. Her mother had given it to her as a gift when she turned four years old. Long before she was able to understand the contents, and several more years before she was able to read it herself. During this interval, her mother had squeezed into the single child-sized bed next to her to read her the stories.

The dedication read:

To my daughter, Sofia, on her fourth birthday. Here are some tales of wonderment for you, my wonderful girl. I hope they fill you with enough magic to cast the spell you need on the world. I look forward every day to seeing the woman you will become. I know it will be as surprising to me as my path was to my mother. Hold true to your own path, and never let anyone lead you astray. Not even me, my love!

WHAT CAME FIRST,

THE MOTHER OR THE EGG?

As Clara Bottom and her daughter, Sofia, were walking, they came across a man being taken out of his apartment. He was struggling. His body was recoiling from the car as though he were to be thrown off the side of a ship. Although cars were invented for movement and travel, the car was the opposite of that now. It would take you nowhere. It would drive you to nothingness.

She took her mother's hand in hers and squeezed it. It was a simple way of communicating what she was feeling. She thought her heart might explode from the effort of keeping it to herself. And her mother squeezed back. And she knew her mother was feeling the same weight. They were feeling it together. They could carry the heaviness of it together.

There were days when the Enemy became more violent. So Clara and Sofia hastened their steps to get back to their apartment. As they were walking down the street, only two blocks away from their building, they passed by a large group of soldiers. They looked Sofia's mother up and down, as though they knew she was hiding something.

There was something about her that was of interest, but they could not determine what.

Sofia often remarked to herself that the soldiers seemed older from afar. When she got close to them, they seemed surprisingly young. They were little more than teenagers. They formed a circle around Sofia's mother. She froze, not saying anything. They began to whistle and blow kisses and say things that, although in the Enemy language, were clearly sexually suggestive.

Her mother did not say anything. She looked at them blankly, as though she had never said anything of any importance in her life. She made eye contact with the leader. Sofia was not used to this. Her mother was never one to be at a loss for words. She particularly enjoyed eviscerating men.

Sofia and her mother walked on without saying anything. But there was tension all around them. Her mother's high heel shoes seemed to be knocking, banging against the ground, as though it were ice and they might finally crash through it. Then she took Sofia's hand as soon as they turned the corner and pulled her into the lobby of a strange building.

Sofia did not know where they were. She looked around the lobby to see whether anything was familiar. It was a typical lobby for an Elysian building. They were often unique and very pretty. The floor was covered with turquoise ceramic tiles. A long row of gold mailboxes was set into a light pink wall. There was a mural of roses that had been painted on the walls and stretched up to the ceiling.

Her mother let go of Sofia's hand and leaned against the mural. She had an expression on her face that Sofia could not recall having seen before. It looked blank. She looked vulnerable.

It made her seem younger. The wrinkles and creases around her eyes and mouth disappeared, and her face seemed porcelain. Her face up against the roses on the wall made her look like a statue of the Virgin Mary in a grotto. Sofia was unclear what she was looking at. She had never seen her mother that way.

And then she began to weep. For a moment, she allowed herself to be just like everybody else's mother. Sofia did not even know that adult women cried like that. Particularly not her mother. She didn't think she had ever seen her mother cry before.

Then Clara Bottom stopped crying, and she stood in front of the window pane of the building door for a moment. She looked at her reflection, which appeared superimposed on the glass, as though she were a ghost. She stood there for what seemed a prescribed amount of time, waiting for her eyes and face to look like she hadn't been crying. She seemed to know the exact time this would take, as though she were boiling an egg.

"Come along," she finally said, as though nothing had happened.

Seeing their mothers cry was something most children experienced when they were younger than Sofia. Clara Bottom was a stoic and proud woman, after all. But now it was happening to Sofia too. It is the first time you understand that your mother is not immortal. The red lipstick on her lips is death. The stain on the sole of her nylon stocking when she takes off her shoes is death. The ring left in the bar of soap on the side of the sink is death. And at this point, every child realizes what a fool they are. What a fool they have been to invest all their time and belief and trust in this person. Who is a charlatan who is as mortal as anyone else.

"The Capital is filled with death," Clara said then. "We will find a way to get you out safely."

• • •

This moment came to Sofia as she read the inscription. This moment and this life in their apartment before the war and during the war. The many days of them together. And she realized that her mother had not used her to get her book out of the country, but had given it to her as a means of protection. It would have made people look out for her and after her. And in some ways, it had saved her life. And perhaps that was the main purpose of it.

Being back in her apartment after such a long absence made her see it in a completely different way. It made her memories and estimation of it suddenly different. It was like returning to a problem after you had put it to the side and gained clarity from the distance.

She realized that part of the reason she had managed to survive all this time was that her mother had always taught her a woman had to make something of her life. She had never believed a woman should be passive. It was necessary to be present. You could not follow others around. You had to forge your own destiny. And she would have to forge one apart from her mother.

Sofia looked out the window at Rosalie. She was speaking to a group of soldiers and laughing. She wondered if, when the country truly became occupied, Rosalie would lose the freedom she had here. She belonged to nobody. She had no morals. She did everything she needed to do to make herself happy. She put herself first. But she was free in a way Sofia didn't want to be free.

She had a strange intuition. And the intuition filled her body with fear. Rosalie was being wonderful and generous to Sofia at this moment because it was something forbidden. Friendships and associations made during war were volatile. They were based on survival—she realized that Rosalie might turn on her at any minute.

Rosalie could have simply left her family. She did not have to give them up just to force herself to leave. She had given in to vengeance. Who could say what she might do next? She had been born with the temperament of a soldier.

Sofia did not always want to be at war. She wanted to be somewhere where she could build relationships again. She wanted to have colleagues she cared for and admired. She might want to have a family of her own. She was not like Celeste, who wanted a baby in order to give her life meaning. And so that she was weak and would be cared for by a man.

Sofia could not stay here. She would see the city only for what it used to be. She would be like a hundred-year-old lady reminiscing about old times. Even if she could manage to learn the language. She would always be living in a sort of palimpsest. Where out of the corner of her eye, she would see people she knew living a life that had disappeared.

She wanted to find a place where she belonged, the way her mother had. She suddenly had a vision of having a little girl of her own. One she could impress with her accomplishments. One she could tell fables to. And at night, they would find themselves in the land of make-believe and battle for meaning together.

Sofia noticed a small glass vial lying on the floor. She picked it up. It was filled with her milk teeth. Her mother had collected and kept them, as was the Elysian tradition. The words you use as a child fall out of your mouth like milk teeth.

In her folktale book, milk teeth were always magical. There was a tale about a girl who did not want her stepmother to have her milk teeth. So she buried them at the foot of a tree in the forest. When she awoke, she found the tree's leaves had turned to silver. There was a girl who hid her milk tooth in a barn. And in the morning, a small white calf was standing in the yard. She put a leash around its neck and held a glass under its teat whenever she was hungry. There was a little girl who planted her milk tooth in a small clay pot. An oleander sprouted out of it. She would take off a petal and put it in a cup of tea to poison her enemies.

Sofia would find a different land to plant her roots in. Whenever she went or wherever she settled down, a new tree would spring out of her, one whose leaves whispered in the voices of schoolchildren, and whose birds sang songs that sounded like lullabies your mother would have whispered to you, like a child.

She was alive. She was actually alive. She knew she was going to make it out alive. She knew because every cell in her body seemed to be preparing for a greater adventure. For a long future. This was the end of the war, but it was the very beginning of her life story.

She contained inside her all the joys and history and successes of the Capital. Now that the Capital had been destroyed, she was the Capital. And even if she was the Capital—and contained all of its history in her own history—she was still so much bigger than all that. There was an unknown country inside of her.

She realized she was never meant to spend her life in the small country she was born in. She was meant to leave it. That was only the first chapter of her life.

She would go to Paris. She didn't tell Rosalie about her ambition. She simply took Rosalie's hand as she stepped out onto the street. "I want to leave the country."

"Yes," said Rosalie. "I know. Don't worry."

And then Rosalie said something that her mother had also said. She hadn't understood it when her mother told her. And she thought it was one of her mother's more radical ideas that nobody else shared with her. But when Rosalie said it, it resonated differently with Sofia. And she thought there was some truth to it. And even though it didn't entirely make sense to her now, she had the feeling it would come to make very much sense to her in the future.

She said, "Sometimes a war can set a woman free."

ACKNOWLEDGEMENTS

Jennifer Lambert
Emily Griffin
Amy Baker
Jonathan Burham
Janice Weaver
Claudia Ballard
Elias Harb
Patrick Watson
Hamlet and Moppet O'Neill
and Arizona O'Neill

Everyone at HarperCollins Canada and HarperPerennial US.

Merci!

Don't Miss Heather O'Neill's Stunning Debut

lullabies for little criminals

A NOVEL

HEATHER O'NEILL

Scotiabank Giller Prize short-listed author of *Daydreams of Angels*
and *The Girl Who Was Saturday Night*

TENTH ANNIVERSARY EDITION

INTERNATIONAL BESTSELLER

"A beautiful book, all the more remarkable because its harrowing tale is (virtuosically) told without a trace of self-pity or bathos. There are phrases in here that will make you laugh out loud, and others that will stop your heart. A definite triumph." —David Rakoff, author of *Love, Dishonor, Marry, Die, Cherish, Perish*